I0761680

KOKUN

Nahoko Uehashi

KOKUN

Volume One
The Girl from the West

Translated from the Japanese
by Cathy Hirano

Europa
editions

Europa Editions
27 Union Square West, Suite 302
New York NY 10003
www.europaeditions.com
info@europaeditions.com

This book is a work of fiction. Any references to historical events, real people, or real locales are used fictitiously.

Original Japanese edition published by Bungeishunju Ltd., in 2022.
English translation rights throughout United States of America and Canada reserved by Europa Editions, under the license granted by Nahoko Uehashi, Japan arranged with Bungeishunju Ltd., Japan.
First publication 2026 by Europa Editions

Translation by Cathy Hirano
Original title: 香君（上）西から来た少女 *(KŌKUN Vol. 1. Nishi kara kita shōjo)*

Library of Congress Cataloging in Publication Data is available
ISBN 979-8-88966-158-0

Uehashi, Nahoko
The Girl from the West

Cover design by Ginevra Rapisardi

Map by Yukiko Saito / Bungeishunju Ltd.

Cover illustration by mia

Prepress by Grafica Punto Print – Rome

Printed in the USA

CONTENTS

KOKUN

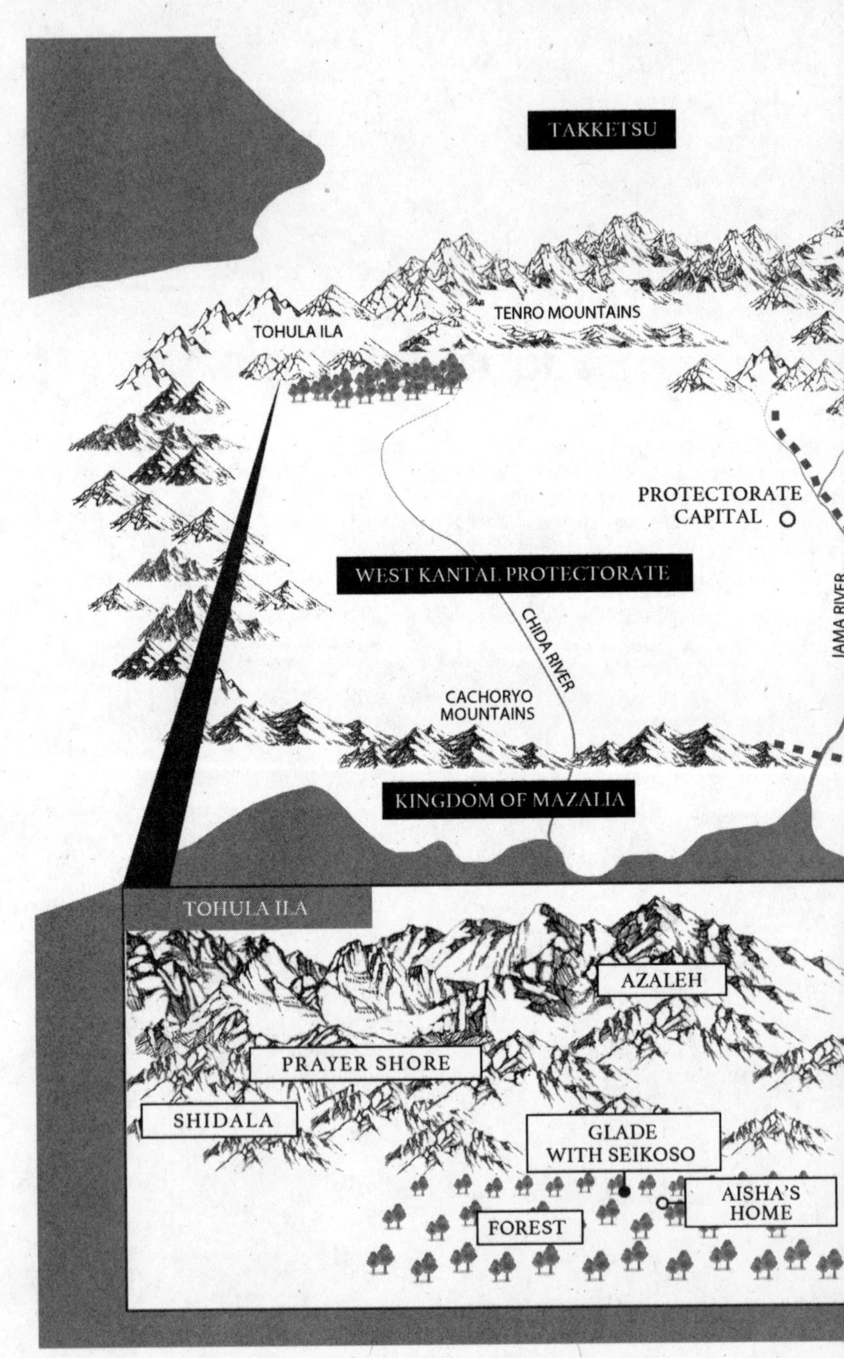
TAKKETSU
TENRO MOUNTAINS
TOHULA ILA
PROTECTORATE
CAPITAL
WEST KANTAL PROTECTORATE
CHIDA RIVER
IAMA RIVER
CACHORYO
MOUNTAINS
KINGDOM OF MAZALIA
TOHULA ILA
AZALEH
PRAYER SHORE
SHIDALA
GLADE
WITH SEIKOSO
AISHA'S
HOME
FOREST

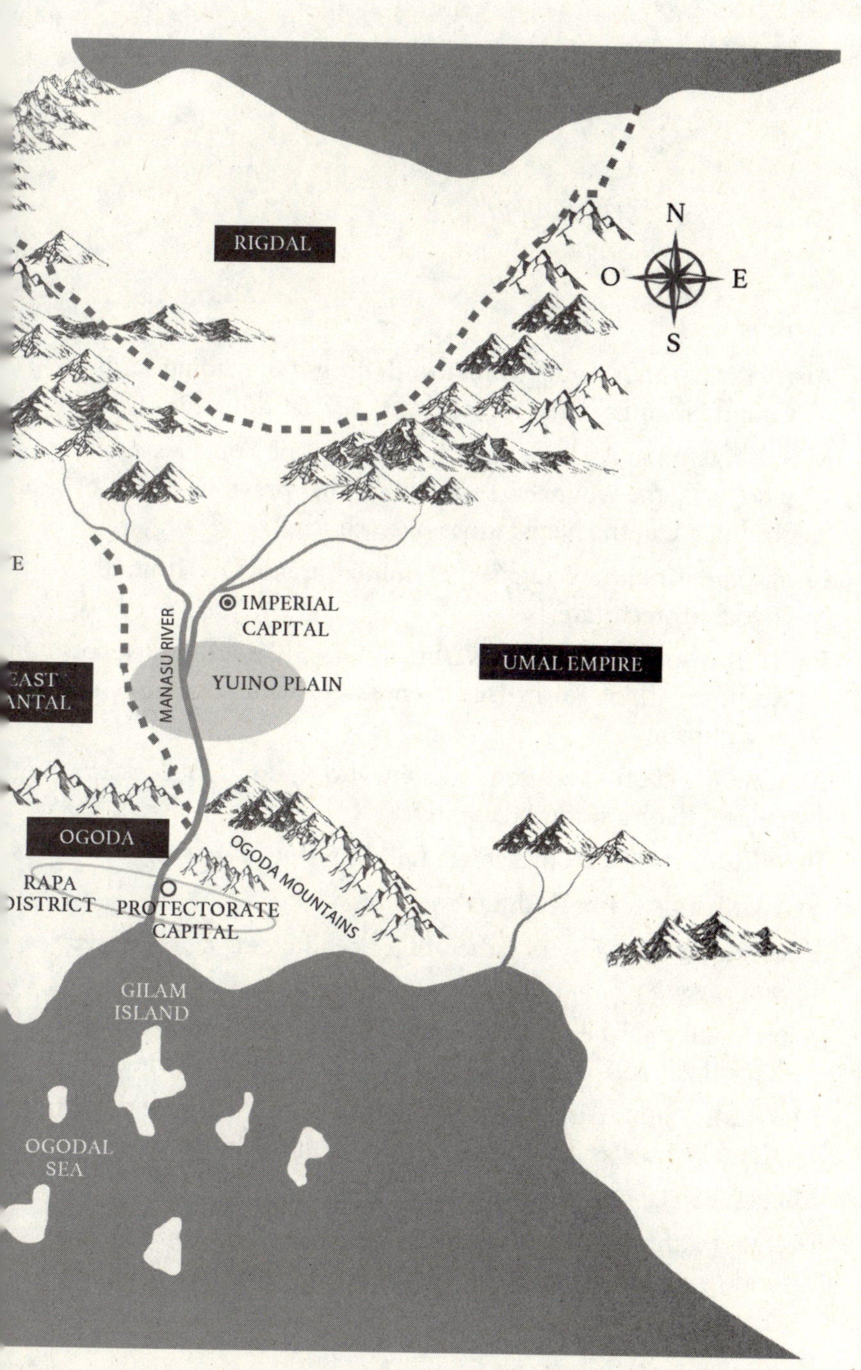
RIGDAL
N
O
E
S
IMPERIAL CAPITAL
MANASU RIVER
YUINO PLAIN
UMAL EMPIRE
OGODA
RAPA
DISTRICT
PROTECTORATE CAPITAL
OGODA MOUNTAINS
GILAM ISLAND
OGODAL SEA

List of Main Characters

Aisha Keluahn: A young woman with the gift of reading scents. Granddaughter of the former lord of West Kantal.

Masyu Kashuga: An imperial inspector. Son of Yuma Kashuga, who was the younger brother of the previous head of Kashuga Lai, the New House of Kashuga.

Olie: The Kokun. Daughter of minor aristocrats from the Rigdal protectorate.

Raoh Kashuga: Head of Kashuga Oi, the Old House of Kashuga, Chief Koshi (scent emissary) who supervises all other koshi.

Mijima Olu Kashuga: A senior koshi who works at the Kokun's palace. Raoh's second daughter.

Iilu Kashuga: Head of Kashuga Lai, Minister of Wealth.

Yugil Kashuga: Iilu Kashuga's son.

Yuma Kashuga: Masyu's father. Has been missing since Masyu was seven.

Amil Kashuga: The man who, with the first emperor, brought back the first Kokun from Ohaleh Mazula, home of the gods.

King Keluahn: Aisha's grandfather. Former king of West Kantal who was driven from power by his own people.

Milucha Keluahn: Aisha's younger brother.

Uchai: Faithful retainer of King Keluahn. He raised Aisha and Milucha as their foster father and guardian. They call him Jiiya.

TAK: Raoh's cousin who lives in Yugino Lodge with his wife Laina and their twin sons.

URAILI: An imperial protectorate inspector and Masyu's colleague.

OLAM: A senior koshi related to Kashuga Lai.

OLOKI MUA: A dog handler who works for Masyu.

ALIKI: Former Chief of Pest Control. Highly trusted by Raoh, she continues to research insects.

OILA: Chief of Pest Control who studied under Aliki.

MILIA: Royal Mother of Ogoda, mother of Agua, lord of Ogoda.

JOOKUCHI: Lord of West Kantal.

ODOSEN: Crown prince of the Umal Empire, who succeeds his father Orulan as emperor.

Prologue: Blue Flowers

The wind whistled in Aisha's ears and whipped at her hair. A passing shower had swept through in the early afternoon, dampening the ground below and making the cliff face to which her hands and feet clung as cold as ice.

"Aisha!"

A patter of soil followed the shrill cry. Aisha jerked one hand off the cliff and reached up to steady her brother's boot where it gleamed palely in the fading light. As her palm found his heel, her body swayed, and her other hand almost slipped. She fought to retain her grip, barely managing to right herself. She let out a deep breath, and her legs began to tremble.

If we fall, we're dead.

Clenching her jaw, she supported her brother's foot until he managed to wedge it into a hollow in the stone. Even once she knew he was alright, Aisha remained frozen in place. She waited for the dizziness to pass, gasping for breath.

There was probably no future for them even if they made it to the top. She'd known that for a while now. The pungent smells of leather, iron, and sweat rolled down from the clifftop, making her gag. She'd been told that this route wasn't well known. If there were warriors lying in wait, it could only mean that Jiiya had been caught. She couldn't believe their elderly guardian, who had acted as a decoy so she and her younger brother could escape, would have given them away. Clearly the warriors had anticipated which route they'd take and were heading them off.

Maybe I should just let go . . .

She caught sight of her brother's muddy boots above her. Recalling how he'd beamed with joy when he first got them, her face twisted.

The wind parted the clouds, and the world around them suddenly brightened. The last rays of the sun as it sank behind the shadowed mountains illuminated the rock face. In that unexpected light, Aisha spotted a plant rooted in a crack just above her handhold. The wind tugged at its small blue flowers, but couldn't tear them off.

Its scent spoke to her, faint but sure, riding the wind like a thread. In time, an insect would pick up that voice and weave between gaps in the wind, following the thread to the flower.

Once again, she heard her brother call out. "Aisha . . ."

On the icy wind, she smelled his fear, a scent like a cowering puppy.

"Milucha! Pull yourself together!" she shouted. "Grip the rocks and climb! If you start to slip, I'll help you!"

They were almost at the top. Her brother started climbing again, and she inched up the cliff after him.

Chapter I
First Encounter

1
Litaran

The light of the torches, which just a short while ago had been invisible, stood out clearly in the blue twilight. Countless tents had been set up in the camp. The wind that had set them flapping noisily had lessened, and smoke rose above them, wavering and dissolving into the night sky. The aroma of food cooking wafted faintly on the air.

"The foot soldiers will eat sooner than us tonight," Uraili grumbled into his beard. He was sitting on a folding chair in the company of several rugged-looking men.

Masyu glanced at his companion and laughed. "You could leave, you know. One observer is surely enough."

Uraili looked like he was about to make a flippant retort, then cast his eyes toward the plain. "If only I could," he muttered.

Pine torches flickered in the hands of a dozen or so horsemen who were galloping across the grassy plain toward the camp. Behind them, the majestic Tenro Mountains sank into dusk.

Uraili craned his neck to look at a man standing behind him. "Oloki," he said. The hunting dog at the man's feet perked up its ears, as if it thought it was being addressed.

"Yes?" Oloki said, placing a hand on the hound's head.

"The boy's about eight and the girl's fifteen or sixteen, right?"

"The heir is nine years old, and his older sister is fifteen."

Uraili nodded and sighed. "What's the point in capturing them?" he muttered. "Why can't Jookuchi just leave them alone?"

He looked up at Masyu. "Don't you agree? It'd be different if someone were trying to use them to take over West Kantal, but they're descendants of Keluahn—a ruler so despised that his own people drove him from the throne! His grandchildren don't have any power. Why else would Jookuchi have left them alone up to now? What made him change his mind? And why now, in the middle of a war?"

Masyu kept his gaze fixed on the approaching horsemen. Ignoring Uraili's question, he murmured, "So they *are* coming from that direction."

Uraili frowned. "Who is?"

"The horsemen. If they're coming from that direction, it means their prisoners—Keluahn's grandchildren, were trying to escape to Tohula Ila, the great ravine in the Tenro Mountains."

Uraili rose and stood beside Masyu. "Sounds like you expected them to come from there. You guessed that?"

Masyu flicked Uraili a quick glance. "Because it's the only way to escape."

"Surely not. They were hiding in the forest, right? It would be a lot easier to flee east than to take that treacherous mountain route."

"Despite the risks, they must have believed fleeing into the mountains would give them a better chance at survival."

"Why?"

"As you pointed out, Keluahn was despised by his own people, but even so, there're some in those mountains who didn't hate him."

Uraili's expression turned grim. "I've never heard that before. Some clan living in the Tenro Mountains? Which one?"

Masyu continued to gaze at the horsemen, who were now clearly visible. "You aren't the only one who didn't know," he said. "In fact, few people do."

Uraili's eyes narrowed. "When did you find out?"

Masyu shifted his gaze to Uraili. "Me?" he said quietly. "I've known since I was a boy."

A man emerged from the large tent that served as the field office of Lord Jookuchi, ruler of West Kantal. It was one of Jookuchi's aides. He peered through the twilight, as though searching for someone. Catching sight of Masyu and Uraili, he moved purposefully toward them. "Inspectors," he said, crossing his arms across his chest and bowing deeply. "The prisoners are expected to arrive soon, and Lord Jookuchi humbly requests your presence in the main tent."

Masyu nodded. "We'll be happy to comply," he said.

The aide bowed once more, then turned to lead the two men toward the large tent.

Imperial inspectors served as the emperor's eyes and ears in the four outlying protectorates of the Umal Empire. The Umalese word for "protectorate" was *rachi*, meaning to enclose and guard. All four had once been independent kingdoms, and they retained some degree of autonomy even after joining the empire. Their borders now represented the empire's frontiers, and in exchange for protecting these, their rulers were given some control over affairs within their own territory. None of them, including Lord Jookuchi, was permitted to hide anything from imperial inspectors such as Masyu and his companion.

Leaving their personal guards behind, Masyu and Uraili strolled toward the bright entrance of the large tent, a slice of light that stood out in the blue darkness.

* * *

The tent was more spacious inside than it appeared from the outside. A large smoke vent opened in the ceiling, and a hearth glowed red in the center of the floor. Lanterns had been placed here and there, illuminating the expressions of the vassals and clan chiefs who sat along the walls of the tent.

An altar beautifully adorned with vermillion, blue and gold stood at the far end facing the entrance. Sitting in a large chair with his back toward the altar was Lord Jookuchi. He was talking in a low voice to his advisers who sat on either side of him, but when Masyu and Uraili walked in, he rose and greeted them, beckoning them to sit in chairs off to one side.

Despite the chill wind outside, the interior was hot and steamy. A small table had been placed before each guest with a bowl of fermented mare's milk to slake their thirst and a plate of nuts and dried fruit to satisfy their hunger.

Soon after Masyu and Uraili had taken their seats, a gong announced the arrival of the prisoners. The murmur of voices stilled, and the tent grew silent.

Jookuchi took his seat and, taking a cloth from an attendant, wiped the sweat from his forehead and neck. He was a large man, well-toned and darkly tanned, with thick arms and legs, but it was his big round eyes and thick eyebrows that were particularly arresting. His penetrating gaze could unsettle the most intrepid men.

Although royal blood ran in his veins, it was only from some distant collateral branch. He was, however, gifted with a keen instinct for military strategy. After Keluahn was driven from power, Jookuchi had borrowed imperial troops with the promise that he would defend the empire's borders when called upon. He'd used them to overthrow Keluahn's successor, who had failed to control the skirmishing clans. In this way, Jookuchi had become the lord of West Kantal.

Although one clan continued to resist, Masyu was sure that if Jookuchi kept on the way he was going, it wouldn't be long before he subdued that last clan and gained control over the entire region. The emperor hoped he would bring West Kantal under his sway as soon as possible, and so did Masyu.

The cold night air swept into the tent as the flaps covering the entrance were raised to either side. Cloaked in a gust of wind, two powerful warriors strode through, each grasping a prisoner—a boy and a slender young woman—by the arm. Neither prisoner was bound, but the warriors' grip held them fast.

One of the men placed an arm across his chest in salute. His voice rang through the tent. "We have brought the descendants of Keluahn, as commanded."

Jookuchi nodded. After thanking them, he motioned for them to withdraw, but the men stayed put, their expressions uneasy.

"What is it?" Jookuchi asked. "I said you can release them."

"By your leave, my lord," one of them responded. "The girl refuses to show due respect. We cannot be sure what she might do should we set her free."

Jookuchi cocked a bushy eyebrow. "I see. I guess I'll have to be careful then. Let them go."

The men bowed and released their grip. Although they stepped back a pace, they watched the girl, ready to seize her at any moment. But she didn't budge, not even the twitch of an eyebrow. She simply stood staring at Jookuchi, her eyes as black and motionless as stone.

Returning her gaze, he said, "So, you're Keluahn's grandchildren, Milucha and Aisha?"

"I have no name to give a usurper," the girl responded, her voice hoarse, yet firm.

Jookuchi sighed. "I see what they mean. You lack due respect."

He rose slowly and glared down at her. From the stand beside him, he pulled a long sword, scabbard and all, and struck the floor sharply with the end of the sheath.

The men assembled in the tent started, and the two children flinched. The boy's face crumpled, and he began to sob.

"Look. Your brother's crying," Jookuchi said, glowering at the girl. "You should consider your situation more carefully before opening your mouth. How you behave will determine whether I lop off your brother's head before your eyes."

The girl's face paled, and she glared up at him. "That's . . . a lie," she gasped faintly.

Jookuchi raised his thick brows. "A lie?"

She nodded. "That how I behave will determine our fate."

Jookuchi's eyes widened. He looked at her intently, then the corner of his mouth twitched. "If not that, then what?"

Masyu thought she would need time to answer, but she replied instantly. "Whether it's to your advantage or not."

A murmur spread through the assembly. Masyu shifted his gaze from the girl to Jookuchi. *Let's see how he responds to that*, he thought.

Jookuchi regarded the girl silently for some time, then heaved a sigh. "Whether it's to my advantage, huh? Well, I suppose you're not far off."

He sat down heavily in his chair. Grasping a bowl adorned with gold lacquer from a side table, he gulped down the milk liquor. An attendant offered him a cloth, and he dabbed his lips with it, then used it to wipe the sweat from his face and neck.

Turning back to the girl, he said, "You're not far off, but you're not right either. It's not me you pose a threat to but the empire."

The boy looked up at his sister questioningly, but she kept her eyes fixed on Jookuchi.

"You were heading for the Tenro Mountains, weren't you? Or, more accurately, for Tohula Ila, the great ravine."

Seeing the look on her face, he added, "Don't get me wrong. The old man didn't confess. He's admirably loyal. He resisted with a strength that made it hard to believe his age. But we were warned from the outset he might be a decoy and split our men into two parties."

The girl's face tensed.

Jookuchi watched her as he continued. "It wasn't the old man who tipped us off to where you might run. It was an imperial inspector."

Uraili jerked. Although he wasn't so indiscreet as to glance Masyu's way, Masyu could feel the shock emanating from every inch of his body. Without a flicker of expression, Masyu kept his eyes fixed on Jookuchi and the girl.

"Your existence, you see, is a hindrance," Jookuchi said flatly. "Not just to West Kantal, but to the Umal Empire itself. Can you guess why?"

The blood drained from the girl's face. She must have realized there was no way out.

Jookuchi's voice was the only sound in the large tent. "Your grandfather was a foolish man. Many people starved to death because of him. Half the people in West Kantal loathed him, including me."

The girl's eyes wavered. Her face was now chalk white.

Jookuchi gestured for an attendant to fill his drinking bowl and drained it noisily. "But apparently, there are some in this frontier land who still revere him, and therefore you, as his descendants," he said. "The People of the Ravine who call themselves the Makishi. Thus far, we've let them be. They're few in number and have no ambition to rule the region. But now their presence is a problem. The territory they control is in a most inconvenient spot."

Masyu heard Uraili murmur, "So that's why."

The clan that Jookuchi's expedition had come to subdue controlled the area along the western edge of the Tenro Mountains. Their influence, however, didn't extend into the mountains themselves, and they couldn't withstand Jookuchi's forces for long on their own. But if they managed to enlist the support of Takketsu, a kingdom on the other side of the mountains, they might succeed in turning the tables.

Curving along West Kantal's north and west borders, the Tenro Mountains were steep and rugged, with only a few passes wide enough for a large army to cross. These were defended by forts jointly manned by soldiers from the empire and West Kantal.

There was also a mountain trail leading from Takketsu through Tohula Ila, a large canyon in the western region of the

Tenro Mountains. This path could be navigated by small contingents of experienced warriors, but no fortress guarded it. Riddled with hidden cavities that could claim the lives of unsuspecting travelers, the steep valley was impassable without a guide.

Unless they won the allegiance of the Makishi, who knew the valley like the back of their hand and controlled it and the surrounding area, invaders from Takketsu could not hope to descend the mountains into West Kantal. Neither could they subdue the Makishi, because bringing in a large army was impossible. Therefore, neither the ruler of West Kantal nor the emperor had viewed defense of this region as a priority.

But the situation could change drastically if the one clan that remained hostile to the empire were to get hold of the girl and her brother, whom the Makishi viewed as the heir of their rightful king.

From the expressions on their faces, it was clear that some of the clan chiefs were only now grasping the significance of Jookuchi's words. Those from the southern and eastern regions of West Kantal, who had just recently declared their fealty, were unfamiliar with the situation in the area on the western edge of the Tenro Mountains. Jookuchi had probably intentionally kept the details from them until now so that they wouldn't start getting ideas.

"You're like an ant nest in the wall of a dike," Jookuchi continued. "Ordinarily, there'd be no harm in letting you be. But if a storm came, that nest could cause the dike to collapse, bringing disaster to the whole country.

"I'm not without compassion, you know. I'd rather not kill you just because you happen to be Keluahn's grandchildren. But it can't be helped. There is the option of keeping you with me, but you'd still represent a risk."

Fatigue spread across his face. "So, that's how it is. If you need to blame your fate on something, blame your lineage."

He gestured with his chin, and the two warriors stepped forward to seize the prisoners' arms. The boy cowered and reached out for his sister. She grasped his hand tightly, then looked up at Jookuchi. A flicker of hesitation crossed her pale face. She opened her mouth as though to speak, then sealed her lips, as if thinking better of it.

Jookuchi's eyes narrowed suspiciously. "Is there something you want to say?"

She thought for a moment, then seemed to make up her mind. "You're being poisoned," she said.

Jookuchi's brows snapped together. He glared at her, wiping his face and neck again. He was perspiring so profusely it soaked his skin at an alarming rate evident even to the eyes of others. "What?"

She regarded him with an unreadable expression. "You smell of chitcho. Someone's poisoning you."

Consternation swept through those gathered, and some half rose from their chairs.

Wiping the sweat from his eyes, Jookuchi grinned triumphantly. "Ha! What's poisoned is your tongue, young lady. While I salute your spirit, if you must lie, you should pick something more convincing."

"I'm not lying."

"Of course you are. The poison extracted from chitcho root has neither smell nor taste."

Understanding dawned in her eyes. "If that's what you think," she said with a sigh, "then let's leave it at that." Putting an arm around her younger brother, she turned her back on Jookuchi and stepped toward the entrance. The warriors jumped forward and grabbed the prisoners by the arm to escort them from the tent.

"Wait!" Masyu said, rising to his feet. The girl and her brother halted and looked around. Masyu could feel the questioning eyes of Jookuchi and everyone else in the tent boring into him.

"Lady Aisha Keluahn," he said. "What about me? Do I smell of anything?"

She gazed at Masyu intently, her eyes like obsidian. She took so long that he thought she wasn't going to answer, but then, with a slight frown, she spoke.

"Are you a litaran?"

Masyu's eyes widened. A chill spread from between his eyes over his entire head, and his heart beat so rapidly it hurt. Through numbed lips, he whispered, "What makes you say that?"

Still frowning, she said, "You smell like seikoso, fragrant blue grass."

Masyu stared at her dumbfounded.

"What's all this about?" Uraili demanded. Ignoring him, Masyu strode swiftly to Jookuchi's side.

Close up, he could see that something was very wrong. Jookuchi's eyes were glazed. Turning to one of the lord's attendants, Masyu barked, "Summon the healer and tell him to bring kaful! Make no mistake. Tell him kaful! And get lots of water! Hurry!"

Then he called out to the warriors holding the prisoners. "Take those two away and confine them securely!"

There was a dull thud, like a heavy bag of flour sliding to the ground. Turning, Masyu saw that Jookuchi had slipped from his chair and lay sprawled on the floor.

The men in the room jumped to their feet, all babbling at once. In the midst of the confusion, Masyu hurried to Uraili's side and murmured in his ear. "Go with the girl and her brother. Take our guards with you, and don't let anyone touch them. Make sure no one tries to poison their food or the smoke smudges used to keep away insects. After that, send Oloki to me."

Uraili nodded wordlessly and hurried after the two prisoners as they were escorted out of the tent.

2
Odorless Poison

It was not until dawn the next day that Jookuchi's condition stabilized, and he was out of danger.

During the long night, his vassals and the clan chiefs had come one after another to his tent, but Masyu had only allowed them to look from the entrance, refusing to let them in. Some were visibly incensed, but as the would-be assassin had not yet been found, Masyu's decision was clearly a wise one, and no one insisted on being let through.

The one man allowed in was Oloki. Masyu gave him detailed instructions, then sent him off to the camp with his dog trotting after him like a shadow.

It was only once Jookuchi was out of danger that Masyu, who had spent the whole night watching over him with the healer, finally spread out a sleeping mat in a corner and dozed off.

When he woke, it was a little before noon, and Jookuchi was still sound asleep, his breathing quiet and regular. Masyu rose to his feet, stepped outside and inhaled deeply. The air smelled of rain-wet grass. He vaguely recalled the sound of raindrops pelting the tent while he had lain dreaming. The region was prone to sudden showers at this time of year.

A strong wind swept the leaden clouds before it, and with each rent it made in the clouds, sunlight poured through, illuminating the Tenro Mountains with startling brightness.

They must be cooking the noonday meal, Masyu thought. He smelled smoke mingled with the savory aroma of rice-flour tapa.

He turned at the sound of feet treading the grass and saw Oloki and his dog approaching. "How'd it go?" Masyu asked.

"Just as you thought," Oloki replied.

"So, you found one?"

"Yes."

Masyu smiled as he listened to Oloki's detailed report. "Well done," he said. "Go get some rest."

Oloki bowed, clicked his heels together, and turned away.

"And be sure to give that friend of yours a special treat," Masyu called after him.

Glancing over his shoulder, Oloki cracked a faint smile and nodded. His dog wagged his tail slowly, perhaps realizing that Masyu was talking about him.

With a deep breath, Masyu turned back to the tent. *Now then, one more job to do.*

When he stepped from daylight into the dim interior, he was momentarily robbed of sight. As his eyes adjusted, he could make out the figure of Jookuchi lying on a quilt by the hearth with the healer at his side. The scent of smoke mingled with that of medicinal tea.

Jookuchi's eyes opened a crack as Masyu approached, perhaps woken by the sound of his footsteps. He motioned for water. The healer lifted Jookuchi's head and brought a bowl to his lips. Jookuchi sipped noisily, and the healer's face relaxed, presumably relieved that his lord drank without choking.

After clearing his throat a few times, Jookuchi raised his head and looked at Masyu. The strength had returned to his eyes.

"Was the poison really chitcho?" he asked hoarsely.

Masyu looked at the healer, an experienced and competent man. "There's no proof," said the healer, "but I believe so. The symptoms are very like those that appear with chitcho poisoning, and when I administered the antidote, it was very effective."

Jookuchi frowned. "But chitcho is odorless, right?"

The man nodded. "Yes, my lord."

Jookuchi shifted his eyes to Masyu. "If so, then why did that girl say I smelled of it?"

Masyu had been pondering how to answer this question all night as he tended Jookuchi, but had failed to find a satisfactory response. Now that the time had come, however, he felt no hesitation. He flicked his eyes to the healer. "Lord Jookuchi's symptoms appear to have improved significantly. Do you think it would be all right for me to be alone with him for a while?"

Still on his knees, the healer moved toward the patient and took his pulse, then nodded. "If it's just a short while, it shouldn't be a problem."

"Then why don't you have a rest? If there's any change in his condition, I'll let you know immediately."

The healer bowed and left the tent. Masyu waited until he could no longer hear the man's footsteps, then turned back to Jookuchi.

"In answer to your question, I believe the girl could indeed detect the scent of chitcho. I think she must have a greater sensitivity to smell than others."

A harsh light glinted in Jookuchi's large eyes. "Why would you go to all the trouble of sending that man away if you're just going to speak nonsense? What I want to know is why she bothered to tell me at all. She knew I was being poisoned, which clearly means she's connected to the person behind it."

Masyu shook his head slowly. Jookuchi scowled, irritation written on his face. "You think I'm wrong? How so?"

"She's not connected to the one who poisoned you."

"How can you be so sure?"

"For the very reason you doubt her: because she told you herself that you were being poisoned."

Jookuchi looked at him blankly.

"It was totally unnecessary," Masyu continued. "If she was part of the plot to poison you and thought by doing so that she and her brother would be saved, surely she wouldn't have uttered a word." He sighed. "She held herself together well, but she's only fifteen. If she'd remained silent, it would have meant someone's death. That's probably what made her tell you."

"But she knew I was going to kill her."

"Even so, some people can't bear to stand back and let others die."

"But chitcho—"

"You're focusing on the fact that chitcho has no taste or smell, but there are other signs of poisoning. I could see that you were sweating heavily, and it would've been even more obvious to her, because she was right in front of you."

Jookuchi stared at him glumly.

"A ruler is always at risk of being killed," said Masyu. "So, those around him become well-versed in different methods of assassination. She's the granddaughter of Lord Keluahn. It makes sense that she would've been taught everything she needed to know about poison. She could have guessed you'd been poisoned with chitcho because you were sweating profusely and your eyes were glazed."

Although he looked partly convinced, Jookuchi's expression was still troubled. He opened his mouth, but before he could speak, Masyu continued, "I don't think the person who tried to poison would've known the value of Keluahn's descendants."

Jookuchi's eyes widened. "You know who did it?"

Masyu nodded. "The chief of the Lima clan."

Jookuchi stared at Masyu. "Laleeha? You have proof?"

"The cloth his servant used to polish the drinking bowls. He was in charge of polishing the bowls in the great tent last night."

Jookuchi sighed and shook his head. "If that's the reason you suspect him, then I'm afraid you're wrong. I wash and polish all my dishes myself, and always put them where I can keep an eye on them. He couldn't have smeared poison on my drinking bowl."

Masyu smiled. "It wasn't poison that was found on the polishing cloth."

Jookuchi stared at him.

"He smeared kaful sap on everyone else's drinking bowls," Masyu said bluntly. "Because you fear being poisoned, you only drink from the same flask used to serve everyone else. If Laleeha was going to poison your liquor, he'd have to drink the poison too. Although he could have chosen to kill everyone in the tent except himself, that would have aroused the enmity of the other clans."

Surprise suffused Jookuchi's face. "I see! So, he used the fact that I polish my own bowl to his advantage."

Masyu nodded. "That's right. The poison in chitcho is vulnerable to kaful sap. Once exposed, it loses its toxicity. The antidote your healer administered was also made from kaful sap."

"And the kaful smeared on the drinking bowls protected everyone else from being poisoned?

"Yes. One of my men spent the entire night searching for someone who had a polishing cloth that smelled of kaful sap." Masyu's lips twitched briefly. "He didn't use his own nose to sniff it out though. His dog did that."

Jookuchi groaned, then hung his head as if lost in thought.

Stroking his chin, Masyu said, "It will be very difficult under these circumstances to punish Laleeha. We'll have to consider the best solution carefully before taking action."

"Yes, there's that too," Jookuchi muttered, then, raising his head, he looked at Masyu. "But what should I do about the girl?"

"Because she saved your life?"

Jookuchi nodded. "Maybe we could spare her and just kill the boy—"

Masyu shook his head. "No, you mustn't do that. If you kill her brother, she'll bear a grudge against you for the rest of her life. You'll just create a breeding ground for future trouble." Seeing Jookuchi's grim expression, Masyu added, "If you want to show compassion, you can have them killed by poison instead of beheading them."

Jookuchi frowned. "Wouldn't that be even more painful?"

"Not if you choose the right poison. Some kill so painlessly that dying is just like falling asleep."

Masyu met Jookuchi's gaze in silence, watching the conflicting emotions reflected in his eyes.

3
Hirin, Ice Weed

Aisha and her brother Milucha were confined to a tent set apart from the rest of the camp in the middle of a grassy field. Anyone approaching could be easily identified. The guards who had accompanied Masyu on this expedition kept strict watch both inside and outside the tent, examining any food or change of clothing before giving it to the prisoners.

In the early afternoon of the day Jookuchi recovered, Oloki came to the tent and summoned Uraili. After a whispered consultation, he took three of the guards with him and disappeared. Other than that, there was little movement.

In addition to the smoke hole in the ceiling, the tent had two small windows for ventilation, and Milucha peered out of one of these whenever he heard the shouts of soldiers training or other sounds from the camp. His sister never budged from the middle of the tent where she sat working on a piece of embroidery given to her to pass the time.

When the sun had set and the soldiers had finished their meal, servants brought a late supper to the two prisoners. Behind them came Masyu and two of Jookuchi's aides.

Raising the tent flap, a guard murmured to someone inside, and Uraili came out. His face froze when he saw Masyu and the others behind the servants. Masyu put a finger to his lips, and Uraili indicated with his eyes that he understood.

Bearing large trays of food, the servants ducked through the tent flap. Masyu went behind the tent to one of the windows, while the two aides went to stand outside the other. It was already dark, and the lights of the camp were far enough away that it would be difficult for those within the brightly lit interior to see the faces of the men outside the windows. Even if their shadowy figures were visible, the prisoners wouldn't be aware that anything was different because guards were usually stationed there anyway.

The dinner was more sumptuous than the fare served to the soldiers. There was roast mutton, soup with stewed vegetables, and fruit. The thin flatbread called tapa had been spread with butter and sprinkled with precious sugar. There were even mugs of milk liquor.

The boy must have been hungry. His face brightened at the sight of all the food placed before them. But his sister hadn't looked up, even when the servant entered. Masyu's eyes narrowed as he watched her. Her shoulders were tensed, as if she were nervous.

She's noticed then.

The boy reached out his hand and, grasping a piece of flatbread drenched in butter and sugar, popped it in his mouth. He consumed it with a raptured expression. The girl began to eat quietly. Like her brother, she started with the tapa, and then moved on to the mutton and soup, savoring them slowly. She ate everything, right down to the last piece of fruit.

When her brother was done, he reached out his hand to pick up his mug. His sister froze and looked at him.

Will she stop him? Masyu leaned forward without thinking, his eyes intent on her profile. Her hands were trembling, and her slender neck was taut, the tendons like rigid cords.

The boy grasped the double-handled mug with both hands and brought it to his lips. His sister watched him steadily without trying to stop him.

He gulped the contents down, then placed the mug on the floor and stretched his hand towards a piece of fruit that still lay on his plate. But before he could reach it, his head drooped, and he fell forward.

His sister caught him and laid him on his side with his head resting in her lap. Something glistened on her cheeks.

She stooped over her brother, cradling his listless head in her hands, then straightened and reached for his mug. Grasping one of its handles, she hurled it toward the window outside which Masyu stood. It hit the side of the tent with a dull sound, and Masyu jerked his head back.

Uraili jumped to his feet, but the girl didn't even glance at him. Keeping her eyes fixed on the spot where Masyu was, she grabbed her own mug and drank the contents down. Her dark eyes gleamed fiercely as she glared at the window.

Masyu's stomach clenched as he gazed back at her. *That's right. I'm the one who poisoned your drink.*

Heat rose in his chest, and he began to tremble from head to toe. *You picked up the scent of my fingers in it, didn't you? And the owner of that scent standing right here.*

A smile spread across his face, although he was unaware of it. His body felt like it was on fire. He kept his gaze fixed on her face until the strength drained from her eyes and she fell forward.

* * *

Jookuchi emerged from his tent, flanked by aides. A large rug lay on the grass before him. In the dim light of the soldiers' torches, he could make out the bodies of the girl and her brother sprawled upon it. The paleness of their faces was evident even in the darkness, and they looked smaller than when they'd been alive.

He gazed down on them for some time, then knelt and placed a hand in front of the boy's mouth to make sure he wasn't breathing. After doing the same for the girl, he gently touched her cheek, then snatched his hand away as though startled.

"They're so cold. They haven't been dead that long, have they?"

From where he stood on the other side of the rug, Masyu said quietly, "I used hirin, ice weed."

Jookuchi nodded. Rising to his feet, he sighed and flicked his eyes to the soldiers. "Wrap them in woolen shrouds and bury them," he said. Then, turning on his heel, he went back into the tent.

It was the custom in West Kantal to bury children under a yugi tree. According to local folklore, a mother bereaved of her child had thrown herself into a river in her grief and drowned. When her body washed up on the river bank, a yugi tree grew from it, and so people believed that if they buried dead children under a yugi tree, its spirit would gently guide the children's souls to heaven.

The soldiers who had been sent out before sunset to find a suitable burial spot had already returned, and they swiftly loaded the bodies onto a cart and carried them across the meadow into the forest. They buried them in a hole dug at the foot of a yugi tree along the bank of a stream.

Being family men with children of their own, the soldiers didn't dump the bodies into the grave, but instead wrapped them carefully in woolen shrouds to keep them from the cold and laid them gently at the bottom of the hole. After filling this with earth to keep wild beasts from getting at them, they bowed deeply toward the grave. Only then did they return to the camp.

No sooner had the clip-clop of their horses' hooves receded into the distance than three figures leaped from the darkness of the trees and began frantically digging up the grave. Hauling out the bundled corpses, they placed them on the grass beside the hole and hastily removed the shrouds that covered them from head to toe.

After wrapping the bodies in woolen blankets, one man

picked up the girl while the other picked up the boy. Together, they melted back into the forest. The third man placed the shrouds in which they had been wrapped back into the grave, reshaping them to look like the bodies were still there. He filled in the hole, restoring it to its former state, while the light of the setting moon gilded the tips of the branches in the forest.

4

Scent Voices

A delicious aroma wafted on the air.

Jiiya's baking tapa. It must be time to get up. I'd better wake Milucha.

With that thought, memory cracked through Aisha's mind like lightning. Pain stabbed her chest, then spread like bitter water through her throat and into her head.

She opened her mouth and gasped achingly for air. The breath whistled in her throat, and with it, scents assaulted her nostrils: tapa baking, woodsmoke, two men, and a dog.

Within that flood of smells, she detected the scent of Milucha. She could feel his warmth where their arms touched.

He's alive!

She opened her eyes to look at him, but the world spun around her so viciously she closed them again and waited for the dizziness to subside.

She heard one of the men say, "She's coming to." She struggled desperately to sort through the confusion in her brain and grasp what was going on.

I drank milk liquor laced with hirin.

She had watched Milucha drink down the poison and then drunk her own.

So why?

Though her eyes were shut, she sensed one of the men rise and draw near. She knew without seeing who he was.

"You're awake, aren't you, Lady Aisha Keluahn?"

She opened her eyes slowly and looked at him. Although she

was still slightly dizzy, she could see his features clearly. Dark eyes in a handsome, tanned face regarded her steadily.

"Why?" she croaked.

He turned and called over his shoulder for water, perhaps noticing the hoarseness of her voice. When a jug of water was brought, he slipped his hand under her head, gently raising her. His large hand felt warm and strong.

Water was poured into a bowl. She sipped it, and smelled old cedar. It must have been carried in a wooden barrel. Still, it slipped deliciously down her parched throat. After draining the bowl, she handed it back, and the man took it silently.

Aisha looked up at him. With each movement he made, the scent of seikoso grew stronger. He must have kept it in his cloak for a long time. Although the smell had merged with and been transmuted by his own scent, it was definitely fragrant bluegrass.

"Why?" she repeated, but he shook his head.

"There's no time to explain right now. I'll tell you tonight. Until then, rest here."

She turned her head, trying to see her brother. The man rose to his feet. "Your brother's fine," he said. "He woke up a little earlier but fell asleep again. He's wrapped snuggly in wool blankets so he shouldn't catch cold. You should warm yourself too. I'll leave my man here to guard you. If anything should happen, do as he says."

With these words, he strode over to the fire, handed the wooden bowl to the other man and grabbed a flatbread from a pile on a plate. Shoving this into his mouth, he walked off into the trees.

The dog lying beside the fire at his master's feet kept its eyes trained on Aisha and her brother.

"If you're feeling well enough to get up, would you like to come sit by the fire and have some tapa?" the man said. His face was slender, but his eyes had the keen glint of a hunter.

Aisha pushed her hands against the ground and sat up slowly. Her head swam a little, but the dizziness soon passed. She walked to the fire and sat down. As the warmth seeped into her skin, she realized she was chilled to the core.

Hirin freezes the body.

If eaten by mistake, the weed chilled a person so rapidly they died without feeling any pain, as though they'd gone to sleep.

So why am I still alive?

Grasping the fragrant tapa between his finger tips, the man deftly flicked it from the griddle onto a plate and slathered it with butter and honey before passing the plate to Aisha. As the warmth seeped through the wooden plate into her palm, the hard shell that had encased her heart cracked and crumbled, and the realization that she was alive spread through her.

She had thought there was no escape, that this was the end of her life.

Expecting to be beheaded, she'd been relieved to learn they'd be killed with ice weed instead. At least they could die more easily. Waiting for death had been bone-shaking terror, but when the moment arrived and she watched her brother drink the poison, her fear vanished. The whole world turned black. Darkness swallowed her, her brother, her whole life.

When she'd caught the scent of that man's fingers in milk liquor, a fierce rage had pierced her brow. To be sentenced to death just because of their lineage. It was so unfair. Fury at her inability to right that injustice seemed to burn right through her.

Slowly, she picked up the thin round tapa from the warm wooden plate and folded it into a manageable size before popping it in her mouth. The rich, salty flavor of the butter mingled with the sweetness of the honey. The taste was so familiar.

The tapa they'd been served during their imprisonment had smelled different. This one, however, was the kind she'd always eaten, and as the aroma penetrated deep into her nostrils, tears welled in her eyes. Averting her gaze so the man wouldn't see her weep, she devoured the warm, fragrant flatbread.

The dog rose slowly and slunk over to her side, placing its cold snout against her elbow.

"Hey you! Sit! You'll get yours later!" the man said. The dog gave him a disgruntled look and sank down beside Aisha.

"Where are we?" Aisha asked.

"Near Green Water Canyon."

Aisha looked around her in surprise. They were so close to home . . . although there was no home for her there now. A pang of sorrow followed on the heels of that thought. "Why are we here?" she asked.

The man shook his head, spreading more oil and batter on the griddle. "I'm just following orders. I don't know anything. You'd better ask Sir Masyu when he comes back."

Aisha blinked. "Masyu," she repeated. "His name's Masyu?"

The man nodded. "Yes, Sir Masyu Kashuga."

It was a long time before the man named Masyu returned. In the meantime, Milucha woke up, gobbled down the supper cooked by the man with the dog, asked Aisha to explain what had happened, peppered her with questions she couldn't answer, then curled up beside the fire and went back to sleep. Aisha felt so drained herself that she lay beside him and closed her eyes, even though the sun hadn't set. She slept fitfully, however, waking frequently to make sure she and her brother were really alive before sinking back into oblivion.

Sometimes a scent slipping through the underbrush on the wind woke her. Smells emitted by vegetation usually subsided after sundown, but when chewed by insects or other creatures, plants cried out in the language of scents.

Could you please be quiet, just for a little? Aisha silently begged an ainala tree. It had been sending out a distress call for some time, and she guessed that insects, a lot of them, were consuming its leaves.

Such calls began as a slow murmur but went on for ages. Surrounding trees responded, emitting acrid warnings in all directions. These odors became quite distressing once Aisha noticed them. What was worse, plant scents slid down and rolled along the forest floor, fanning outward, so that when she slept on the ground like this, she felt them more acutely.

If it had been daytime, birds and other natural enemies of the pests would have responded eagerly to the tree's summons, but now that night had fallen, nocturnal insects ruled the world. Some insects hid in the soil during the day, only appearing at night to feast on leaves while their enemies slept.

It wasn't just plant scents that bothered Aisha once they caught her attention. Animals also gave off odors intense enough to jolt her from sleep. That's why at home she'd always slept on the second floor with the windows shut.

During the day, she was so used to the clamor of scents that she could tune them out, much like the bustle of the marketplace, which overwhelmed her whenever she left the quiet forest, but then faded quickly into background noise. At night, however, the abrupt squeal of a mouse accompanied by the stench of terror and fresh blood just as she was falling asleep would startle her and set her heart pounding, keeping her awake. Nocturnal beasts had heavy odors, which made ground-level scents particularly annoying at night. Although they still reached her on the second floor, carried by the wind, they were much noisier near the ground.

She'd tried to explain this to Jiiya, but he'd laughed and looked puzzled. "Noisy?" he'd repeated doubtfully. "Smells?"

Watching his face, she'd ached with the loneliness that comes from never being understood. "Noisy" was the best word she could think of to describe her experience; nothing else quite captured what she felt.

Ever since she was born, she'd been able to pick up the scents of the living things around her—and all the interactions that took place through them. To her, smells were like words conveying meaning. It wasn't that beasts or plants spoke like humans, but when chewed by an insect, a plant's scent felt like it was shrieking, "Ow! That hurts! A bug's eating me!" The same way a bell clanging in a fire tower seemed to shout, "Fire! Fire!" or Aisha's mother's sigh and wry smile seemed to say, "Aisha! Honestly!"

Unlike human voices, smells lingered. They were always there, but those that wafted from the forest at night were far more disturbing. Night-blooming flowers began emitting their fragrance at dusk, drawing moths and other nocturnal insects with their scent. Though powerful, those smells were pleasant, like a love song. But there were other scents that rose from the night forest, and when tinged with the sharp scent of creatures being harried and killed, they sometimes swelled to a cacophony that pressed against Aisha's chest and set her on edge.

The only person who had ever understood this was her mother. Although Aisha's younger brother shared her sensitivity to smell to some degree, it didn't seem to bother him as much, perhaps because he was more easygoing by nature. Her father hadn't understood at all. Neither had Jiiya. Although she'd tried many times as a child to explain, each time, Jiiya had just laughed uncomfortably.

A bleak loneliness spread through her at these memories, as though her heart were sinking to the bottom of the night. Even now, with her brother right beside her, this loneliness was always there. It had lurked coldly inside her ever since she could remember.

Her mother had carried it too. She recalled her mother's pale, fever-ridden face gazing up from the bed in the dimly lit room that smelled of medicine. She heard the whisper of her voice coming back to her now as if pulled by a thread.

"You're lonely too, aren't you?" she'd murmured as she reached out to brush a lock of hair from Aisha's forehead. "So am I. This loneliness never leaves, no matter who I'm with. I can think of lots of reasons for it, but maybe there's really no reason at all. I'm just lonely."

Aisha remembered the dry heat of her mother's fingers; the scent of her skin; her voice, weak and delirious with fever as she whispered, half talking to herself.

"All creatures are lonely," she'd continued. "That's why we call out. We shout futilely into the emptiness, without even realizing we've raised our voices."

Mother . . .

Aisha had been too young to understand then, but now she understood all too well. Every living creature bore this loneliness. Which was probably why they constantly cried out, unconsciously releasing their scents.

These scent voices had filled Aisha's world all her life. Hearing them was normal. When had she first realized that it wasn't normal for others?

Even Jiiya, who was quick to understand everything else, had been unable to grasp that scents could speak.

Jiiya . . .

His face rose in her mind, and her heart constricted. Rugged yet kind, he'd cared for her and Milucha not just out of the loyalty of a family retainer, but as their foster father when they lost first one parent and then the other to illness.

Where he is now?

Was he imprisoned somewhere in the same camp where she and Milucha had been held? Or had he already been killed?

Pain shot through her chest at this thought. She couldn't bear to think of life without him. Of all those who had served her family, he was the only one who'd stayed, standing by them faithfully even after her grandfather was driven from the throne. As a child, she hadn't understood the implications, but now she knew just how rare and precious his loyalty had been. Keluahn had not simply been deposed. As Jookuchi had said, he'd been so reviled by his own people that they'd dragged him from the throne.

Keluahn's subjects weren't the only ones who'd despised him.

Father hated him too . . .

Although she tried hard to ignore it, Aisha knew that within the shadows of her own heart, she also harbored a bitter resentment toward her grandfather.

Her memories of their escape from West Kantal were fragmented, but she could still recall the smell of her father's back and the freezing cold of the blizzard. Her clearest memory was of hunger. Even though she'd cried and pleaded for food, she'd been given none.

The few provisions they'd managed to bring with them were quickly exhausted, and any villages they happened to stumble upon while wandering in the mountains were stricken by such severe famine that their inhabitants had nothing to spare for outsiders. Even now, the gaunt faces and huge eyes of the starving children in those villages haunted Aisha's dreams. Nor could she forget how her mother, pregnant with Milucha, had gritted her teeth in pain as she walked. The grimace on the face of one who'd always been so kind and strong had frightened Aisha.

There'd also been the rush of joy at her first sip of the hot soup the Makishi had fed them when she and her family had finally reached this land. But their days together didn't last long. Hunger and the arduous journey had eroded her mother's health, and after Milucha's birth, she was often laid up with fever. Still, she carried on, raising Milucha and Aisha with love and affection until she could no longer get out of bed.

Aisha saw the figure of her father slumped by her mother's sickbed in the dimly lit room, heard his voice, lamenting, "If only you hadn't been pregnant at that time, if only you'd had enough food and sleep, it wouldn't have come to this. If only you hadn't married me . . ."

Her mother's scent sprang into her nose. With it came an image of her mother's face, which was now beyond her reach.

Mother . . .

How she longed to see her again. To hug her and feel her arms around her. Wrapped in the moist forest air, Aisha thought of her parents, remembering their scents, their faces, their voices.

We had happy times too. They didn't last long, but we had them.

The firelight flickering on her mother's face as she sat embroidering beside Aisha's father, the smells in the room, remained engraved on her memory. But all of that was gone, lost in the past.

The black despair that had engulfed her as she'd watched Milucha raise the cup of poison to his lips had been tempered by the thought that they could now join their mother and father. But when she'd smelled that man's scent from the drink, a burning rage had flared inside her.

They weren't leaving this world by choice. They were being snuffed out because they were in the way. At that thought, everything she'd kept inside had erupted.

You're like an ant nest in the wall of a dike. Ordinarily, there'd be no harm in letting you be. But if a storm came, that nest could cause the dike to collapse, bringing disaster to the whole country . . . If you need to blame your fate on something, blame your lineage.

They'd done nothing wrong. Yet their mere existence meant trouble. That's all they were—in the way.

So . . . why are we still alive?

Cloaked in the scent of the night air and filled with anger, futility, and confusion, Aisha stared into the darkness behind her eyelids.

* * *

The touch of a hand on her shoulder jolted her awake. For a moment, she couldn't remember where she was.

"I'm sorry to wake you, but now's the best time to talk. Do you still want to know more?"

Rubbing her eyes, Aisha nodded and sat up. She reached over to wake Milucha, but Masyu touched her hand and shook his head. "Let him sleep. You can explain later."

The fire had died down to embers, and both the dog and the man were gone. There was just Masyu, kneeling by the fire and stoking it with twigs. Aisha went over and sat by the firepit, watching Masyu and the flames. Once they blazed strong enough, he settled himself on the ground. "Well then, where shall I start? What would you like to know?"

"Why are we still alive? Even though we drank hirin?" Aisha asked, her voice hard. She fixed her eyes on his face, remembering his scent rising from the poisoned mug. Up close, she realized he was younger than she'd thought. "You're the one who put the hirin in our drinks, right?"

Masyu shot her a crooked smile. "That's why you threw the mug at me, isn't it?"

Aisha nodded slowly, her eyes still watching his face. "You poisoned our drinks and we drank them," she said. "The fact that we're still alive can only mean one thing. You gave us the antidote. But why? And how?"

Masyu stretched his hands toward the fire. "Did you know that the effectiveness of ice weed depends on how much you use?"

Aisha gave a short gasp. *So that's it! He didn't give us the antidote. He adjusted the dose.*

Jiiya had once told her of a boy who'd accidentally eaten hirin. He'd stopped breathing and had no pulse. Believing him dead, his weeping parents dug his grave and laid him out in it, but when they began filling it in, the boy woke up. He survived because the amount he'd eaten was small. Aisha's mother had told her hirin was an unusual poison. For those who survived, recovery was surprisingly fast.

Aisha frowned. "But . . . how could you know? We're not even the same size or build."

Masyu kept his eyes on the fire. "To be honest, it was an extremely risky gamble. But it was the only way to save your lives." He raised his eyes to her face. "I had to use hirin to convince Jookuchi you'd died."

Aisha stared at him. His tanned face glowed faintly in the firelight. "But why? You're the one who told him the route we were going to take. Why save our lives after letting him catch us?"

Masyu gazed silently at the flames for some time, then raised his head and looked at her. She sensed a tension in his eyes. "I let Jookuchi capture you for the reason he told you. In reality, it's unlikely that what he fears will ever happen. The possibility of the Makishi of Tohula Ila turning against the empire is negligible. But one of Jookuchi's informants found out that the hostile clan know the Makishi hold you in high regard and that they hoped to use you to win the Makishi to their side. That really upset Jookuchi. He looks tough, but in reality, he's quite cautious. Although I tried to convince him there were other ways to prevent that, he was adamant we shouldn't let it go if there was the least possibility it could happen."

Masyu's tone was dispassionate. "It's true that nothing's ever certain, and eliminating you would be the safest way. It wouldn't be a bad choice for the empire either, so I guessed that even if I stopped him, he'd likely go ahead anyway."

"That's not what I'm asking!" Aisha snapped. "Why did you help us?"

The look in Masyu's eyes shifted. His scent changed too. The smell of sweat grew stronger, as if his body temperature had risen slightly.

"Because . . ." he said huskily, "my mother is a Makishi."

5
Ohaleh Rice

Aisha opened the shutters on the carriage window and gasped.

It's so bright!

A sea of golden grain spread as far as the horizon. With each passing breeze, waves of light rippled across it and the scent of ohaleh washed over Aisha. She'd been aware of it for some time—an extraordinarily powerful scent, unlike that of any other plant.

Beside her, Jiiya said, "Ripe ohaleh, ready for harvest. Spectacular, isn't it?"

"What? What? Let me see!" Milucha bounced off the seat on the other side of the carriage, pushed past Jiiya and tried to stick his head out the window.

Jiiya grabbed him hastily. "You mustn't do that, my lord! You'll unbalance the carriage. Please go and open the other window. You can see the same scenery on the other side."

Jiiya watched Milucha climb back on the seat and open the shutters on the other window. "There are many ohaleh fields in this region," he said, "so the scenery is pretty much the same from here on. Once we enter the empire proper, we'll come to the Great Yuino Plain. Ohaleh has been grown in the empire since ancient times, so it covers a vast area. It's quite an impressive sight. Most of the seeds distributed to the protectorates come from there."

Aisha could hear the pride in Jiiya's voice. He'd been to the empire proper when he was engaged in trading.

Ohaleh . . .

The precious grain brought from Ohaleh Mazura, the land of the gods, by the Kokun, the Scent Goddess, to save the starving people long ago when the land was colder and the crops failed to ripen in the parched soil. The grain for which Aisha's grandfather Keluahn had been driven from his throne.

The Lady Kokun was always reborn and so, never died. Even now, she lived in the Kokun Palace in the imperial capital. Knowing all things through their scent, she used her wisdom to guide the people. Ohaleh was also the staple food of West Kantal, where Aisha had been born and raised, and if a village had enough money, it would send a representative to the capital at the beginning of the year to pray at the palace for a bountiful harvest.

Although Aisha had seen ohaleh sold at the local market, she'd never been to any fields where it was grown, even those near the marketplace. This was her first time to see the ripening grain.

Bobbing in the breeze, the heavy-laden ears looked charming, but their scent voices made her frown. As the carriage passed through the fields, she found the monotonous drone of ohaleh's fragrance disturbing and oppressive, like an ache in the center of her forehead, just between her brows. It was very different from the scents she was used to picking up from field and forest.

Fragrances that wafted from wild woods and meadows were boisterous, as if carrying on lively conversations about this or that. When she stepped from a forest into a farm field or vegetable plot, those voices scattered and faded, and the quietness of the neatly organized rows made her feel a little sad. Yet even then, she could still pick up faint scents—a yelp when being chewed or a sigh of contentment in the warm sun. As a child, she'd often crouched down in the vegetable patch just to hear those little voices.

But ohaleh didn't smell like any of those. Its scent voice seemed alien—hushed and repetitive, like something breathing, in-out, in-out, yet strangely intimidating. It exuded the stillness of pent-up anger, a stifled longing to cry out, as though each grain shook with suppressed emotion and one day might crack to emit a bloodcurdling scream.

It made Aisha uncomfortable, and she gently closed the shutter and stared at the pattern of light and shadow that fell through the slats. Words from the Ode to the Kokun popped into her mind.

Ohaleh in the wetlands, ohaleh where the wind blows,

To every land, our compassionate Lady Kokun grants the precious gift of ohaleh.

As the ode said, ohaleh was now cultivated in every part of the Umal Empire, including the protectorates. Where paddy fields weren't possible, it was grown as upland rice in dry fields, and it was now rare to see any other type of rice, or even other grains, being cultivated.

As Aisha thought of ohaleh, the scent of her father came back to her—the way he'd smelled when he'd talked about her grandfather, Keluahn.

Keluahn was a wise man, a hero who'd managed to quell civil unrest and establish a stable government in West Kantal despite relentless inter-clan conflicts. Recognized by the empire for his capacity and character, he'd succeeded in making West Kantal a protectorate without fighting any battles. He'd worked hard to extend the network of underground aqueducts and improve maintenance methods, thereby expanding the amount of arable land. Even so, with its nutrient-poor soil and wide stretches of wasteland, West Kantal frequently suffered from famine. Yet, for some reason, her grandfather had declined to introduce ohaleh, although the right to cultivate it was granted to all subjects within the empire.

Ohaleh was a miracle grain. It could be grown several times

a year, even on land that was unsuited to other types of rice or in cold regions with poor soil, and the yield was at least twice that of conventional grains, or even three or four times if conditions were right. It was resistant to cold and drought, and pests avoided it. Weeds didn't grow where it was planted either, saving farmers the arduous job of weeding. Even with dry rice farming, it didn't cause the kind of problems that normally occurred with continuous cropping.

The only place it didn't grow was by the sea, but that drawback was of no concern to landlocked West Kantal. The sea was far away in the kingdom of Takketsu on the other side of the Tenro Mountains and the kingdom of Mazalia on the other side of the Choryo Mountains, which spread like a long wall along West Kantal's southern border.

And ohaleh rice was delicious. It had just the right chewiness and could be used in a variety of ways. The West Kantalese, who were used to making tapa with wheat flour, were soon captivated by the taste of rice flour tapa, and eagerly adopted this along with steamed rice, pounded rice cakes, and other rice dishes learned from the Umalese.

It was said that eating ohaleh made people physically stronger and more fertile. In other countries, it was treated as a medicine and prized for bartering. Many of the clan chiefs in West Kantal had declared allegiance to the empire precisely because they wanted ohaleh, and they were alienated by Keluahn's stubborn refusal to introduce it. When a terrible famine struck the land, the people's anger reached its peak, and they drove Keluahn from power.

Keluahn did not accompany Aisha's family on the journey she remembered as one of bitter cold and hunger. Afraid of exposing his family to danger, he rejected her father's pleas and remained behind in the capital of West Kantal. In the plaza where starving citizens gathered to get rations, he took his own life.

Her father's scent when he'd told her this was still fresh in

Aisha's mind. "I think it was his way of apologizing to those who would have lived if he'd accepted ohaleh and all those suffering from starvation. But I also think he still believed his decision was at least partly justified."

Conflicting emotions—anger and resentment, love and affection—swirled in her father's scent. "He called ohaleh the rice of joy and sorrow," he said. "Kantal was poor. There isn't much land for farming in the mountains, and the lowlands are full of rocks and poor soil. When my father ruled, neighboring East Kantal was the first to declare allegiance to the empire and become a protectorate. The soil there is even poorer than ours, and they often suffered from famines and had to turn to us for aid. That's how poor they were. But once they became a protectorate and started growing ohaleh, they prospered. The transformation seemed truly miraculous. When they saw this, the people of West Kantal naturally wanted to grow ohaleh too, but my father wouldn't allow it."

The sorrow in his eyes deepened. "Ohaleh is indeed a miracle grain. It thrives even in poor soil and can be planted several times a year. It's pest resistant, and replanting doesn't deplete the soil or cause other common problems. It even tastes good. The only drawback is that farmers can't produce their own seed rice."

Oddly enough, grains from harvested ohaleh wouldn't sprout when planted. The empire's Ministry of Wealth provided each protectorate with all the seed rice it required for the next harvest in accordance with the amount of tax paid to the empire.

"Your grandfather used to say, 'It's the perfect yoke,'" said Aisha's father. "Ohaleh frees us from the fear of starvation. It can make our people fat and rich. But the price is servitude."

He shook his head. "I know his feelings were noble. He wasn't motivated merely by a desire for political autonomy. He was afraid we wouldn't be able to grow other crops if we started cultivating ohaleh. And of what would happen if ohaleh failed once we'd become dependent on it. But I can't believe anything matters more than the lives being lost right in front of us."

With a harrowed look, he said, "You remember, don't you? The agony of starvation. The burning hunger and the despair that makes everything seem futile. I've lived through that repeatedly, ever since I was a child, and it still gives me nightmares. If I were the one faced with that choice, I wouldn't have chosen the path my father took."

Bitterness filled his eyes. "I couldn't dissuade him. I couldn't convince him to save his people. Aisha, I bear a great sin. I committed an unpardonable crime, one that resulted in death for many people. I wanted to stay behind and take my own life to beg their forgiveness. But I couldn't."

Her father had chosen to flee to save the lives of his family—his pregnant wife and Aisha. Because of the guilt he bore, he never ate ohaleh. Which was why neither Aisha nor Milucha had ever tasted it.

Aisha had never found this a hardship as the young men from the Makishi clan that lived in Tohula Ila brought them things like buckwheat, beans and wheat, carrying supplies down every ten days from the mountains.

The soil was too poor to grow rice in the Tenro mountain region where Tohula Ila was located, and the people who lived in the foothills had always survived on wheat and buckwheat. But ohaleh flourished even where other types of rice wouldn't grow, and it was now being farmed extensively even in the foothills. For some reason, however, the Makishi called it the "cursed rice" and stuck to growing the same crops they'd always cultivated. For this reason, they called Keluahn, who had refused to introduce ohaleh into West Kantal, the "true king" and took in Aisha and her family and helped them survive.

Aisha recalled the darkly tanned faces of those young men as they descended the steep mountain path bearing a load that must have been at least half their height. The image called forth Masyu's face where he'd sat by the campfire.

She had laughed at him when he'd told her his mother was Makishi. "Don't tell me lies even a child could see through," she'd said.

"What makes you so sure I'm lying?"

"You belong to the House of Kashuga. You really think I'd believe the mother of someone from an imperial clan came from the remote depths of the Tenro Mountains?" Her sarcastic grin faded, however, at the sudden strength of his scent. The smell of anger.

His expression hadn't budged, but she knew he was holding back his rage.

"If you don't believe me, fine. I know it must sound incredible." As his voice overlayed his scent, Aisha realized his anger wasn't directed at her.

He dropped his eyes to the fire but seemed to be seeing something else. "My father was the younger brother of the previous head of Kashuga Lai, the New House of Kashuga. He was a bit different. Despite being born a Kashuga, he had no interest in politics. From the time he was in his teens, he traveled throughout the empire with the koshi when they inspected cultivated areas. Eventually, he extended his travels to the frontier lands and met my mother in a remote part of the Tenro Mountains."

Illuminated by the fire, his face twisted slightly. "My father kept wandering even after marrying my mother, so for fourteen years, she raised me as a Makishi in Tohula Ila."

For some time, Masyu remained silent watching the crackling wood and the flickering flames. Aisha couldn't guess what he was thinking, but she could tell from his scent that his anger was under control.

He raised his eyes and looked at her. "My cousin delivered supplies to your family."

Aisha gasped. "Really?"

Masyu nodded. With the heavy accent of the People of the Ravine, he told her that her mother had always given his uncle and cousins tea and sweets when they took wheat and beans to her house. The way he seemed to swallow his words sounded exactly like the Makishi. He grinned. "I was seventeen."

He paused, looking at her with a soft expression, but a moment later his smile faded. "Two years before that, when I turned fifteen, my father told me I must live as a man of the Kashuga family."

Aisha gazed back at him silently.

"My father's elder brother had three sons, but two of them died of illness, one after the other, leaving only the youngest. My grandfather decided this one should have a foster brother to assist him, and he ordered my father to give me to his older brother, my uncle, as a foster child."

He ran a hand over his face. "That's how it happened. Are you satisfied?"

The Makishi didn't like outsiders, and Aisha had heard they had strict rules around marriage. It seemed strange that a Makishi woman would marry an outsider and bear his child, but she didn't know them well enough to say it could never have happened. And Masyu spoke the Makishi dialect so perfectly, she doubted he'd learned it by studying.

"Is that why you saved us?" she asked quietly.

"It's one of the reasons," he said. "I'm an imperial inspector, the emperor's eyes. I observe the situation in each protectorate while considering the empire as a whole. Unlike Jookuchi, who only thinks of West Kantal."

He nudged a piece of wood in the fire with a stick and added some kindling. "If the balance of power in West Kantal were to shift—if, for example, Jookuchi were to get sick and die a few years from now—your existence might become important."

He looked at her and said in a low voice, "Things can change at any time, and in many different ways. I try to save lives that don't need eliminating and hang onto potentially strategic pieces we might regret losing. That's my job."

The carriage continued to sway as they sped along the road. Milucha, probably bored by the endless sea of ohaleh, was curled up on the seat asleep. Jiiya, who had been watching the boy's sleeping face, raised his eyes and looked at Aisha.

"It feels like a dream," she said with a little sigh.

Jiiya heaved a deeper sigh. "Truly. When I saw you both, I told myself that if this were a dream, I didn't want to wake up."

The night Masyu had talked with Aisha by the fire, he'd told her that Jiiya had been freed. Jookuchi, he said, had decided it couldn't be considered a crime for a loyal retainer to protect his lord, and now that his lord was gone, there was no need to fear rebellion. Aisha had trembled with relief and joy at the news.

At dawn the next day, the man with the dog had brought Jiiya to Aisha and her brother. When he'd stepped from the mist that was drifting among the trees, she and Milucha had run up and clung to him, sobbing.

The carriage was rolling along much more smoothly than when they'd traveled through West Kantal. *The roads here must be well maintained,* Aisha thought. It was far more comfortable.

The early afternoon light fell softly on the seat beside her. In its gentle glow, Jiiya's face turned somber. "We may not be able to talk privately again," he said. "My lady, there's something I wish to say while we still have the chance."

He paused as though searching for words. "I am deeply grateful to Sir Masyu—and I mean that sincerely, but . . . I don't know quite how to put this . . . something about him makes me uneasy."

6
Bearer of Fragrant Blue Grass

Aisha kept her eyes on Jiiya's face, waiting for him to continue, but he remained silent. "Me too," she said with a sudden rush of irritation. Although she also found it hard to read Masyu, to hear Jiiya doubting him bothered her. "I think there's a lot he's not telling us. I also think he helped us for some reason of his own . . . but . . ." She faltered, not sure where this was going.

Frowning, Jiiya rubbed the back of his neck. "Actually, I don't believe he was being cold and calculating when he rescued you. It seemed to me he genuinely wanted to save you."

Aisha blinked and stared at him. "You think so?"

Jiiya nodded.

"Why?"

He sighed. "Because he let me go. Of course, rescuing you was likely to his advantage, but if he had just wanted to use you for his own ends, it would have made more sense for him to get rid of me. Me being alive could cause problems later. What Jookuchi said when he freed me suggested it was because of that man's advice. I'm guessing that's probably the case, but I'm not sure why would he have gone to all that trouble. It would have been much easier to kill me than to make Jookuchi let me go. And safer too."

Aisha tilted her head. "I'm not so sure. If you were executed, then both Milucha and I would have hated him. I'm grateful we were saved, but he was the one who gave Jookuchi the information that got you captured. If he wants to use us, making us hate him wouldn't be a good plan."

"But that is exactly the point. Consider carefully. Milucha is young and could easily be won over and controlled, but the same is not true for you, my lady. That means he cares about what you might think. I can't help but feel his choice was governed by consideration for your feelings."

Jiiya shifted his gaze to Milucha, who was sleeping peacefully. "He said he'd arranged for me to work on a farm in the southern part of the imperial capital and told me to raise Milucha there. I don't know what kind of farm it is, but my guess is that it will be run by a good-natured farmer and our lives will be comfortable. Knowing that Milucha is in such a place will ease your mind."

Jiiya continued slowly. "Even if Masyu is hiding his intentions, it will be a much better life than living in fear of being killed by Jookuchi or anyone else who wants to gain control over West Kantal."

Aisha frowned. "Then what's bothering you?"

Jiiya raised his eyes and looked at her. "What bothers me is . . . I think the person he wants to use is you, my lady, not Milucha."

"Me?" Aisha said, startled.

"Yes."

Aisha laughed and shook her head. "You've been thinking too much. I've got no value as a pawn at all. If I did, it's only because I'm Milucha's older sister. He just wants to tame Keluahn's blood kin, to keep us as pieces he can use if the political situation in West Kantal changes."

Jiiya stroked his beard thoughtfully. "Yes, that is certainly part of it. He told me he made it look like you'd both died because he knew that under the current situation, Jookuchi might kill you. He also told me to raise Milucha well, because once West Kantal has been securely unified, Keluahn's achievements might be reconsidered."

His gaze shifted back to Milucha's sleeping face. "Considering the state of West Kantal, that sounds like a very plausible reason. But I have this gut feeling that's not all."

He raised his eyes again and said, "If it were, then it would have made more sense to entrust not just Milucha, but you to my care as well. So why is he separating us and sending you somewhere else?"

I've arranged for you to live at Lia Garden.

When Masyu had told her this, she'd wondered why she was the only one being sent there, but she'd assumed it was because separating them posed less risk and had thought no more about it.

"Maybe he separated me because it will be safer if the three of us aren't together. People come to the capital from West Kantal, and if someone who knew us saw all three of us together, they might notice."

Jiiya shook his head slowly. "Yes, that is true, but . . ."

"But what?"

Jiiya looked troubled. "During our lessons on the empire, do you remember what I taught you about the House of Kashuga? That it's divided in two?"

"Yes, it's split into the old and the new."

Jiiya nodded. "That's right. And do you know to which house Masyu belongs?"

"The New House of Kashuga."

"That's right. He belongs to Kashuga Lai."

Aisha's eyes narrowed. Now she could see what was bothering him.

Jiiya lowered his voice. "While people think Lia Garden belongs to the House of Kashuga, in reality, it belongs to Kashuga Oi, the Ancient House of Kashuga, not the new house. Although the two houses are allies, not enemies, Lia Garden is run by people the Kashuga Lai must be wary of, a place where they can't let down their guard. At the same time, the direct descendants of the head of Kashuga Lai must study at this garden for a fixed period. That's the rule. So, while there's nothing going on at the garden that needs to be concealed from the Kashuga Lai, it's unheard of for someone who doesn't belong to either of the two houses to be allowed to work there."

Aisha stared at him wordlessly.

"For him to send you there is an extraordinary exception. Why would he go to such lengths for you? What does he want from you? That's what makes me uneasy."

It's a beautiful garden surrounded by hills and fields and run by people I know. It may seem hard at first, but once you get used to it, you should be able to live there quite peacefully.

That's what Masyu had told her, but what had he been thinking? Staring vacantly at the fading light, Aisha rubbed her arms. She'd known that there were two Houses of Kashuga, so why hadn't she remembered at the time?

While he was talking . . .

She'd felt at ease. Because he smelled calm and peaceful.

And also . . .

Because he'd been cloaked in the scent of seikoso, fragrant blue grass. She'd instinctively felt he wasn't wicked.

Whenever she smelled fragrant blue grass, it conjured up an image of an elderly man dressed in ragged clothes. A man with a staff striding off into the forest until he disappeared from sight.

She'd encountered him a few months after she'd started living in the foothills of the Tenro Mountains. It must have been late spring or early summer. It was an unusually hot and muggy day, and she'd gotten the urge to go to the river. Although she'd been strictly warned never to go alone, she snuck off when the adults weren't looking.

There was no breeze, and the air felt sticky even in the usually cool forest. The smells around her didn't move, and it was so stifling that she wandered absently and lost track of where she was. No matter how long she walked, the deep forest seemed to go on forever.

Just when she felt like bursting into tears, a refreshing scent wafted toward her; one she'd never smelled before. It felt like a cool breeze stroking her cheek, and she pushed her way through the underbrush until she stumbled into a sunlit glade.

In the middle of the grassy clearing was a spring. Clear water gurgled from it, spilling onto the grass and running off in a little stream out of the glen. Around it, blue flowers bloomed, trembling in a barely perceptible breeze.

Aisha staggered over to the spring, knelt beside it and scooped up water in her hands. The icy coldness soothed her parched throat.

Her memory of what happened next was patchy. She remembered feeling dizzy and guessed she must have passed out by the spring. Through a hazy dreamlike stupor, she recalled someone bending over to look at her. He smelled like the flowers blooming beside the spring. Picking her up, he carried her over to the shade of a tree and laid her down on the cool grass. She woke at the sensation of a cold cloth being placed on her forehead and neck, but although she tried to rise, her body felt so heavy, she couldn't sit up.

In a gruff voice, the man told her to stay there; that help would come soon. She dozed off for a moment, and when she opened her eyes again, the man who'd been kneeling beside her was gone. Turning her head, she saw him striding off into the deep forest. The white sunlight falling through the leaves dappled the back of his worn clothes.

The next time she woke, she saw a Makishi woman who often brought fruit and other things to her family kneeling beside her. At the sight of her face, deep relief washed through Aisha.

The woman gently raised her to a sitting position and gave her cold water to drink. "Goodness sakes! Did you walk all this way by yourself now? Everyone's worried sick about you. I'll take you home, dear, don't you worry."

She slung Aisha lightly onto her back as if she were a knapsack and set off. Her clothes smelled of sunshine.

Lulled by the motion, Aisha started to doze off when she suddenly remembered the man who had picked her up and carried her into the shade.

"Who was that man?" she asked.

The woman paused in her stride for a moment, then carried on. "Ah, so you remember that, do you now? And did you see his face then?"

Aisha shook her head. The sun had been behind him when he'd bent over her, leaving his face in shadow. She'd gotten the impression he was old because of the way he walked when she saw him from behind.

When she explained this haltingly, the woman said, "Good." She sounded relieved.

"Good? Why?"

"He's a litaran."

"Litaran?"

"Uh-huh."

"What's that mean?"

The woman was quiet for so long, Aisha thought she wasn't going to answer, but then she began to speak slowly. "Litaran are seekers. They're seeking answers. They make a vow to the gods of the mountains and fields, the wind, sun and water, and ask for guidance."

Her voice grew husky. "Most of them are sad. They run into some kind of trouble or bad luck and don't know what to do, so they ask the gods for help. They're sad, but they're straight and true inside, and they stick to that path because there's no other."

She kept talking, rocking Aisha on her back. "They bear a sprig of seikoso in their clothes as a sign of their vow. And they never take a wife or make a family. They keep to themselves and live alone."

An image of dappled light dancing on the old man's back as he made his way deep into the forest rose in Aisha's mind. "So they don't like people looking at them?" she asked in a hushed voice.

The woman sighed. "Mm, maybe it's not the looking they mind. Maybe they just don't like people saying things like, 'That man there's a litaran.' Their vows are made in secret, so maybe they don't want people talking about them."

When they drew near Aisha's house, her mother ran towards them shouting and waving her arms. For a long time, she held Aisha tightly without saying a word, tears pouring down her cheeks. Then she gave Aisha a good scolding, but for some reason what stuck in Aisha's mind more than the scolding was the look on her mother's face when she'd told her how she'd been rescued by an elderly litaran in a glade with a spring surrounded by pretty blue flowers.

"Ah," her mother had murmured. "So that's why you smell of fragrant blue grass."

When Aisha had smelled fragrant blue grass in Jookuchi's tent, she'd been overcome with a strange feeling. Cloaked in that fragrance, Masyu had stood out from everyone there. Although he was surrounded by a crowd, to Aisha, he seemed to be standing alone.

Masyu. What's he seeking? What kind of trouble has he run into?

And what does he want from me?

As she listened to Jiiya hesitantly voice his fears, Aisha thought of the fresh smell of the spring and the fragrance of seikoso that glowed like blue light.

Chapter II
Olie

1
The Kokun's Palace

As Aisha stepped down from the carriage, the wind ruffled her hair and tugged at her clothes. It smelled of earth and trees. Although acrid smoke and the odors of iron, horse and man came mingled with it, the wild scent of the mountains was a welcome relief from the insistent smell of ohaleh that had pervaded the long road to the capital.

Aisha walked around the back of the carriage and gazed up in amazement at the imperial palace. On the other side of a deep moat, the enormous structure soared toward the blue sky; its walls were so white they seemed to blend into the peaks behind, which were still snow covered despite the season.

The palace was set on a large, gently sloping hill, and, judging by the formidable stone rampart that encircled it at the midway point, the hill was an integral part of the imperial compound. Black, ant-like figures—most likely soldiers—scurried along the top of the rampart, but the wall was so huge they looked too small to be human.

The stone steps leading to the main gate were wide enough for several dozen people to climb abreast. Spear-bearing guards, their armored helmets gleaming, stood on both sides of the staircase at intervals of several steps.

On the western edge of the palace complex rose a white tower. It was too far away to see clearly, but whatever stone it was made of seemed to give the structure a luminous blue tint.

Aisha's companion had been talking to the coachman, but she returned now. "That's the Tower of the Scented Wind," she said evenly. "The Lady Kokun frequently ascends it to read the fragrances carried by the wind and identify any changes in the weather in each region. Beside it lies her palace, where she resides. We'll enter through the main gate, so please follow me."

With that, the woman, whose name was Mijima, set off across the drawbridge over the moat.

After reaching the capital, Aisha had spent four days at the farm where Milucha and Jiiya would live. There she'd rested to recover from the long journey, but with the arrival of Mijima last night, she'd suddenly become very busy.

Mijima had appeared at the door of the farmhouse just as the sun was setting. Small in build but quick and agile in her movements, she was so darkly tanned that Aisha thought she must be a trader come to sell her wares.

"I am Mijima Olu Kashuga," she said, dispelling Aisha's first impression instantly. Her crisp, concise language marked her as a capable official, and her surname, Olu Kashuga, showed she was from a collateral line of the House of Kashuga.

"I serve the Kokun palace as a senior koshi, a scent emissary," Mijima continued. "Masyu commanded me to take you under my wing until you enter Lia Garden. To work at the garden means to serve the Lady Kokun. Therefore, you must first present yourself to her ladyship. I have prepared clothes for the occasion as you must purify your body and dress appropriately to express reverence. I will teach you the proper etiquette that must be observed."

Once they were alone, Mijima instructed Aisha thoroughly in the workings of the Kokun's palace, how to pay her respects appropriately, and what work she would be doing at Lia Garden.

"There is one additional point. It is extremely important, so please keep it firmly in mind. You are Aisha Loliki of the Makishi, Masyu's cousin on his maternal side."

When Aisha gasped in disbelief, Mijima said slowly and

deliberately, "Lia Garden is off limits to all but the kin of the House of Kashuga. To be related to Masyu's mother is just barely acceptable. But . . ." She lowered her voice. "There is one thing you must be very careful about. This is a sensitive matter, so I must ask that you never mention it to anyone else. Sir Iilu, the head of Kashuga Lai and the Minister of Wealth, does not think well of his younger brother, Sir Masyu. Or perhaps it would be more accurate to say that he is wary of him. If it is necessary for you to know the reason, I am sure that Sir Masyu will explain it to you, but if anyone from Kashuga Lai asks how you came to be at Lia Garden, tell them you have come from West Kantal to study, and say no more. If they ask any further, try to give them the impression you know nothing."

Aisha thought she could guess what Masyu intended. "In other words, you want them to think he sent me to Lia Garden as part of his work as a protectorate inspector. Is that right?"

Mijima raised her brows. After giving Aisha a long, appraising look, her stiff and formal demeanor dissolved and her face softened. "Yes, it is just as you have guessed. To put it simply, we must bring the Makishi, who have stubbornly rejected ohaleh, over to the empire's side. If the Kashuga Lai believe you were brought here to help achieve that aim, it will allay any other suspicions they might have."

Aisha nodded. "I understand. But in that case, I'd like to know more about the background. Otherwise, I can't lie convincingly."

Mijima smiled. "Indeed. I will share with you any points that seem necessary. Oh, and I should warn you that from here on, I will no longer use deferential language toward you as I will be considered higher in rank than you. I hear you are a member of the royal family of West Kantal, and so I apologize if that seems disrespectful."

Aisha shook her head. "You needn't worry. Almost no one

used polite forms of speech when speaking to me in my homeland either."

Aisha followed Mijima across the drawbridge over the deep moat and up the stone stairs. As they climbed, she heard a bell ring from below.

"Aisha, stop there and kneel," Mijima said. Aisha knelt on the cold stone. Two large horse-drawn carriages had pulled up on the other side of the moat. On one rested a palanquin covered in cloth embroidered with glittering gold thread. While servants removed it and placed it on the ground, a nobleman descended from the other carriage. The servants helped him into the palanquin and raised it onto their shoulders, then carried it across the bridge and up the stone steps. As they passed, Aisha caught a whiff of an unfamiliar fragrance mingled with the sweat of the servants. She bowed her head and waited for the palanquin to pass.

The bearers stopped at the main gate, but the guards merely glanced briefly at the passenger, bowed and allowed them to pass. After making sure the palanquin had disappeared inside, Mijima led Aisha up the stairs. When they drew near the gate, the guards on either side of it gestured for them to halt.

Mijima climbed the remaining stairs and showed them a thin metal plate that hung from her neck while she explained the purpose of their visit. One of the guards came down to Aisha and stood in front of her. "Raise your arms and don't move," he said. Quickly but thoroughly, he ran his hands over her body. Even though Aisha knew she carried nothing dangerous, being searched like this made her nervous, as if he might find something, and she fought to keep her face composed.

At last, the guard said, "All right. Proceed."

Once she'd climbed the rest of the stairs to stand beside Mijima, she let out the breath she'd been holding.

They passed through the gate, beautifully decorated with mother of pearl, and were enveloped by a soft breeze. It was a welcome change from the wind outside. Before them spread a wide, verdant garden. Water sprayed from two large fountains, one on either side, and droplets sparkled in the sunlight.

Although she'd heard of them, this was Aisha's first time seeing a fountain. She paused, spellbound. Why the water pumped from underground and spewed into the air didn't overflow the basin and flood the garden was a mystery to her.

High walls surrounded the garden on all sides, shutting out the chilly wind, and sunshine poured into the space, gleaming on the foliage.

Although they were already through the main gate and within the palace grounds, the imperial palace still seemed far away. Now that she could see it in its entirety, Aisha's eyes widened in surprise.

From below, the building had looked as white as snow, but now she saw that the lower half was covered in a delicate gold pattern. Although still some distance from it, she could see ripe golden ears of grain depicted with such skilled artisanship that the white palace seemed to be floating on a sea of rice undulating in a gentle breeze.

The garden that spread before them was as large as the marketplace in Aisha's hometown, and the people walking there appeared small, like insects. The palanquin that had passed them on the stairs had been set down a little inside the main gate, and the nobleman was now climbing into a carriage that had been waiting for him. The carriage set off along a broad avenue that traveled straight down the middle of the garden, and people walking beside the road stopped and bowed their heads or knelt until it had passed.

"That was Sir Iilu Kashuga," Mijima murmured.

Surprised, Aisha stared after the carriage that was heading toward the palace. Although she'd only caught a glimpse of him, the gentleman was nothing like what she'd imagined. Tall with aquiline features, he did, however, resemble Masyu.

"I thought he would be much older," she said.

"He's still in his thirties. A very shrewd and able man." Mijima set off again, urging Aisha to follow her.

They turned off the road to the imperial palace and onto one that led toward the Kokun's palace, eventually coming to a blue gate. Once they passed through it, the scenery changed yet again.

A variety of flowers, shrubs and trees grew along both sides of the road, and bees and other insects flitted among them. The fragrances that wrapped themselves around her made Aisha feel safe and secure, as though cloaked in a familiar robe. Perhaps it was because the trees here resembled those that grew in her homeland.

The garden of the Kokun's palace was vast and so thick with vegetation that it seemed they were walking in the woods rather than in a garden. Here and there a sunny glade appeared, and in each of these there were always people robed in white and bowed in prayer facing the direction of the Kokun's palace. These were pilgrims who had traveled from every part of the empire to pray for a bountiful harvest. Aisha guessed that some were from West Kantal as well. Coached in advance by Mijima, she averted her eyes and passed them silently.

Even though she sensed the presence of many people within the palace grounds, it was so hushed Aisha began to find the silence oppressive.

The fragrances changed abruptly, as if she'd walked through an invisible wall. Before her, the road forked into three paths, each disappearing among the trees.

Mijima stopped in front of Aisha and bowed her head.

Ah, so this is the place.

Aisha remembered what Mijima had taught her the previous night at the farm. *At a certain point along the way, those who make pilgrimage to the Kokun's palace for the first time must choose their own path.*

Known as the Quiet Way, the path to the palace branched off in many places, but Mijima had told her not to worry because all paths eventually led to the same place. Aisha had asked why they did it this way, but Mijima had merely said it was the rule of pilgrimage.

Aisha passed Mijima, who stood with bowed head, and set foot on one of the paths. Mijima followed.

Aisha had chosen the path without hesitation. Because from somewhere along it came the scent of fragrant blue grass. It was faint, as if from flowers blooming a long way off, but it rode the wind like a glittering spider thread, fluttering through the trees. Not only the flowers but also the stems and leaves exuded a refreshing scent, one that she could never forget.

As she moved farther away from the neighboring paths, the scent grew stronger. Just as she realized the types of trees were changing, the path branched in three directions. Once again, she chose the one that smelled most strongly of fragrant blue grass.

Eventually, she came to a glade filled with sunshine. A small spring gurgled in the middle, surrounded by a patch of flowers. Their pretty blue petals shone in the pool of sunlight.

Fragrant blue grass . . .

The path continued past the glade and deeper into the trees. As she followed it, the fragrances changed. In the dancing light that sifted through the leaves, Aisha moved as if in a dream.

Myriad scents wafting from every species of tree, plant, moss, and mushroom wove together, their conversations creating a pleasant harmony that enveloped her, caressing her skin. It was so tranquil, so serene.

Once she passed that spot, a few discordant notes interrupted the tranquility, only to merge into another indescribably pleasant place. This happened repeatedly, and each time Aisha came to a fork in the road, she chose the one that exuded a calm, pleasing fragrance, until she finally emerged into the light.

The area before her was covered in white sand, in the middle of which reared an enormous, chalk-white building with a roof rounded like a hill. Beside it rose a tower that glowed with a bluish tint.

Aisha's eyes were drawn first to the tower, but when she directed her gaze to the building below it, she gasped in surprise. Just as the walls of the imperial palace had been decorated with golden rice, a colorful pattern adorned the lower half of the white walls of the Kokun's palace. Depicted there was a profusion of blue flowers on green stalks that conjured up an image of the glade Aisha had seen as a child.

She turned to ask Mijima if the flowers were seikoso, but froze when she saw her expression. Mijima was staring at her, the color drained from her face.

Aisha opened her mouth to ask if she was all right, but then hastily swallowed her words. She remembered that, having entered the garden of the Kokun's palace, she was forbidden to speak unless asked a direct question.

Mijima took a deep breath, as if trying to pull herself together, then walked silently past Aisha and began leading the way.

As they drew closer to the Kokun's palace, Aisha sensed the fragrances receding. Unlike the blissful, harmonious hush of the forest, the stillness here resembled the total absence of sound.

Because it's surrounded by sand, Aisha thought.

The sand had been neatly swept and cleaned, and she could see not even the smallest movement. Within this space devoid of living things, fragrances were very quiet. This made her happy, although she wasn't sure why.

I wonder if the Kokun also finds scents noisy.

She had lived so long without anyone understanding how she felt. She'd thought she was just peculiar, but if the Kokun also felt this way, then Aisha was not alone in her sensitivity.

When they finally reached the entrance to the Kokun's palace, it seemed strangely small compared to the size of the building. The door was firmly shut. Stepping forward, Mijima pulled the rope hanging beside it, and a voice inside asked who was there.

"Mijima Olu Kashuga," she answered.

The door creaked open, and two women appeared. They bowed and led Mijima and Aisha inside.

The entranceway was simple, with a space on either side of the door for the guards and a narrow corridor stretching beyond. The two women stood aside, heads bowed, as Mijima, followed by Aisha, passed between them and proceeded down the corridor.

When she stepped into the hall beyond, Aisha's jaw dropped. The chamber before her was huge.

Light—soft yellow, pale blue and green—poured through stained glass skylights far above. As she passed beneath them, Aisha felt like she was walking along a forest floor bathed in dappled light falling through the canopy.

There were no furnishings of any kind, except for a floor-to-ceiling bamboo blind that hung in front of the dais at the far end of the hall. Smells were faint and monotonous, which made anything with a clear scent stand out. From the moment she'd entered the building, Aisha had been aware of the scent of seikoso, and it pervaded this hall as well.

Mijima came to a halt and knelt. Behind her, Aisha followed suit, placing her forehead on the cold stone floor.

The scent drifting from the screened area wavered, indicating that a door had opened somewhere behind it. Instantly, the smell of seikoso intensified. As clearly as if she could see behind the bamboo screen, Aisha sensed a figure haloed in that scent walk slowly to the dais and sit on a chair.

A goddess goes there.

With this thought, Aisha began to tremble. She felt as if her stomach had risen into her throat, and a cold numbness spread from her scalp down to her toes.

A bell rang, and Mijima spoke. "Oh, thou, compassionate goddess, Lady Kokun. I, the koshi Mijima, beg leave to speak with your Majesty."

Her voice echoed hollowly and was swallowed by the shadows. The figure behind the screen gave no reply, but the bell sounded again.

Mijima continued in a ringing voice. "Prostrated behind me is Aisha Loliki. She has come to work at Lia Garden. I have brought her here to venerate thee."

The scent behind the bamboo screen shifted slightly. Until then it had been tranquil, but now it suggested a sudden interest.

The goddess looks at me.

Aisha shivered at the touch of that invisible gaze.

The sound of Mijima's finger tapping the floor jolted her back to her senses, and she slowly spoke the words Mijima had taught her.

"Compassionate goddess, Lady Kokun, I, Aisha Loliki, beg the honor of an audience."

Once she began speaking, the confusion in her mind stilled. She listened to the sound of her own voice echoing faintly across the hall as she spoke.

"It is my ardent wish to dedicate myself to conveying your blessings to the people that they may be saved. I beg permission to serve thee."

As these words left her mouth, she was struck by a strange feeling. She'd thought she had come to get permission to live at Lia Garden, to hide there, and so survive. But now, without warning, a clear and completely different thought welled from her heart.

I was born to walk this path.

She was painfully aware of the Kokun's gaze boring into her, but there was only silence from the other side of the bamboo curtain.

Finally, the bell rang three times, signaling that the Lady Kokun had accepted the offer of service gladly.

When the reverberations rippling through the space had faded, Aisha felt the Kokun rise and leave. Even after the door had closed behind her, the scent of seikoso remained, wafting gently through the shadowed hall.

As they left the Kokun's palace, Aisha suddenly felt drained, and she plodded after Mijima, staring vacantly at her back.

Her spirits began to revive only after they'd exited the palace gardens. It was then that she noticed Mijima's scent; something was troubling her. Even after they'd stepped through the main gate and left the imperial palace grounds, Mijima remained silent, her expression hard, and she exuded a sharp scent.

Once they'd climbed into their carriage and were sitting across from one another, Aisha mustered the courage to speak, but Mijima cut her off before she could start.

"Did Sir Masyu teach you how to navigate the Quiet Way?"

Aisha blinked, struggling to comprehend. "No," she said. "No one taught me anything."

Mijima's eyes narrowed. "Then why did you choose that route?" Her face was stern, but her scent conveyed fear and suspicion, rather than anger.

Aisha gazed back at her and said, "Because I caught the perfume of a flower I like."

" . . . a flower you like? What flower?"

"Seikoso."

"Sei . . . koso?"

Mijima's response perplexed Aisha. "Don't you know seikoso, fragrant blue grass?"

Mijima shook her head. "No, I don't."

"Really? But I thought those were the flowers depicted on the outer walls of the Kokun's palace."

"Is that what you're talking about?"

"Yes, they look exactly the same. When I saw that mural, I wanted to ask you . . ."

Mijima's scent deepened. Her heart must be pounding, Aisha thought.

In a level voice that belied the excitement betrayed by her scent, Mijima said, "Those are teardrop flowers. They're said to have sprung from the tears the first Kokun shed for the starving people. But I've never seen real ones."

"Teardrop flowers?" Aisha cocked her head. Is that what they're called here, she wondered. "Do you remember the spring we passed on the way?"

"Yes."

"They were blooming in that glade. The blue flowers. Didn't you notice them?"

Mijima shook her head. "No, I never noticed. And I've never taken that path before."

She fell silent for a few moments, then narrowed her eyes. "But those flowers were blooming quite close to the Kokun's palace, weren't they? You couldn't have smelled them when you chose the first path, could you?"

The thought that Mijima would say this had occurred to Aisha even before she spoke. The first fork in the road was likely too far from the flowers for Mijima to have smelled them. If so, then she probably wouldn't believe her.

But Aisha hated to lie about why she'd chosen that path. It was truly a "quiet way." Just the memory of it filled her heart with a pure light: it had been exquisitely peaceful.

Aisha looked Mijima in the eye. "Even so," she said, "I could smell it. The leaves and stems, as well as the flowers, give off a distinctive fragrance. I merely chose the paths that smelled like seikoso."

Mijima remained silent, staring at Aisha with unseeing eyes. What she was thinking, Aisha couldn't tell. "Did I do something wrong?" she asked.

Mijima slowly shook her head. "No." Her voice sounded strained.

"If not, then what worries you?"

Mijima remained silent for a long time, but at last she spoke. "You chose that path with such confidence I thought Sir Masyu must have broken the rules and given you directions."

Then she smiled, relaxing the rigid muscles in her face. "I'm sorry. Don't worry about it. You haven't done anything wrong." She sighed. "You must be tired. So am I. Let's rest until we reach the farm."

So saying, she sank back against the seat and closed her eyes. She kept her eyes closed for the rest of the journey, feigning sleep, but her body continued to give off a strong scent of confusion and concern.

2
Olie

Shall I place it here, Lady Kokun?" The servant, who bore a specimen box, kept his eyes averted as he asked this question.

"Yes, that will be fine," Olie answered.

The servant bowed deeply, then retreated toward the door, being careful not to turn his back toward her.

"Oh, before you leave," she said, "could you please open that window up there? The one on the east side."

Perhaps startled by the politeness of her request, the servant glanced at her with a jerk of his head, but then quickly looked down at the floor again.

He must have started working here recently, Olie thought. He was young, and it was the first time she'd seen him.

"As you wish, Your Holiness," he said, his voice cracking.

He picked up a long bamboo pole with a hook on the end and went over to the window. Raising the pole, he tried to slip the hook into the iron ring on the window frame, but the tip of the pole shook so much, it wouldn't catch. The metal hook bumped against the frame.

"Relax," Olie couldn't help saying. "There's no hurry. Just take it slowly."

"Yes, Your Holiness! Begging your pardon, Your Holiness!" the youth exclaimed, his voice squeaking.

He wiped the sweaty palms of his hands on his clothes, then raised the pole once more. When the window finally opened, he breathed a sigh of relief. Olie exhaled right along with him.

"That was hard work, wasn't it?" she said.

The boy flushed crimson and apologized again.

"There's no need to apologize for something like that," Olie said.

He bowed and stammered, "Would there be anything more, Your Holiness?"

Olie smiled. "That will be all."

The high window on the west wall was slightly open, and the wind blew in, bearing the fragrance of senzako flowers.

"Ah, isn't that a lovely scent," she murmured.

The servant froze, as if uncertain whether he was expected to say something or could now make his escape.

Taking pity on him, Olie said gently, "You may leave now."

The servant bowed and backed out of the room. Once he was gone, the large room was quiet.

The early afternoon light slanting through the high window illuminated the specimen box on the long table. Olie stood with her hand on the lid for some time thinking about the young servant's confusion and nervousness.

She'd watched people tense up like that for so many years, she should have been used to it by now. There were only a handful of people who didn't get nervous. Yet even so, it made her feel guilty and uncomfortable whenever it happened.

Olie had been born into a noble family in the Rigdal protectorate. Her father was a minor aristocrat who governed a small mountain valley called Teela, and her mother was a village woman who'd served his household.

Although Olie's mother had died of illness when Olie was five, her father was a kind man, and the woman he later took as his official wife was generous and had raised Olie with loving affection as if she were her own child.

The climate of Teela was harsh, but the bonds among its

people were strong, and together they overcame the hardships of life in the valley.

As a child, Olie had spent much of her time playing in the woods with the other children. From the age of seven or eight, she had joined the adults when they went hunting for herbs and had helped them with their work.

All this came to an end when she turned thirteen.

In the fall of every year, a troupe of traveling performers came to Agaboi, the capital of Teela. Despite being the capital, it was a small town, not much larger than a village, but when the traders brought their wares for the autumn festival, people flocked to the market from nearby villages. Attracted by the crowds, the traveling performers turned it into a lively event.

Olie's thirteenth year coincided with the thirteenth year since the living goddess, the Kokun, had left the world—the year of her return. Consequently, the autumn festival was much larger than usual. Rumors had it that noblemen from the imperial capital might come, and the town was bustling with excitement.

When did Father tell us about the message from the Kokun's palace, Olie wondered. *Maybe just two or three days before the festival.*

The message had ordered him to gather every girl who turned thirteen that year and present them to an imperial emissary, who would be sent to conduct the Ritual of Return.

Although flustered at the short notice, her father had remarked that, considering how far Teela was from the Kokun's palace, they were lucky the message had reached them when it did. At least he would have time to notify everyone.

As if it were an afterthought, he'd turned to Olie and said, "You turned thirteen this year, too, didn't you?"

"Oh, my! You're right!" her stepmother had exclaimed. "Festival clothes won't do then." She turned quickly to her maidservant. "Go and take Olie's formal robes from the trunk and hang them out to air."

It was a fine day, and the clear autumn sunlight poured through the open windows onto the living room floor.

Now that Olie thought about it, her father and stepmother must have known why thirteen-year-old girls were being gathered, but they'd never mentioned it.

She doubted it was because it would have been inappropriate to speculate about a message from the Kokun's court. It was more likely that they were simply unconcerned. It would never have occurred to them that it could impact them personally; their focus was solely on making sure this important event was brought to a successful conclusion.

On the day of the festival, a dozen thirteen-year-old girls, including Olie, gathered in the town square. Olie knew most of them.

The festival was in full swing, and a large stage—decorated with flowers, chestnuts, and autumn fruits—stood in the center of the square. A bundle of silver grass had been tied to the top of a straw pillar in the middle of the stage to summon the god of the land. Each time the wind blew, the feathery grass swayed, glittering in the light.

Normally stalls selling various wares would have surrounded the square, but on this day, they'd been moved to a vacant spot along the main road to leave the area looking neat and tidy. The square had been swept and purified, and a rope barrier had been strung around it to keep back the crowd.

Olie's father, stepmother and siblings, as well as her father's retainers, were seated under a canopy, and the girls were lined up in front of them. Their faces showed a mixture of nervousness and excitement.

As they whispered among themselves, wondering if they would be asked to do something or given something, the sound of a flute came from afar, riding on the wind.

As it gradually drew nearer, a procession came into view and passed through the onlookers lining the road. It was led by a flagbearer with a magnificent banner embroidered in gold and silver thread depicting some kind of flower. This, Olie later learned, was the Kokun's banner.

The procession seemed to brighten everything it passed. As it entered the square, her father and stepmother emerged from under the canopy to greet the guests, who were all garbed in clearly opulent clothes the like of which Olie had never seen.

She didn't remember the long ritual that followed—except for one part that was imprinted indelibly on her mind.

The emissary from the Kokun's court called on those who were thirteen to step forward, and Olie and the others moved to the spot to which he was pointing. His servants murmured instructions to the girls, and they lined up obediently. The emissary then handed each girl a narrow strip of cloth.

Just as Olie was wondering what it was for, he announced in a ringing voice that carried to all those assembled, "The Search for the Departed Spirit will now commence. Stay where you are without speaking. The ceremony must be observed in silence!"

To the girls he said in a low voice, "Cover your eyes with the cloth and tie it behind your head."

Olie's hands trembled as she blindfolded herself. Someone approached her and checked the knot. She felt a hand wave in front of her face, but couldn't see anything except perhaps a slight wavering of the darkness.

Once again she heard the emissary's sonorous voice. "Oh, living goddess who saves the masses. Oh, Lady Kokun. Thirteen years have passed since thou didst cast off the body of one generation to abide within the womb of a woman and be born again into this world. Thou hast grown healthy and strong, awaiting the summons. With this familiar scent, we call on thy beloved spirit to wake!"

As his voice faded and silence cloaked the square, Olie felt someone approaching. A dignified voice said, "We will place something before each of you. You must smell it and tell us what it is."

Olie heard the girl beside her gasp and almost gasped herself, but managed to catch herself in time. She'd never dreamed this is what they would be asked to do.

She recalled something her father had told her long ago: When the living goddess at the Kokun's palace in the imperial capital grew old, she abandoned her body and entered the womb of a good woman to be reborn garbed in a new physical frame.

"Like she's shedding her skin?" she'd asked her father, and he'd scolded her severely, warning her not to say something so blasphemous.

No one, he explained, knew where the Lady Kokun would be reborn, but in the Year of the Return, when the reincarnation of the Kokun reached the age of thirteen, the chief koshi would search for her in an area revealed to him in a dream.

When the Kokun reaches the age of thirteen . . .

Olie's pulse quickened. Her skin prickled and grew taut with the realization that the living goddess might appear within one of the girls gathered here.

Amazing! Who could it be?

"Lady Kokun."

A voice from behind jerked Olie back to the present. She turned to see Master Raoh, a gentle smile lighting his face.

"Oh! You startled me!" Olie said, pressing her hands against her chest. "You're stealthier than a cat!"

Master Raoh laughed as though pleased. "Is that so? I'm grateful for your praise. That means I haven't lost my touch yet."

Olie hadn't heard the door open, which meant that Raoh had been somewhere in this vast room full of specimens all along.

"How long have you been here?" she asked.

Raoh waved a hand at a pile of specimen boxes in a corner of the room. "I've been right there ever since this morning. I was planning to greet you once you were alone, but—"

He paused and peered closely at her face. "It's been some time since you came to this room. Is there something bothering you? You seemed to be lost in thought."

Olie smiled. "No, nothing really. I was just remembering the past."

Raoh gazed at her for a moment longer, then shifted his eyes to the specimen box in her hands. "Those look like yoma specimens. Why those ones?"

Yoma were the only insects that ever ate the pest-resistant ohaleh. Although they clung to the seedlings, most succumbed to the effects of ohaleh and died by the time the plant matured and ears of rice appeared. They rarely caused much damage, but they still had to be exterminated because they could kill off weaker ohaleh plants.

There were several types of yoma, such as the smaller koyoma and the red-winged akayoma. Staring at the specimens in the box and the accompanying illustrations depicting their characteristics, Olie sighed. "I saw some eggs at the base of an ohaleh stalk. They looked like yoma eggs, but were much bigger than anything I've ever seen. I wondered what kind of yoma might have laid them, but couldn't find anything like them."

Raoh raised his brows. "Where did you see them?" he asked.

"I noticed them during the last Rite of the Green Rice Wind."

"Then it must have been in the fields of Rapa in Ogoda."

"That's right."

Performing the rite was one of the Kokun's important duties. When the rice plants began sending up green shoots, she would walk slowly through the ohaleh fields and smell the wind to detect impending disasters and warn people of danger. Each year she visited fields in a different area, not only near the capital, but also in the distant protectorates.

Olie had returned three days ago. This year she'd inspected the rice fields of Rapa in the Ogoda protectorate. She'd been so overcome with fatigue upon her return that she'd spent the last two days soaking in warm baths. It was only this morning that she'd regained her energy and been able to eat a substantial breakfast.

If I could really smell the wind to warn people of potential dangers, I probably wouldn't get so tired.

During these rites, Olie closed her eyes and addressed the people as though speaking from some inner inspiration. In reality, however, she was reciting a script on farming prepared for her in advance.

The first draft was submitted to the Kokun's court by the Ministry of Wealth and carefully examined by a group of senior koshi who served the Kokun. They revised it and sent it back to the Ministry of Wealth. After further review by the Ministry, the script was then submitted to and approved by the emperor and returned to the Kokun's court. Only then was it presented to Olie.

The Ministry of Wealth, an enormous organization that oversaw every industry in the empire, had been established upon the abolition of the Ministry of Agriculture, which had been run by the Kokun's court. The commander in chief, the Minister of Wealth, had always been the head of Kashuga Lai.

Under the first Kokun, everything to do with farming had been overseen by the Kokun and the Ministry of Agriculture, but with the establishment of the Ministry of Wealth, the administration had been split between this Ministry and the Kokun's court, and responsibilities had been tacitly divided. The Ministry of Wealth formulated basic policies that reflected the will of the emperor, and the Kokun's court considered and advised on those policies.

This didn't mean that the Kokun's court had fallen into decline. The emperor still valued its advice, and the Minister of Wealth took into consideration its opinions when administrating agricultural affairs.

Most people believed the Kokun's palace was merely the place where the Lady Kokun was enshrined. In fact, however, her court was the central organization responsible for examining all agriculture-related information gathered by the koshi, the scent emissaries, who were dispatched to every region of the empire. The Kokun's court used the information collected to forecast yields for the coming year and to develop countermeasures for any foreseeable problems, advising the Ministry of Wealth on how to respond. The Kokun's court was led by the chief koshi, Master Raoh Kashuga, who was also the head of Kashuga Oi.

The House of Kashuga had two lineages: Kashuga Oi, an ancient distinguished family line founded by Amil, who had brought ohaleh rice to Umal; and Kashuga Lai, a new branch established many generations later by Makiya, the second son of the House of Kashuga. Makiya was revered as a hero because his innovative agricultural policies had dramatically increased the empire's wealth within his lifetime.

It was Makiya Kashuga who advised the emperor to abolish the Ministry of Agriculture under the Kokun's court and establish in its stead the Ministry of Wealth to oversee the empire's various industries, including livestock farming, fishing, and trade. His proposal was approved, and he became the first Minister of Wealth.

Since that time, Kashuga Lai had managed the Ministry of Wealth, while Kashuga Oi had overseen the Kokun's court.

"I'm just a decorative lantern swinging between the two Houses of Kashuga," Olie sometimes complained.

Each time, Master Raoh laughed and shook his head, saying, "That's not true, as you well know. The reason the people do as they are told, even when those instructions seem harsh, is because the directions come from the Lady Kokun."

During the many years she'd lived in the palace, Olie had come to realize these words were not flattery but truth—that this was the very meaning of her existence. Which was why she somehow managed to keep her expression detached and lofty whenever she saw people tremble before her as they paid obeisance.

"About those insect eggs."

"Yes?"

"Would you be able to draw me a picture of their characteristics?"

Olie smiled and pulled a folded piece of paper from her robe. She spread it out before him. "I already did. Because I wanted to compare them to the specimens here. The drawing is the actual size."

"Wonderful!" Master Raoh took the drawing.

He removed his glasses and placed them on the table, then brought his face up close to the picture to examine it. His eyes widened slightly, and he froze, staring at the eggs in what appeared to be disbelief.

"Can you tell what insect it is from the picture?" Olie asked quietly.

Master Raoh blinked and tore his gaze away from the drawing. Even so, his eyes remained unfocused for a moment, as if his thoughts were elsewhere.

Recollecting himself, he looked at Olie. "Pardon me. What did you say?"

"Oh, um, I asked if you could tell what kind of insect it was from the drawing."

Master Raoh shook his head slowly. "I believe it must be some kind of yoma, but I can't tell for certain without investigating further."

His eyes rested on Olie, but his gaze went right through her, as though he was seeing something else.

His behavior seemed so unlike him that Olie opened her mouth to ask what was wrong, but before she could, he smiled brightly and began to speak, preventing her inquiry. "Your eyes are very sharp, Lady Kokun. Regardless of what it is, if it's a type of yoma, it's better to be cautious. I will ask the koshi to look into it right away."

With that he bowed deeply and headed for the door. Watching his receding back, Olie placed a hand to her heart.

So . . . those eggs . . .

She had hoped they were not what she feared. But if Master Raoh had reached the same conclusion, then her fears may have been justified.

With the sun streaming through the window onto her face, Olie felt her heart thudding against the palm of her hand.

3
The Secret of the Fertilizer

When the servants opened the large doors to let in the guest, a cloud obscured the soft sunshine that had been falling through the skylight.

Odosen looked up from the letter he was reading and faced the man crossing the carpet toward him. The man placed the fingertips of both hands to his forehead and bowed deeply.

"Your Highness, Crown Prince."

Odosen inclined his head and gestured toward the chair opposite him. "Welcome, Iilu Kashuga. Come warm your throat and stomach with some chieka wine."

Iilu smiled and bowed again, then sank onto the chair the servant had pulled back for him. The capital was blessed with a relatively mild climate, but when it clouded over, it was chilly even in early summer. A small charcoal brazier was kept beside the chair, but as this time of year was usually warm, no coals had been lit in it.

Once the servants had filled the wine glasses, Odosen signaled for them to leave, and they withdrew. As the heavy doors closed behind the servants, silence filled the large study.

Odosen raised his glass slightly in acknowledgement of his guest, took a sip, and waited until Iilu had done the same.

"Were you able to have an audience with His Majesty, the Emperor?" he asked.

"Yes, he appeared a little better today," Iilu responded.

Odosen's face brightened. "You thought so too, did you? It would be wonderful if he continued to recover. He doesn't have much appetite yet, which is worrisome, but the new medicine the doctor has been giving him seems to be working, and that should speed up his recovery."

Iilu observed with mixed feelings how this thought brought a smile to the young prince's face.

The emperor Orulan, who had always been robust, had collapsed at the end of the previous year, and Iilu fervently prayed for his recovery.

Prince Odosen's base was not yet secure. If Orulan were to die now, his younger brother Ragalan, who had many supporters, might try to instigate an uprising and usurp the throne, throwing the imperial court into chaos. At this time, when not all the protectorates were necessarily loyal, the resulting confusion could destabilize the empire.

Fortunately, the emperor had survived the year and was showing signs of gradual improvement. Although he was still confined to his bed, he could converse quite normally.

Even so, while keeping an eye on the balance of power within the court, Iilu had already begun preparing for the emperor's death to prevent any chance of disruption. The crown prince and the emperor's younger brother were pretty much equal in influence. Iilu was constantly mulling over which one should be placed on the throne in the event of the emperor's death and how to go about it. As well as what to do with the one who wasn't chosen.

The crown prince Odosen had turned twenty the previous month. He was a careful, intelligent young man, but Iilu worried that his character was too pristine, lacking any shades of gray.

It's helpful that his thoughts are so easy to read, but . . .

He didn't have the depth or breadth of experience needed to rule the sprawling empire of Umal. In contrast, Ragalan was old and cunning with a strong ambition to rule. But unlike previous emperors, he might not be content to follow the House of Kashuga's lead in governing.

Iilu put down his glass. "Are you aware of what is troubling His Majesty?"

Odosen raised an eyebrow and gave a crooked smile. "I'm sure many things trouble him, including my ineptitude. But if you mean what's bothering him right now, I would say it's this." He flicked his eyes toward the letter lying on the table.

Iilu nodded. "So, you already have a copy. Your Highness is very fast indeed."

"One of the Listeners memorized it and wrote it down for me," he said. He began reading the document aloud.

"'Pirate raids on ships carrying chichiya through the Ogodal Sea have been increasing. Efforts to eradicate pirates and prevent any further incidents must be expanded. We therefore respectfully request the dispatch of imperial warships. If this is not possible, then we humbly request permission to build two naval vessels of our own.'"

Odosen rapped the document with his knuckle and grimaced. "Ogoda's arrogance has become quite blatant. They know that for the last year increased tension with the southern continent has hampered our ability to dispatch imperial warships. It's all too obvious they're using this as an opportunity to boost their own naval power, yet they've got the audacity to send us this petition."

Iilu smiled wryly. "They are likely flushed with their good fortune at discovering a rich chichiya deposit in their recently acquired archipelago." Chichiya—the Umal term for guano—was a valuable ingredient in the fertilizer that the empire distributed to the protectorates. "However, I suspect they are also in a hurry to bring more islands under their control while the empire is distracted by the southern continent."

"Do you think this tale of pirates is a ruse too?"

Iilu gazed at Odosen. "What do the protectorate inspectors say?"

"My father has commanded them to look into it, but it seems they've yet to report."

Iilu's eyes narrowed. "It might be prudent to check whether there truly has been no report."

The smile faded from Odosen's face. "You already have proof, don't you?"

Iilu nodded. "I came today to inform His Majesty of that very fact." He continued in an even voice. "The forces Ogoda claims are pirates transfer their cargo onto warships waiting out at sea. From these, the cargo is transferred yet again to two trading vessels that take the contents to two different ports and pass them off as legitimate trading goods."

"Two ports?"

"Yes. The ports on Nagi Island and Migalan Island, located in an archipelago in southwest Ogoda. They use a special processing method to make wine jugs from chichiya. The jugs are filled with a specialty wine produced in Nagi and exported to another protectorate."

Surprise crossed Odosen's face. "Another protectorate? Where?"

"Rigdal."

Odosen's lips parted, and he stared at Iilu for a moment. Then, with a grim look, he pressed his fist against his forehead.

"I see . . . So that's what's going on. You're right. I should check whether the inspectors were really unaware of this. The case being what it is, they may still be investigating it carefully, but if that information didn't reach me, it means that either the Listeners were sloppy or my uncle interfered . . ."

Odosen bowed his head and clicked his tongue in disgust. "But still, Rigdal! Why would they do something so ill-advised?"

Iilu took a sip of wine, then placed his glass on the table. "I expect Rigdal is in a hurry too."

Odosen looked up. "I know that. Marrying my older sister off to East Kantal is just the kind of equalizing strategy my father would take. For the lord of Rigdal, it must have been a shock that her hand was granted not to his own son but to a prince of the protectorate on his very border. I can imagine he must have felt anxious and impatient. Still, how could he do something like this when he was awarded the highest honor of having the Lady Kokun chosen from his realm!"

Iilu blinked. "I beg your pardon. My explanation seems to have been insufficient. That is precisely why I said Rigdal is in a hurry. Because the Lady Kokun was chosen from their land."

Odosen looked puzzled.

"Fifteen years have passed since the Lady Kokun ascended the throne."

A light kindled in Odosen's eyes. "Ah, I see. So that's the source of their anxiety."

Iilu nodded. "Yes. Through the bounty of the Kokun's selection, Rigdal profited from increased ohaleh production and saw a significant leap in its population. Over the last few years, however, ohaleh yield has begun to wane. The imbalance between population growth and the distribution of profits has widened the gap between rich and poor. Discontent smolders among the masses."

Odosen curled his lip. "True. The lord of Rigdal chose the wrong people to serve as his officials. With bureaucrats that are so corrupt, there's no way profits can be distributed fairly."

Iilu sighed. "We were also a little too slow to act. We should have intervened earlier."

"The situation in Rigdal is troublesome, but what about Ogoda? If they're lying about the volume of chichiya extracted, then they're probably trying to produce their own fertilizer, right?"

Iilu smiled thinly. "I asked His Majesty to overlook that for the time being."

"Why?"

"Because this is an excellent opportunity to determine where Ogoda is selling the guano and identify how it's being distributed. Of course, once we find out, it will be necessary to punish them severely in a way that makes it very clear we were just keeping them on a leash."

"That's certainly one approach . . . But isn't it risky?"

Iilu answered with unruffled confidence. "Fertilizer suited to ohaleh cultivation cannot be manufactured just by obtaining guano. If someone ignorant of the correct ratio mixes the fertilizer, ohaleh yield will decrease."

Odosen scowled. "I'm well aware of that. We've gone to great lengths to keep the secret of ohaleh fertilizer production strictly guarded; it's what underpins this empire. But nothing in life is absolute. It's your confidence that worries me. How can you be sure it won't become arrogance and blind you to the truth? A long time has passed since the empire began distributing fertilizer to the protectorates. It wouldn't be surprising if someone figured out how to mix and produce it to increase the yield."

Iilu said calmly, "Knowing the kind of person I am, I cannot guarantee that my eyes will never be blinded by pride. That risk was there for my father, my grandfather, and all our ancestors who passed down the secret."

"Well, then—"

Iilu cut him off casually. "At this point in time, I can say with certainty that the secret has not been revealed to any of the protectorates."

"How can you be so sure?" Odosen demanded irritably.

Iilu smiled. "The fact that Your Highness is asking me this very question is proof."

Odosen frowned. "What is that supposed to mean?"

Iilu's smile vanished. He fixed his eyes on Odosen, who pulled in his chin slightly. "Your Highness would never have asked me that question had you been privy to what lies at the root of the secret."

A cold light gleamed in Iilu's eyes. "How could those in the protectorates possibly know something that Your Highness, the Crown Prince, does not, when you are first in line to succeed His Majesty the Emperor, and are informed by the Listeners and a network of intelligence through the Ministry for Protectorate Inspection?"

Odosen stared back at Iilu silently. Finally, he said in a low voice, "What did you mean by 'the root of the secret'?"

His eyes still fixed on Odosen's face, Iilu answered, "That is a secret known only to His Majesty the Emperor himself and the Lady Kokun."

Anger kindled in Odosen's eyes, but it quickly turned to a dark smile. "I see. Just the Emperor, the Lady Kokun . . . and the House of Kashuga."

Iilu bowed his head silently.

Odosen stared at his implacable face for a moment, then sighed and changed the subject. "What shall we do about Rigdal then?"

Iilu raised his face and brushed a lock of hair from his forehead. "Their crime is related to that of Ogoda, so it will be necessary to punish both at the same time. This issue, however, strikes at the very heart of protectorate management, so punishment alone won't be enough."

"What exactly are you thinking of?"

"There are several factors involved, so I am still considering this question carefully. It is not that urgent, which is why I asked His Majesty for more time."

Odosen's lips crooked. "Knowing you, you already have several strategies up your sleeve."

The cold smile faded from his lips, and his expression turned serious. "Still, I can understand why you wish to exercise caution. To punish Rigdal ineptly could damage the authority of the Lady Kokun."

Iilu nodded. He glanced out the window, squinting as if it were too bright. "Very true," he said, his expression unreadable.

* * *

When Iilu left Odosen's hall, he was met by a young man. They climbed into the sturdy carriage together. As soon as the horses set off, the youth asked impatiently, "Father, how was your meeting with His Highness, Odosen?"

"Pretty much as I expected," Iilu replied, then frowned. "For the sake of the future though, I'll have to find him a good assistant. That he lacks even a shred of doubt about the secret of the fertilizer shows that those who serve him aren't capable. Although I suppose his character may be part of the problem."

The young man, who seemed to have been thinking about something as he listened, now said gravely, "Father."

"Mm?"

"Do you think we can continue to guard the secret of the fertilizer?"

Iilu looked at his son. "What do you think, Yugil?" he asked.

"To be honest, I think it's in danger of being exposed."

"Why?"

Yugil gazed back at his father. "It's really just a grand deception. Although to unravel it would require a shift in thinking, even the most insignificant thing could trigger that."

His well-shaped brows drew together. "I've been worried about this ever since Ogoda was brought under the empire's rule. It's a prosperous maritime protectorate with a flourishing sea trade. It was only a matter of time before it would discover a chichiya deposit on an island within its own territory, and I feared that once they found one, they'd be able to figure out how to make fertilizer."

Iilu listened silently.

"Until now, there was no opportunity for any of the protectorates to try making their own fertilizer. Guano is strictly controlled and can only be obtained as part of the fertilizer mix supplied by the empire. That's why we could keep the secret of how it's made for so long. Now, however . . ."

Yugil paused and looked at his father. "Ogoda has gained a source of guano that it can use freely. Quite likely, they're already attempting to make their own fertilizer. And once they do, they'll use it to grow ohaleh."

A strong light glinted in Yugil's eyes. "Once they start trying to cultivate it on their own, they're bound to realize that there's no special secret to imperial fertilizer; that anyone can make it as long as they know the ingredients and the correct amounts."

Iilu smiled faintly. "You're right. They're bound to notice. But even if they do, they'll still be powerless."

Iilu looked out the window and watched the townscape passing by. "You call it a grand deception, but the empire has never declared there to be any secrets concerning the fertilizer. That's just a story fabricated from the assumptions made by the people who use the fertilizer we supply. Although it helps to reinforce the sacred nature of ohaleh, it has no other meaning. Even the crown prince, however, seems unaware of that fact."

Iilu sighed. "The secret that must be preserved at all costs is how the seeds sprout, not how the fertilizer is made. Even if people learn how to make the fertilizer, as long as the seeds won't sprout, there's no way to escape the empire's yoke."

With each building they passed, a thin shadow flickered across Iilu's face. "Fertilizer is just a means for controlling the growth of ohaleh rice. What we teach the people is the optimum amount to use. Too much fertilizer suppresses the growth of ohaleh and reduces the yield, while too little makes it too toxic to eat, even though it increases the yield. So just being able to produce one's own fertilizer doesn't make it possible to do anything more."

Yugil's face clouded. "That's true, but . . ."

Iilu shifted his gaze back to his son. "At the same time, your fears are not unreasonable. The Ogoda don't lack ability. They're likely aware that fertilizer must be applied in the right amount and that applying extra won't increase the yield. If so, the reason for producing their own fertilizer is not to increase the yield, but to allow them to cultivate ohaleh on their own—without the empire. It's meaningless to try because they still won't be able to produce their own seed rice. But the fact that they have such ambitions makes them dangerous."

Iilu paused and smiled. "How would you resolve this?"

Yugil rubbed the thumbs of his clasped hands together. "They'll have to be punished. Otherwise, they'll think the empire doesn't realize they're extracting and trading chichiya and will be emboldened to disregard imperial authority."

Iilu nodded. "Exactly. I have just told His Majesty the Emperor the same thing."

Yugil's eyes dropped to the floor, and he spoke slowly, "But it will be difficult to punish Ogoda, won't it? It only became a protectorate recently. And if Ogoda is punished, Rigdal will have to be punished too."

He raised his head, as though a thought had suddenly occurred to him. "Speaking of Rigdal, I hear that Uncle Masyu is back. To report on the situation in West Kantal to His Majesty." Yugil's eyes shone. "Apparently, he brought back a refugee from the old royal family. A young girl, who he intends to harbor at Lia Garden. Although I wonder why. There are lots of other places here he could use."

Still smiling, Iilu said, "You're very well informed, aren't you? Where did you hear that?"

Yugil flushed. "I just happened to overhear it."

"You happened to overhear it, did you?"

Iilu regarded his son's face silently for a few moments, then said in a quiet, measured tone, "You were talking of Rigdal before you mentioned your uncle. What made you connect Rigdal with Masyu?"

Yugil's head jerked back slightly, and a look of dismay crossed his face.

"Tell me the truth."

Blinking, Yugil said, "At the Kokun's palace, I once heard the maidservants talking about him."

"What did they say?"

Yugil's face turned bright red, and he said nervously, "That . . . Uh-uncle Masyu and the Lady Kokun were once on intimate terms. They said that's why he was relieved of his position as a high-ranking koshi and joined the army."

Iilu said nothing.

Yugil hesitated for a moment, then blurted out, "Father . . . is that true?"

Iilu gave a snort of laughter. "Ridiculous. If that had happened, the Kokun would be dead." His voice turned hard. "Besides, Masyu's not that naïve. He's far more dangerous than you imagine. The Lady Kokun's unparalleled beauty coupled with Masyu's aloof charm are just feeding the fantasies of the inner court maidens who crave romantic tales."

He gave a deep sigh. "However, it's a bad sign that the maidservants are still gossiping about that. The Lady Kokun is kind, which makes some people forget their place."

He looked his son over with cold eyes. "Keep that in mind. The Lady Kokun is not a human being."

"I see . . ."

"Don't answer lightly. As the eldest son of the head of Kashuga Lai, you're in a position to know what's going on behind the scenes, so somewhere in your heart, you think of her ladyship as an ordinary person."

Yugil paled and shook his head, but Iilu's expression remained hard. "No, you do. If you didn't, you would never have believed that tale about Masyu being the Kokun's lover."

Iilu glared at his son. "Remember. Even an infinitesimal change in attitude on your part can cause everything to unravel." He lowered his voice. "I have shown you my gentle side so far, but I am the head of Kashuga Lai. For the sake of the empire, I wouldn't hesitate to kill my own son. Should you become the seed of its destruction, I will disown you, cut out your tongue and chop off your hands myself, so that you can't share your secrets with anyone."

The color drained from Yugil's face at the sight of his father's expression. Even his hands had paled. He pressed his lips firmly together, suppressing a shudder. Bowing deeply, he said, "I will engrave those words on my heart."

4
A Figure in the Moonlight

Chee-chee-chee!

The shrill call of a bird jolted Olie awake. Two shadows flitted across the window. One of the birds must have been defending its territory; its warning shrieks penetrated even the thick glass windowpanes.

She'd been reading but seemed to have dozed off. The shadows of the desk and chair stretched across the floor. She must have slept for quite a while.

Lately, she'd been waking frequently at night, perhaps because she was worried. Once she was awake, with her pulse racing, sleep fled, so that often she tossed and turned in her bed until morning. That was probably why she'd dozed off in the middle of the day like this.

With a sigh, she stood up and went over to the window. The room was on the third floor, and she could look out over the vast garden planted with various vegetables and herbs as well as to the forest beyond. The lush green foliage shone in the sun.

Perhaps Master Raoh had perceived the deep fatigue that permeated her mind when he'd suggested she leave the palace and spend time in Lia.

When she'd first become the Kokun and moved to the capital at the age of thirteen, she'd been exhausted by the unfamiliar life and plagued by nightmares. Concerned, Master Raoh had invited her to this garden in his homeland of Lia territory and let her rest and recuperate. Ever since, it had been one of the few places where she could find peace.

No one here knew she was the Kokun. They believed her to be a noblewoman who was under Master Raoh's protection for some confidential reason and whom he occasionally brought with him. They could guess by the way he treated her that she was of high rank, and so they also treated her with deference, but they weren't so awe-struck that they couldn't even look her in the face. Thanks to this, Olie could relax more while she was here.

The sun shone gently on the garden, and she could see people busily at work. Although it was a vegetable garden, the plants grown here were not sold but were instead used for research. Botanical experts called Garden Masters grew plants gathered from every region and examined them daily to study such things as how to improve yield and prevent pest damage.

The Garden Masters instructed experienced staff known as Gardeners, who did the actual work of cultivation, and these were assisted by workers known as Farm Children. Tending the garden required heavy labor, but the workers weren't children of nearby farmers. They were all young men and women rigorously selected from families related to the House of Kashuga.

Although the garden was run by Kashuga Oi, even members of Kashuga Lai were required to study here at least once for a fixed period. In the same way, members of Kashuga Oi had to apprentice at Loa Factory, which was run by Kashuga Lai, so they could learn how to make fertilizer.

This system, which had been created when the House of Kashuga first split in two, not only ensured that those born into the House of Kashuga would learn everything they needed to know, but also served as a mutual monitoring system that prevented the two branches from keeping secrets from one another.

On the first day the Farm Children began working at the garden, they stood before Master Raoh, head of Kashuga Oi, and vowed never to reveal the knowledge gained here or at Loa factory to outsiders. If they broke this vow, they would pay for it with their lives, a rule that applied even to the children of the heads of both houses.

Despite the harsh system that governed work at the garden, life was surprisingly peaceful, and the young people who worked and studied here were cheerful and carefree. Selected by Master Raoh, each was endowed with different capacities and, within a few years, would become Gardeners. The most talented would go on to become Garden Masters or scent emissaries.

As Olie observed the garden from above, she noticed a girl she hadn't seen before. She was slender, and her hair was tied back with a thin blue ribbon. She appeared to be learning how to care for potted plants from a senior Farm Child.

There were only about twenty young people working at the garden, so Olie knew all their faces, but she didn't recognize the girl whose gaze was fixed intently on her instructor.

Oh . . . that's right.

Someone had recently come to request her permission to serve. She recalled the clear, resonant voice on the other side of the bamboo curtain.

So, you've already started working here, have you?

Last night, one of the maidservants had mentioned that a new Farm Child recommended by Master Raoh had joined the garden. The maid had seemed slightly puzzled by this. Although they needed replacements for two young women who had recently quit to get married, the new girl was from one of the protectorates, and it was highly unusual for someone with that background to be selected for Lia Garden.

As Master Raoh hadn't mentioned it to Olie, she'd been a bit surprised, but guessed that he didn't want to bother her because she'd come to rest. She'd decided to ask him later and had forgotten about it until now.

Master Raoh will be working at the palace today and tomorrow. She decided to ask him the day after.

A bell rang hesitantly outside her door.

"Please come in. I'm already up," she said, and a maidservant opened the door.

"It is almost time for tea, ma'am. Shall I bring it to you now?

Olie smiled. "Yes, please do."

* * *

People who worked at the garden went to bed early. After supper, everyone—except for the guards—took a bath and called it a night, and a hush fell over the building.

Olie went to bed early too, but sleep wouldn't come. *Probably because I took such a long nap this afternoon,* she thought. It was agony to lie in bed tossing and turning when she couldn't sleep, so eventually she gave up and rose with a sigh.

The night air felt chilly when she threw back the quilt, but it wasn't frigid. Normally, nights at this time of year were freezing, but tonight a light robe over her pajamas was enough.

The room was surprisingly bright. She'd forgotten to close the curtains when she went to bed, which was probably one reason she hadn't been able to sleep.

You've been doing that kind of thing a lot lately. You should be more careful.

She swung her legs over the side of the bed, shoved her feet into her slippers, and walked over to the window.

The night sky was a clear indigo. The full moon floating within that indigo sea cast a brilliant silver glow over the garden, as if the ground was covered in frost. The fields on either side of the central path glittered white.

In the middle of the silence, Olie sensed something moving and peered through the window.

Someone's in the garden.

Her first thought was to call the guards, but when she realized the shadowy figure was a young woman, she stopped and stared.

What on earth could she be doing?

The figure was crouched in the field on the right. After some time, she stood with something in her hand, carefully shook the bottom of it, and crossed over the path and into a field a little farther away on the left side of the path where she crouched again.

She's transplanting something.

Olie's knees went weak, and she gripped the window frame with her hands to steady herself. Her heart beat painfully fast.

Long ago, she'd watched someone else do the same thing. When he was a youth. He'd risen in the middle of the night while everyone lay sleeping and gone out to move plants.

Am I dreaming?

Her forehead felt cold and numb, and her chest tightened. Although she knew she was awake, she couldn't shake off the feeling that this was a dream.

When he finished, he rose and smelled the wind.

Just as this thought flitted through Olie's mind, the figure stood and turned her face to the wind, as though sniffing it.

Olie pressed her trembling hands over her mouth and stared down at the garden until the figure returned inside.

* * *

After a shallow, dream-riddled sleep, Olie woke, still tired and groggy. Even once she'd washed her face and breakfast had been brought to her room, she was plagued by the dazed feeling that nothing before her was real.

The maidservant was setting breakfast on the table. It was another fine day, and the clear morning light shone on the rim of a glass pitcher full of fresh milk.

If I see that person in the garden again tonight . . .

She would go out and see who it was. It was probably just one of the Farm Children who couldn't sleep and was playing some kind of prank in the garden.

Don't be hasty or overthink things, she reprimanded herself as she reached for a warm buttered tapa. At that moment she heard voices raised outside.

"What's that?" Olie asked, turning toward the window.

The maidservant looked outside. "Someone appears to have collapsed."

"Collapsed? Who?" Olie started to rise from her chair, but the maidservant hastily gestured for her to sit.

"Please stay and eat your breakfast, ma'am. I will go and find out for you."

When the servant left the room, Olie rose and went to the window. Several people had gathered around someone lying on the path and were trying to lift her.

The maidservant appeared, and one of the Gardeners went over to talk with her. Shortly after, the resident doctor came out and pushed her way through the crowd.

Olie watched all this with a fluttering heart.

Soon, the maidservant returned, out of breath. "My apologies for keeping you waiting, ma'am. It was one of the Children. She made a mistake and, when she was asked to explain, she fainted. She'll be taken to the infirmary to rest. It's nothing serious, so please don't concern yourself."

"Nothing serious," Olie croaked. She paused to clear her throat. "That's a relief. Thank you."

The maidservant blushed and bowed her head. "It was nothing. You're welcome, ma'am."

Olie moved back to the breakfast table, only to pause in mid stride. Something still bothered her, and she couldn't get it out of her mind. She knew she shouldn't get involved, but the urge to know conquered her desire for caution.

Taking a deep breath, she turned to the maidservant, who was standing in a corner of the room. "Would you please ask the Gardener, the one who was reprimanding the girl, to come and see me?"

The maidservant's brows shot up. "The Gardener . . . ma'am?"

"Yes, please bring her here."

The woman bowed deeply and hurried away. She soon returned and ushered in the Gardner, a young woman who had not been serving in that position for long. Olie recognized her face but had never spoken to her before.

As soon as she entered, the woman knelt and bowed her head. Olie forced herself to speak calmly. "Please raise your head and have a seat on that chair."

The woman sat down, looking a little nervous.

"My apologies for calling you here when you're busy."

" . . . Not at all." The young woman was clearly puzzled.

With her eyes on the woman's face, Olie said, "I asked you to come because I wished to know more about the Farm Child who collapsed this morning. I was told she'd made a mistake, and I wondered what it was."

The Gardener tensed, probably expecting to be scolded. "It wasn't . . . a mistake. Not really, but she's a new girl and . . . quite different. She keeps doing the same thing, even though she knows she shouldn't, so I had to question her a bit sternly . . ."

"What does she do that she shouldn't?"

The woman blinked. "Well . . . For some reason she goes into the garden at night and transplants things."

She began speaking more confidently. "I first noticed three days ago. Something we'd planted in the growth-inhibiting field had been moved to the growth-nurturing field. I thought this was odd, but just moved it back where it belonged. The next day, however, it had been changed again. I wondered who could be playing such a silly prank when one of her roommates said she'd seen her sneaking out at night. I asked the girl why she moved the plants, but . . ."

Without thinking, Olie leaned forward. "Did she tell you why?

The woman shook her head. "No. She refused to speak and just stared at the ground with a stubborn look on her face. Then, she collapsed."

"You said she was a new girl, didn't you? Was she given special permission to study here?"

"Yes."

"I heard she's from one of the protectorates. Is she having trouble understanding what people are saying?"

"No. Although she's from the mountains of West Kantal, she speaks Umalese without an accent."

Olie caught her breath. *The mountains of West Kantal!*

The woman was beginning to look doubtful. Olie exhaled softly. "I see," she said. She took a deep breath. "I'm sorry to have bothered you. Thank you. You may go now."

5
Olie and Aisha

Aisha dreamed she was sleeping beside her mother. The curtains were drawn so that it was dimly lit even during the daytime, and a medicinal smell filled the room.

She heard the door open and her father entered. She tried to open her eyes but her lids wouldn't budge. A deep exhaustion filled her head, making her too sleepy to pry them open.

She thought she caught the cool scent of flowers, and her eyelids fluttered.

Fragrant blue grass . . .

It wasn't her father who had entered the room, but the Kokun.

Before she knew it, the walls of the room had switched to those of a huge, shadowed hall. Illuminated by the late afternoon sun that streamed through the skylight, the Kokun walked over and sat by her bed.

She had no face.

Aisha jerked and opened her eyes. Her heart hammered against her ribcage.

She was in a dimly lit room, large and empty with a row of vacant beds. It was still daytime. Light glowed faintly behind the curtains.

Someone was sitting beside her.

"Are you awake?" a soft voice asked.

Aisha gasped and turned to stare at the woman who sat there. She seemed to embody the scent of fragrant blue grass.

The Lady Kokun . . . but . . . it can't be . . .

Although Aisha knew it was impossible, the woman sitting there smelled exactly like the one who had been behind that bamboo screen.

People's scents change from one moment to the next. Even so, Aisha could identify someone despite these changes, just as a mother will never mistake her children even if they cut their hair or wear different clothes.

"How are you feeling?"

The woman's voice jolted Aisha from her thoughts.

"Thank you," she managed to croak. "I'm fine. Excuse me, but you are . . ."

"I'm sorry. I forgot to introduce myself. I'm Olie." She paused for a second, then continued, "There's a reason I can't tell you my surname, but I'm staying here thanks to the kindness of Master Raoh."

Aisha's eyes narrowed. "Miss . . . Olie." Her brain had finally switched on, and she began thinking furiously.

This was the person she'd sensed behind the bamboo curtain. Of that, Aisha was certain. Yet it was unthinkable that the living goddess from the palace could be sitting on a chair beside her bed. It was unthinkable, yet this was no dream. The Kokun was here, right before her eyes.

At that moment, a bell rang, signaling the start of the lunch hour.

As the familiar sound washed over her, Aisha's confusion and agitation abated a little. Whether she understood the reason didn't matter. If this woman had decided to call herself Olie and conceal the fact that she was the Lady Kokun, then Aisha had no choice but to accept her as that.

Still, the thought of lying in bed in her presence was unbearable. Aisha threw back the blanket and tried to sit up, but Olie raised a hand to stop her.

"Please. Don't get up."

"But . . ."

Olie smiled. "This is no time to worry about manners. You fainted; you must rest."

Her friendly tone robbed Aisha of speech. Although Olie was an ethereal beauty, she didn't dazzle. Rather, she seemed kind and gentle, yet with an inherent dignity.

"I'm sorry to have surprised you like this. You must have thought it very strange to wake up and find a stranger beside you. It's just that when I heard about how you fainted, I wanted to ask you something."

Aisha kept her eyes respectfully averted. "What would you like to know?" she asked.

"Well, you see . . ."

Olie paused, then said, "There's no need to look away. Let's speak normally, face to face."

After a moment of uncertainty, Aisha raised her head and looked at her.

Olie relaxed visibly. "That's better," she said.

She cleared her throat and started again. "Let me go back to the beginning. I've been having trouble sleeping lately. Last night too. I just couldn't get back to sleep, and it seemed pointless to stay in bed. So, I got up and went to the window. It was a lovely moonlit night, wasn't it?"

Aisha said nothing.

"It was so bright the eaves looked like they were covered in frost. Bright enough that I could see someone moving in the garden."

She looked at Aisha and smiled. "That was you, wasn't it?"

Aisha nodded. "Yes, it was me."

"You were removing a plant and replanting it elsewhere, yes?"

"Yes."

Aisha braced in anticipation of her next question. She knew she couldn't explain why she'd done that. But the question wasn't the one Aisha was expecting.

"What plant were you moving?" Olie asked.

Although puzzled, Aisha answered honestly. "I beg your pardon, but I don't know what it is called. It is not one that grows in my homeland, and I have not yet been taught its name."

A light kindled in Olie's eyes. "You didn't know its name, yet you knew it needed transplanting. Is that right?"

Aisha started to nod, but then froze. The realization of what Olie's words meant struck her like a lightning bolt.

She knows!

She felt like laughing at her own denseness. Of course, she knew. She was the Lady Kokun, the living goddess who could read the scents of all things.

I don't have to hide.

The tension inside her snapped, and she began to tremble. The pain that had been building up ever since her arrival burst its bonds, and she shook uncontrollably.

Olie watched her steadily. There was a strange light in her eyes that Aisha couldn't fathom. Although Olie's expression remained calm, from her scent Aisha could tell that her heart was racing.

"It's just as I thought," Olie murmured. She closed her eyes and took a deep breath.

What she was thinking, Aisha couldn't guess, but for a long time Olie didn't move. Finally, she breathed slowly in and out several times as though to calm herself, then opened her eyes. They were filled with compassion.

"It must have been so hard," she said. She reached out a hand and patted Aisha on the shoulder.

At her touch, Aisha felt hot tears well in her eyes. Unable to hold them back, she squeezed her lids shut and let out a sob.

"You couldn't sleep either, could you?"

With her eyes still closed, Aisha nodded. Tears spilled from beneath her eyelids.

She hadn't been able to sleep. Not at all.

When she'd arrived at this garden, she'd been inundated with the screams of plants. The clamor of smells had been so intense, she'd felt like throwing up.

There was one section of the garden, in particular, where so many incompatible plants had been placed together, she'd wondered why on earth they'd been planted there.

Some species inhibit the growth of other plants. Normally, scent voices are mere whispers compared to the screams and angry shouts of humans, but in that section, certain sensitive plant species shrieked incessantly because of their proximity to plants that hindered their growth. Their anguish, in turn, affected the surrounding plants and trees, causing chaos throughout the garden.

At first, Aisha had tried to adapt. It was her only option for survival. She'd thought that if she could just get used to the scent voices, she could suppress her reaction, like she did in a crowd.

But even when she was inside, the scents that crept into the building were so distressing she lost her appetite. Instead of getting used to the smells, her misery intensified with each passing day.

It was impossible to accustom herself to the tormented voices of plants subjected to such torture. She felt so sorry for them that, after five or six days, she could no longer even sleep.

She thought of running away and joining Milucha and Jiiya on the farm, but decided against it. No matter how small the risk, she couldn't chance anyone finding out they were still alive.

If she were to survive, she'd have to find a solution, yet no one would understand her, even if she tried to explain the idea of scent voices. After agonizing over this for some time, she had hit upon the idea of rescuing the plants by secretly moving them to another part of the garden.

Olie continued to pat Aisha's shoulder. "This is no ordinary garden," she said. "It's a place to experiment."

Aisha's eyes widened. "Experiment?"

"That's right," Olie said gently. "In a normal garden, farmers strive to foster the healthy growth of their plants, but here they also do the opposite. Some sections are used to test what inhibits plant growth. The area of the garden to which you've been assigned is one of those. That's why incompatible plants are being grown side by side."

Aisha stared at Olie. This possibility had never occurred to her. "Why do they need to test that?"

"To understand plants more deeply. If we want to foster plant growth, we need to understand any factors that could hamper it. That includes what stunts them and what kills them. Many different experiments are conducted here to find that out."

Olie spoke in a low voice, but her tone was clear, her words easy to understand. "For example, by trying out many different things, we might learn how to prevent weeds from growing without using weed killers that harm the human body."

She paused for a moment, as if thinking, then said, "You know that some crops wither when grown near ohaleh, right?"

Aisha's eyes widened. An image of the rolling sea of golden grain out the window of the carriage popped into her mind. Along with its distinctive, powerful smell.

I see.

She'd heard from her father that ohaleh inhibited the growth of other crops, but since she'd come to this region, she'd noticed that the soil where ohaleh grew had a peculiar smell, quite different from any other soil. It wouldn't be surprising if other crops couldn't thrive in it.

"Although it's impossible to farm other grains alongside ohaleh rice," Olie continued, "certain vegetables can be grown with it. At this garden, they're studying which plants grow best where and how. Climate and soil conditions differ in each region, and each protectorate has its own indigenous crops. At Lia Garden, they're carefully researching every aspect of farming and plants to promote agriculture and prosperity throughout the realm."

So that's what's going on here.

Aisha suddenly realized she'd stopped trembling. She'd been told she'd be working at a garden, only to discover it was a very strange garden indeed. Olie's explanation had dispelled her fear and eased her mind.

"But—" she began, then checked herself hastily.

"What is it? You've nothing to fear," Olie said with a friendly smile. "Go ahead. Say whatever you like."

Emboldened, Aisha blurted out, "It seems so cruel. Plants can't move. They can't run away when they're in distress. They're screaming in agony . . . and it's not even their fault."

Olie's eyes widened in shock. She sat silently, her mouth slightly open. "Yes . . . Yes, that's true," she murmured finally, then fell silent again, her eyes downcast.

Unable to bear the silence any longer, Aisha sat up.

As if nudged, Olie raised her head and began to speak. "Living here is torture not just for the plants, but for you too. I'll think about whether there's somewhere else we can send you."

Startled, Aisha stammered, "S-somewhere else?"

She was immensely grateful that Olie understood her so well, and joy suffused her at the thought of escaping this place. It seemed like a heavy ceiling that had been pressing down on her had suddenly been lifted. But when she recalled her situation, her face clouded.

"Please. Do not waste your time on someone like me," she said. "I sincerely appreciate your concern, but in my circumstances, I am not at liberty to—"

"Your circumstances?" Olie asked, raising an eyebrow.

"Yes."

"What kind of circumstances?"

Aisha clenched her hands together and averted her eyes.

"It's difficult for you to answer, is it?"

Aisha bowed her head. "Yes. I beg your pardon."

Olie's face relaxed. "That's all right. I'll talk it over with Master Raoh when he comes back. Let's decide after that."

6
The Hidden Room

"I will arrange things just as you suggest. Allow me to prepare everything so that you may depart on the morning of the day after tomorrow."

With these words, Master Raoh rose from his chair and took Olie by the hand, gently leading her toward the door.

"Thank you," she said, smiling a little bashfully. "And my apologies for insisting you let me go too. I know it will make it harder to get ready in time."

"No apology necessary," he said. "You'll be able to rest much better at Yugino Lodge. As for the issue we talked about the other day, I've already taken measures to address it, so rest easy and enjoy your stay."

With a nod, Olie stepped out into the corridor. Master Raoh watched her leave with her maidservant, then closed the door of his study, turned the key in the lock, and hurried over to the back of the room.

He pushed a spot on one of the bookcases, and it moved soundlessly to one side, revealing a small room behind. As Raoh entered the room, Masyu, who was sitting in a chair reading a book by candlelight, raised his face.

"What a rascal you are," Raoh said dryly. "Everything turned out exactly the way you planned."

Masyu glanced toward the study and smiled faintly. "It's a good thing that was Lady Olie. If it had been Aisha, she'd have realized I was here."

Raoh raised an eyebrow. "She's that sensitive?"

"Yes."

"She surpasses even you then."

Masyu chuckled. "I don't even come close."

"If so, isn't it risky for her to stay with Lady Olie?" Raoh frowned.

Masyu shook his head. "It'll be fine. Because it's Lady Olie."

"Yes, I suppose you're right," Raoh acknowledged with a groan. "But still . . ."

Masyu stood, and pulled another chair over, urging Raoh to sit, then returned to his own chair. "Master Raoh," he said quietly. "A door has opened unexpectedly before us. Please don't falter now."

Raoh's brows drew together. "True, it is unexpected. But what on earth do you think that girl can do? Even if she's endowed with . . . the power of the first Kokun, where will that door lead us? I fear it could be the road to destruction."

"I understand your concern. Aisha's existence is exceedingly dangerous. There's no knowing when, where or who might realize her significance."

Raoh glared at him. "More than dangerous. Disastrous. Depending on who realizes the truth, it could shatter the foundation upon which this empire stands."

Masyu held his gaze steadily. "What we're trying to do will shake up the empire one way or another," he said evenly.

Raoh shook his head. "No, Masyu. That's different. Although what we're trying to do will shake the empire to its core, I've no intention of destroying any elements founded upon the Kokun's existence. Those won't be dismantled; we'll maintain them while still making changes. If we don't, the damage will be too great."

Masyu gazed at him. "I'm sure you know I feel the same way. But there's no guarantee that will be possible once things start to unfold."

Raoh grimaced. After staring somberly at Masyu for some

time, he finally said, "And how do you think that girl can avert the disaster you've feared for so long?"

"I don't know. Not yet. But she may be able to put a crack in the wall we're up against."

Raoh remained silent.

"Like her," Masyu continued, "I'm aware that ohaleh gives off a scent markedly different from any other plant. But I don't know what that means. Aisha might be able to find out."

Still Raoh said nothing.

"It was the Kokun who brought ohaleh rice from the land of the gods," Masyu said. "A girl endowed with the power of the first Kokun has appeared. Are you saying we should ignore this and not seek her help?"

"No. I'm saying it's dangerous."

"Master Raoh, we've already discussed this many times, and I'm sure you understood. It's unlike you to rehash it like this."

Raoh sighed and ran a hand over his face, wiping away the sweat. "Before it was just hypothetical. It's different now that I've met her." He fixed his blank gaze on the flickering candle. "To be honest, I didn't really believe what you told me. It was just a theory. I thought if there was someone like that, I'd have to agree. But I never believed such a person really existed."

Raoh shook his head. "The way you transplanted things in the garden when you were a boy was surprising enough, but if she's able to identify people by their smell, even when separated by a bookcase and a thick wall . . ."

He raised his eyes to Masyu's face. "That's far beyond the realm of human beings. There's no way such an extraordinary power can go undetected. Mijima's already noticed. When Aisha walked through the palace garden, she chose the original route made by the first Kokun—the true Quiet Way. And she did so without any hesitation."

There were many paths in the Kokun's garden. All were called the Quiet Way, but only one of them had been made by the first Kokun. The others were added by subsequent Kokun after the number of pilgrims increased to keep the first path from being trampled.

Other than the Kokun, only the emperor and direct descendants of the House of Kashuga knew which one was the true path. They were also the only ones who knew the difference between the first Kokun and those who came after her, knowledge that was passed on to their direct descendants and not to anyone else.

No one had ever correctly chosen the forks in the road that would lead them down the true path without being informed in advance.

Masyu returned Raoh's gaze steadily. "That's precisely why I'm entrusting her to Lady Olie. Olie is wise. Although my older brother gravely underestimates her, I'm sure you realize that."

Raoh absently stroked his beard, which was flecked with white. "Yes . . ." he murmured. After gazing into the air as though lost in thought, he finally shifted his eyes back to Masyu. "Yes. You're right. Considering the situation, keeping her with Lady Olie is probably the best solution."

Masyu nodded. Raising his cup to his lips, he took a sip of his now-cold tea. "It seems there's a high possibility the eggs Olie found were laid by giant yoma."

"Did Mijima tell you that?"

"Yes. I was impressed you ordered a survey to be undertaken just based on Olie's drawing."

Raoh snorted. "It's rare to be praised by you. But to be honest, I was afraid." He rubbed his arms. "It looks like your fears were justified after all. I don't know how many times I've wished the great earthquake had never happened."

Sixty-three years after the death of the first Kokun, a massive earthquake had struck the capital. A huge fire had broken out in the palace, and flames had engulfed the archives, destroying many precious books and documents. Although the Book of

Regulations, which contained the rules and addendum governing the work of the scent emissaries known as koshi, had survived, documents concerning the reasons for those regulations had been lost.

Raoh reached over and pulled the book Masyu had been reading toward him. It lay open at an illustration, and Raoh traced it with his finger. "The only mention of giant yoma is this one recorded here in the Alternate Tales of the Kokun. All it says is that a destructive infestation occurred after the first emperor began cultivating ohaleh in the Amaya wetlands. There's a description of the eggs and of how he paled when he saw them and ordered the whole crop burned. But that's it. There's no record of giant yoma appearing after that."

"Which indicates that the regulations and addendums left by the first Kokun were effective," Masyu said. "She recorded minutely detailed instructions on how to respond to a wide range of situations. Looks like there were good reasons for strictly adhering to them."

Raoh nodded. "Considering what's happened, I'd have to agree with you." He sighed. "Your father kept warning us that revising the regulations could jeopardize our future."

Over the course of the empire's long history, revisions to the regulations had ostensibly been carried out at the Kokun's command; in reality, however, it was the emperor who directed such changes.

Thirty-four years ago, Raoh and Masyu's father Yuma had been involved in one such change: the modification of a directive that koshi must report on climate and pest conditions in every area cultivated with ohaleh.

"We had no choice but to change that rule," said Raoh. "Although in retrospect, if we hadn't, we could have prevented the risk of overlooking giant yoma eggs."

With the expansion of the empire's territory and of land devoted to ohaleh, it had become difficult to keep detailed records of every rice-growing area. Instead, the empire was divided into regions, and the inspection method was modified so that the koshi visited only one selected rice growing area within each region to observe and collect climate and pest data.

Yuma had vehemently opposed this change, but he was only seventeen, and the emperor at that time, as well as the heads of both Kashuga Oi and Kashuga Lai, had ignored his objections. A compromise proposed by Raoh to have the farmers in each area report any changes observed during the year was accepted, just barely, but otherwise the revision was adopted in its entirety.

"I agree it was unavoidable," Masyu said. "Last year's revision, however, should never have been passed."

Raoh remained silent for a moment, then nodded. "You're right. And as I helped revise it, I'll be responsible if the result is the reemergence of giant yoma."

The previous year, the regulations had been revised once again. The instruction to: "add shisha weed to the fertilizer when conditions, such as unusually high temperatures and heavy rain, increase the risk of an explosion in the yoma population" had been abolished. The direct reason for the change was a disease that had wiped out much of the shisha crop, but the decision was closely related to management of the empire.

Yoma was the only pest that ate ohaleh, but as it rarely impeded ohaleh growth, it had little effect on the yield. Many varieties existed throughout the empire proper, as well as in the protectorates, and they could fly considerable distances by riding the wind. Because they were so widespread, modifying the fertilizer mix in warm, wet years, when yoma populations multiplied, had placed a heavy burden on the koshi.

It didn't help that the regulations instructed the koshi to: "mix the liquid squeezed from the roots and leaves." To be used fresh, shisha weed had to be grown on location, even in the protectorates, rather than being supplied by the imperial government like other ingredients. As shisha couldn't be used for food or medicine, the empire had to buy up any surplus.

Not only that, when shisha was added, it dramatically reduced overall yield, which meant that the empire had to implement measures to help affected areas.

The emperor's top priority was the stability and efficient management of the empire. As soon as he'd learned that a disease had affected the shisha crop, he requested that the heads of both Houses of Kashuga consider revising this rule. Through trial cultivation, they confirmed that no issue occurred in areas where yoma proliferated even when shisha wasn't added to the fertilizer, and the rule was therefore removed.

"It's too late for regrets," Raoh said, "but at the time, I didn't think the revision would result in the reemergence of giant yoma. Because of something Master Holam, the previous Chief of Pest Control, once said.

"When we were considering the first revision thirty-four years ago, Yuma was so afraid of giant yoma reappearing that I asked Master Holam if yoma mutated. He said they do. When factors like high humidity and heavy rainfall create favorable growing conditions for the plants yoma eat, they proliferate. When they start running out of food and are massed densely together in one spot, sometimes yoma with bigger wings and stronger jaws appear."

Raoh looked at Masyu. "I asked him what would happen if we weakened the plants they like to eat, such as ohaleh. Would that prevent them from mutating?'"

Masyu's eyes gleamed. "And what did he say?"

"He laughed and said he thought it would do the opposite. A decrease in the nutrient content of their food would probably encourage mutation.

"He said the reason yoma mutate is to survive. They bite each other when they fight, so stronger jaws would give them an advantage and increase their chances of procreating, while bigger wings would mean they could fly to new areas where there's less competition for food. So Holam thought that where there'd been a major outbreak and yoma were densely packed together, weakening the ohaleh might instead promote mutation."

Raoh caught sight of Masyu's expression. "I guess I haven't told you that before, have I?"

"No, this is the first time I ever heard it."

Raoh stroked his chin. "It's hard for me to talk about. I was relieved by what Master Holam said, but Yuma wasn't satisfied, and we almost came to blows. It's not a pleasant memory."

Masyu blinked. "What did my father say?"

"He said human knowledge isn't absolute. We aren't omniscient or omnipotent. We don't know everything about insect behavior or about ohaleh. He said the first Kokun must have had good reasons for making those regulations, and it would be dangerous to alter them without knowing what those reasons are."

Raoh's eyes had a faraway look. "At the time, I told him, it's true we're imperfect. But that's precisely why we should use what we do know as a starting point to figure things out. 'History will show which of us is right,' I said."

He sighed and cast Masyu a rueful smile. "In the end, Yuma was right, but what Master Holam said seemed logical to me. To be honest, I still feel that way. If a large outbreak coupled with scarcity of food is what triggers yoma mutation, then why did the first Kokun instruct the koshi to suppress ohaleh growth by adding shisha? Wouldn't it have made more sense to prevent mutation by making sure there was plenty for the yoma to eat?"

"Forgive me for sounding like my father," Masyu said, "but I think the reason that regulation doesn't make sense to you is simply because there's too much we don't yet know. For example, there may be other things we aren't aware of that encourage mutation. And for sure, there's still plenty we don't know about ohaleh. Livestock grow more robust when fed with ohaleh straw, so maybe it changes the physiology of living creatures."

Raoh groaned. "But we tried growing ohaleh without shisha where there were a lot of yoma, and nothing happened—even though we did that for a whole year. At least some of those yoma must have been eating the ohaleh."

"It's true that the area in which you experimented had plenty of yoma, but not enough to call it an infestation, right? The regulations stipulate that shisha should be added when there are signs of a major infestation, so perhaps it's the combination of the two that makes a difference: a massive outbreak coupled with unsuppressed ohaleh growth."

Raoh frowned. "But there haven't been any reports of a major yoma outbreak in Rapa where the giant yoma eggs were found."

Masyu drew a sheet of paper from his robe and placed it on the desk. It was wrinkled and smudged as though from rough treatment. "This is a page from a miscellaneous report I found in the discard bin of the Rapa district governor's archives. It records the words of a farmer from one of the villages in Rapa."

Raoh picked it up and began reading. His eyes widened. "But this is—!"

Written in the Ogoda language, the report stated, *Days of heavy rain and heat continue. Yoma have bred so profusely, they rise like clouds.*

"In the past," Masyu said, "this would have been given to the koshi. The farmers did indeed report continuous heat and heavy rain coupled with a major yoma outbreak, but the official in charge didn't pay attention."

Raoh closed his eyes. "How could they . . ." he murmured. "So the combination of a yoma outbreak and no shisha weed can trigger the appearance of giant yoma . . ."

Masyu gazed at Raoh. "Of course, we need to further

investigate what caused their reemergance, but there's something else we need to consider. What's happening in Rapa shows that giant yoma could appear anywhere in the realm.

"Even after the revision made thirty-four years ago, the koshi still kept a close watch on yoma populations because they had to modify the fertilizer whenever they proliferated. Farmers reported any outbreaks to the koshi, and the koshi added shisha weed to the fertilizer in accordance with the regulations. Since last year, however, there has been no need to add shisha, and we're seeing the result of that in Rapa."

Raoh nodded, his face grim. "You're right. It's been unusually hot and humid, not just in Ogoda but in East and West Kantal too. We must hurry. I'll tell Iilu first thing tomorrow and reinforce monitoring."

Masyu's lip curled slightly. "I'm quite sure my brother will have a very different opinion when he hears this report."

Absently, he ran a finger over the handle of his tea cup. "He's far more likely to think that if there's a possibility of a giant yoma outbreak in Ogoda, we should just let it happen. Because they've been smuggling chichiya and making their own fertilizer behind the empire's back."

Raoh frowned and opened his mouth, only to close it again.

In a low voice, Masyu continued. "What better deterrent for the people of Ogoda than to believe that the most disastrous pest infestation they've ever experienced is due to their covert experiments to produce fertilizer?

"When the news gets out, places like Rigdal that have been secretly buying chichiya from Ogoda will think twice before trying to do the same thing. And even if giant yoma outbreaks occur in areas that didn't make their own fertilizer, they can be blamed on pests flying in from Ogoda. That would solve a number of thorny issues all in one go."

"You're right," Raoh said with a grimace. "That's what Iilu would probably do. And I was one of those who agreed with his proposal to overlook the fertilizer issue for the time being."

He shook his head and sighed. "All these things coming together at once, it's such bad timing. Although I suppose Iilu would see it as giving us a chance to plan our response."

Masyu dropped his gaze to the illustration in the book. "Have giant yoma eggs been found anywhere else, or just in Rapa?" he asked.

"Just Rapa. To make sure, I sent reliable koshi to each region, and also notified all the cultivation areas in every part of the realm, but no eggs were found. For now, I think we can assume that Rapa's the only place."

"And the fields where the eggs were found have been burned off, right?"

"Yes. We checked the surrounding areas thoroughly too, but found no signs."

"If so, we may be able to buy some time."

Raoh nodded. "And," he said, "if an outbreak only occurs when those two conditions are combined, we should be able to do something about it."

"I hope you're right," said Masyu, "but if giant yoma could be stopped so easily, I doubt the founding emperor would have paled at the sight. Even if there was something we could do . . ."

He shifted his eyes to the crumpled page from the report. "Under the present circumstances, it's going to be hard to monitor conditions thoroughly enough to catch every yoma infestation. And even if we catch them, we can't restore the directive to modify the fertilizer and prevent the emergence of giant yoma—because that revision was made by the Lady Kokun's decree."

Raoh's face tightened.

His eyes still on the report, Masyu continued. "If a giant yoma outbreak occurs, even my brother will likely recognize the importance of shisha weed, yet it still won't be easy to reinstate that regulation. The reason the empire stopped buying shisha weed has already been explained not only to the koshi but also to the farmers producing it in the protectorates. If we start using it again, they'll suspect the giant yoma outbreak is not Ogoda's fault, but rather the fault of the fertilizer distributed by the empire. That will shake their faith in both the Lady Kokun and the empire itself. Neither my brother nor His Majesty, the Emperor, will be quick to conclude that they should revive the use of shisha weed."

Masyu raised his eyes and gazed at Raoh. "For His Majesty and my brother, the current state of the empire is top priority, and therefore, they're likely to see everything through that lens. We, however, must think and act in consideration of the coming years, decades, and centuries ahead."

Emotion flared in Masyu's eyes, perhaps grief or anger. "The two Houses of Kashuga made a terrible mistake, and they've plowed ahead without correcting it. We can't let the empire proceed any further down the wrong path.

"If giant yoma, which were assumed to have disappeared forever, should reemerge and proliferate in the near future, everything recorded by our founding ancestor could come true. If we make the wrong choice now, we'll bear the blame for a crime so grave we can never atone—a catastrophic famine that will bring about the collapse of the empire."

Raoh stared at Masyu for some time. Finally, he said in a low voice, "You've been thinking like that ever since you were seventeen. I've been thinking about it for a long time too, but the urgency you feel has always been far more pressing than my vague premonitions."

Masyu smiled suddenly. "Do you remember the little bug at the bottom of the bath dipper?"

Raoh stared at him.

"Once, long ago, when I was taking a bath, I noticed there was a little bug in the dipper I'd filled from the tub, but I couldn't stop myself in mid-swing and poured the water down my back. The bug probably died instantly, without ever knowing what happened.

"When you heard me muttering about it, you said we're just like that bug. And so is everything else in this world. Even so, you said, some bugs survive, and so have we.

"For me," he continued softly, "to know that the head of the House of Kashuga thought that way was like a light shining in the darkness."

Masyu rose slowly. "Master Raoh, please continue to be my guide and companion."

7
Olie and Masyu

Once Masyu had left, Raoh remained in the hidden room, lost in thought, his eyes fixed on the cover of the book that still lay on the table.

Masyu's a lot like Yuma.

He'd thought of his friend as a younger brother. Seeing Yuma's face and eyes in his mind, he sighed.

Yuma had been a cheerful man, so when Raoh first met Masyu, with his intense, melancholy gaze, he'd wondered if they were really father and son. But as he got to know him better, he realized Masyu and his father were very similar.

Yuma used to get that same glint in his eyes when he argued.

When Yuma was called upon to help revise the koshi regulations, he had only been seventeen, but he'd still argued passionately with his father. Recalling his earnest expression, Raoh reached out a finger and traced the shape of the white mountain depicted on the book's cover.

Did you find it in the end?

Ohaleh Mazula, home of the gods. Not even the emperor knew where it was located, although it had served as the catalyst that transformed the tiny valley kingdom of Umal into a great empire. Nor had anyone found the shining white mountain, Yugila, the gate that stood between this world and the land of the gods.

The only depiction remaining of the mountain Yuma had spent his life searching for was this one, painted long ago by the founder of the House of Kashuga, who'd accompanied the first emperor to the home of the gods. With them, they'd brought back ohaleh rice and the first Kokun.

Yuma had warned him that ohaleh was an aberration. "We who have turned a blind eye to that fact will soon witness the fruit of our own folly," he'd said.

Raoh had wondered at the paleness of his face when he'd declared this. He recognized that Yuma's fears were not unfounded. He wondered himself if it was wise to change the regulations when they didn't know why the first Kokun had made them. He'd even considered the possibility that a disaster might someday occur if they made the wrong choice.

But it was nothing more than a hypothesis, a disaster that hadn't happened yet and might never even occur. How could Yuma find that so terrifying that the blood drained from his face?

When Yuma left the capital to travel around the empire, Raoh had assumed he was trying to prove he was right because he couldn't accept the opinions of the rest of the Kashuga Lai. The dread that drove Yuma was not something Raoh had been able to share.

Even now, when a giant yoma outbreak seemed imminent, there was still a part of him that wanted to believe it was only a passing phenomenon. Masyu, however, was deeply afraid. Like his father, he'd feared this catastrophe ever since he was a youth.

Raoh's eyes narrowed. *He's probably worried about Lady Olie, too.*

If a disaster struck, the people would direct their anger and resentment at the Kokun. What would they do when their hearts turned against the one they'd revered as a living goddess? At this thought, fear seized him.

Lady Olie . . .

He closed his eyes. *I'm so sorry for what I've done to you . . . and to Masyu.*

The Kokun was forbidden to have a relationship with any man, let alone marry one.

Although outwardly no such rule had ever been recorded, after the death of the first Kokun, the heads of the House of Kashuga had been ordered by successive emperors to dispose of the Kokun if she became romantically attached. They were to make it appear that she'd died of illness; then begin selecting a replacement.

The first Kokun had had a lover, a fact known only to her successors, the emperor, and the direct heirs of both Houses of Kashuga. She'd had a long-term romantic relationship with Amil Kashuga, who had brought her back from Ohaleh Mazula, home of the gods. But she never bore any children.

Because she died without offspring, Ramulan, the emperor at the time of her death, decided they should seek out her reincarnation, and the system developed for this purpose was passed down from one generation to the next.

Although not recorded in the official history, within the House of Kashuga, it was orally transmitted that Ramulan was relieved the Kokun did not bear Amil Kashuga any children. He probably feared that if she'd had descendants and their kinship connections had expanded, it could give rise to a faction that rivaled the emperor. It was for this reason that he secretly ordered the House of Kashuga to ensure that future Kokun bore no children.

The idea of a deity incarnate discarding one body and being reborn into another seemed so appropriate for a living goddess that the selection system became instrumental in enhancing the Kokun's divine authority.

It also had another advantage: The search for the reincarnated goddess made it easier to manipulate the protectorates. The empire could choose the next Kokun from a protectorate with which it wanted to reinforce its ties.

It was no easy task to find a girl who was not only the most politically advantageous, but was also endowed with celestial beauty and intelligence coupled with an obedient nature. That the system had worked well up to now was thanks to the myth that it took thirteen years to reincarnate, a belief based on the fact that the first Kokun had been thirteen when she arrived in this world.

During the empire's long history, the system had been threatened just once—when a Kokun had fallen in love and become pregnant. At the command of the emperor, she, along with her lover, had been eliminated by the House of Kashuga before she could bear her child, and the cause of their deaths had been made to look like illness.

From then on, this story was told to every girl chosen as the Kokun when she reached her fifteenth year. By then, she'd had time to understand the true nature of her existence and wasn't surprised to learn this appalling tacit rule.

The empire awarded significant economic privileges to the protectorate from which the Kokun came. Every Kokun was made aware while still in her teens that her role was to bring prosperity to her homeland and stability to the empire—and therefore she could not hope for the kind of happiness enjoyed by ordinary girls.

The Kokun's crown is a disguise for forced surrender.

Olie's words still haunted Raoh. He was the one who'd selected her as a candidate for Kokun. He'd been the chief koshi responsible for all the scent emissaries, and he visited every corner of the chosen protectorate, Rigdal, in his search.

At the time, Rigdal was engaged in a power struggle with neighboring East Kantal, but was in a notably inferior position. If East Kantal were to absorb Rigdal even by legitimate means, such as a marriage between the ruling clans, it would result in the birth of a large power near the imperial capital.

Fearing this, the emperor ordered the House of Kashuga to choose the next Kokun from Rigdal, and Raoh had been entrusted with this mission. For twelve years, he traveled secretly to Rigdal to observe the different girls he'd identified as possible candidates.

Each one was beautiful and intelligent, but Olie was outstanding. Her vibrant cheerfulness and inner radiance captured the hearts of everyone around her, children and adults alike. That she herself was oblivious of this was, Raoh felt, a positive trait.

Above all, she was endowed with good character. She put others before herself and was sincerely kind, which Raoh considered the most important qualification of all. The Kokun had to forget herself and live for others. A girl who put her own selfish interests first could never serve as the living goddess.

Although Olie's father came from a good family, the territory he governed was small, and he was easygoing and content with life. Raoh considered this another favorable factor. Even if his daughter became the Kokun, he wouldn't be tempted to use that for political gain.

Relieved to have found someone so suitable, Raoh chose Olie. Still, he couldn't help but pity her when he thought of the difficult path she would be forced to tread.

She proved to be much stronger than he'd imagined. She'd understood the significance of her role and fulfilled his expectations. But the burden of living as the Kokun ate away at her.

Raoh worried about the subtle physical and emotional changes he saw in her, changes that would have gone unnoticed by those who didn't know her from before. He began to wonder if there was some way to give her a break from being the Kokun, even for brief periods, and ease the burden on her mind.

First, he arranged for her to spend some time away from the palace at Lia Garden. After being there for a while, her spirits revived a little. But there were too many people there for her to completely relax, and although they didn't know she was the Kokun, she still had to pretend to be an anonymous noblewoman.

At the time, Raoh had launched a number of reforms. The construction of Yugino Lodge was part of these, and he'd recently received word that it had been completed. The lodge and adjacent farm would be a base for projects that weren't possible at Lia Garden, and he'd entrusted the work there to his cousin and close friend, Tak, and Tak's wife, Laina.

When Raoh saw Yugino Lodge, located in a remote area where no one else would set foot, he realized that it could be the perfect place for Olie to get the respite she needed.

His guess hit the mark. Tak, Laina, and their two sons all understood Olie's situation. While she was there, she could just be a normal girl. Like a wilted flower exposed to welcome rain, she regained her natural vivacity.

After that, whenever she wasn't traveling or performing her duties as the Kokun, she divided her time between Lia Garden and Yugino Lodge.

Raoh had been relieved. He'd assumed that now she had a refuge, Olie would be able to serve as the Kokun for the rest of her life.

But then a ripple occurred: Olie met Masyu.

Masyu had just arrived at the capital from the distant Tenro Mountains, leaving behind his mother and his clan. Now that he was fifteen, he was to be trained as an assistant to Iilu, the future head of Kashuga Lai, and he applied himself studiously to his training.

When he first came to Lia Garden, however, the Gardeners accused him of being an irresponsible prankster because he moved plants around in the fields at night. They punished him harshly, and Masyu punched them in return, causing a ruckus.

Raoh knew the Gardeners often treated Masyu spitefully because they belonged to Kashuga Oi, and he guessed that this had escalated the incident. Regardless of the reasons, however, Masyu had broken some of their teeth with his fists and would need to be punished accordingly.

When asked why he'd played such a prank, Masyu had refused to answer, glaring at Raoh with a strange gleam in his eyes. This attitude further incensed the Gardeners and the Master Gardeners as well, and Raoh concluded it would be better to remove Masyu from Lia Garden altogether.

However, if he sent Masyu, who was already in a delicate position, back to Kashuga Lai after causing such a commotion, Raoh feared he would be treated even more cruelly, aggravating his already troubled heart.

One night, when Raoh was searching for some way to protect the son of his friend Yuma, Olie came to visit.

"Did you see what that boy transplanted?" she asked.

Raoh realized with a shock that he hadn't even thought to ask which plants Masyu had moved.

Her cheeks slightly flushed, Olie said, "I checked the garden management diagram. Everything he moved had been planted with things that inhibited their growth. He was trying to save them."

Raoh stared at her in surprise.

Masyu had been sent here to learn about plants as part of his training as an assistant to the future head of Kashuga Lai, but lessons on which plants inhibit the growth of other plants would only begin a little later. Having just been posted here, there was no way he could have known that.

"I'll probably sound silly for saying this," Olie stammered. "But I think he may have realized from their fragrance how the plants were affecting each other."

Raoh still remembered the light that had shone in her eyes as she'd said this.

"What makes you think that?" he asked.

The flush in her cheeks deepened, and her voice grew fainter. "I saw him. Replanting them at night. It looked like he was bending down and smelling them."

Raoh wasn't convinced that Masyu could tell which plants

inhibited others and how just by their smell, but he'd been racking his brains to find a way to help the boy. Olie's animated expression inspired an idea: He could send Masyu to Yugino Lodge.

Tak had recently sent word that he needed more help and had asked Raoh to find a reliable young man to join them. It seemed like the perfect plan. He could send Masyu into the mountains and say it was a punishment.

The thought that he might meet Olie there didn't concern Raoh at all. As a direct descendent of the Kashuga Lai, Masyu's rank allowed him access to both the Kokun and any confidential information. So even if their paths happened to cross, Raoh couldn't see it being a problem.

I wonder when . . .

When had the two of them come to care so deeply for one another.

In the beginning, there'd been no sign of any attachment. But when Masyu finished his work at Yugino Lodge and returned to Kashuga Lai just a year later, he'd undergone an astonishing transformation.

The youth, who had been like a sharp blade that cut anyone who touched it, had become a man, taciturn but with an inner strength. The change was so remarkable that the head of Kashuga Lai, Ranosh, had jokingly wished Tak and his wife would teach him how to tame wild horses like that.

Although training to become a koshi normally took three years, Masyu finished in just one year and began traveling around the empire as the Kokun's escort. He was promoted to the rank of senior koshi when he was not yet twenty, an unusually young age, and this position gave him access to a wide range of classified information.

His sharp mind and industriousness were so outstanding that his brother Iilu worried he might usurp his position as heir to the head of Kashuga Lai. Masyu, however, evinced no interest in politics. Instead, he traveled to every corner of the empire as though possessed.

At the time, it probably never occurred to anyone that he cared for the Kokun. He treated her with a cool composure that bordered on coldness, never letting anyone suspect that he loved her.

If that disaster had never happened . . .

Raoh sometimes wondered if the two of them might have succeeded in nurturing their relationship without being discovered.

It was Olie who broke the protective cocoon they'd spun together.

In those days, winters were often longer and colder than they were now. Heavy snows fell in the mountain regions, blocking roads to villages in the valleys and isolating them for months. The advent of spring brought frequent avalanches that could obstruct roads already cleared.

The koshi, who traveled the empire to collect data on the approaching seasons and important stages in the farming year for the Ministry of Wealth, were well-versed in the climate of each area and how to circumvent danger. Even so, they couldn't completely avoid sudden changes in the weather, or avalanches, and occasionally some lost their lives.

Raoh was having lunch with Olie in her palace when he received the news that three koshi, including Masyu, had gone missing while crossing a mountain pass.

During the messenger's report on the harsh conditions at the site, which had been struck by several avalanches, Olie remained motionless, her face frozen, but Raoh clearly remembered her turning as pale as paper.

A search party was dispatched immediately, but avalanches blocked the roads in many spots, and word was slow to reach the palace.

One night, a few days after they'd first received the news,

Olie came down with a high fever. She recovered quickly, by which time news had reached them that Masyu and the others were safe. Raoh breathed a sigh of relief.

Not long after, however, rumors began circulating like ripples among the palace maidservants that the Kokun, in her fevered dreams, had repeatedly called Masyu's name.

When Mijima, who was working as a koshi with the Kokun at the time, told Raoh about the rumors spreading among the palace maidservants, fear knotted his stomach. He recalled the way all color had drained from Olie's face when she'd heard the report.

Collapsing with a high fever and calling out someone's name indicated a depth of concern that was far from ordinary. It was no wonder the servants were gossiping.

While Raoh was agonizing over what action to take, Masyu visited Kashuga Oi, supposedly to apologize for causing everyone so much concern. Once they were alone, Masyu asked as casually as if he were talking about the weather, "So, are you planning to poison the Lady Kokun?"

There was something terrifying behind his smooth composure, as if he were prepared to whip out a blade should Raoh give the wrong answer. In that instant, Raoh knew his feelings for Olie were as deep as hers for him.

After a pause, Raoh said sternly, "Is there some reason she should be poisoned?"

In a quiet voice, Masyu responded, "If you're asking whether we've fallen in love, that question is meaningless. Whether it's true or baseless rumor, the very existence of such a tale puts the Lady Kokun at risk. The fact that I've placed her life in danger is an indisputable fact."

"That's true, but if there's any chance she's with child—"

Masyu shook his head. "There is not."

He gazed steadily at Raoh, a fierce gleam in his eyes. "However, my brother's already searching for proof. If there's anything he can find to use against me, he'll gladly recommend that the emperor do away with me."

True, Raoh thought. Iilu was certain to see this as a gift from the gods. He feared Masyu, so it'd be no wonder if he seized this opportunity to get rid of him, as well as the Kokun.

"I'm going to distance myself from the House of Kashuga," Masyu said flatly. "No matter how frantically my brother may search, I doubt he'll find evidence compelling enough to convince the emperor. But now that he's found a weak point, he'll inflict on me and Lady Olie a level of insidious suspicion and scrutiny we've never experienced before.

"I don't care about myself, but I don't want to subject Lady Olie to a life devoid of any rest at all." His voice cracked as he said these last words.

Masyu rarely revealed his emotions, and the break in his voice pierced Raoh's heart like a needle. Sorrow seeped from the pinprick and spread through his chest.

Olie's pale face rose in his eyes. They'd met when Masyu was fifteen and Olie seventeen. Had they been just a man and a woman, the bond they'd nurtured since that time could have become the greatest treasure of their lives.

But between these two, such a bond could never be.

Raoh shut his eyes. There was no time to regret the past. He had to think ahead and act.

With a sigh, he opened his eyes and said, "I understand how you feel, but if you leave the House of Kashuga now, people will assume the rumors are true."

A smile touched Masyu's lips. "That's why I've come to you, Master Raoh."

Raoh stared at him.

"Could you please explain that you've sent me away as a warning?" he began, the words tumbling from his mouth.

"Whether or not the rumors are true doesn't matter. The fact that those rumors arose, in and of itself, has hurt the Lady

Kokun. Who knows what other rumors might arise should I continue to travel with her as a senior koshi. You can tell everyone that you explained this to me and told me to reflect on how I should conduct myself as a direct descendant of the House of Kashuga."

Masyu concluded by suggesting it would also be helpful if Raoh could tell Sir Ranosh, Masyu's adoptive father and head of Kashuga Lai, that Masyu saw this as an excellent chance to avoid conflict with his brother.

Masyu's explanation was so thorough, it was clear he'd been planning for a long time how to respond to this situation if it arose.

"What will you do once you leave the House of Kashuga?" Raoh asked.

"Enlist in the Five Peaks Army," Masyu replied lightly.

Raoh was stunned by his answer.

The Five Peaks Army, so called because the first emperor had crossed five mountain peaks to pacify the clans, was an elite force that guarded the empire's borders. Unlike the imperial guards, which protected the emperor and the imperial capital, soldiers serving on the frontiers were quite rough, and many were hostile toward the House of Kashuga, which controlled central politics.

"Why would you choose the Five Peaks? Wouldn't the imperial guards make more sense?"

"They're too close to the House of Kashuga."

"But . . ." Overcome with disappointment, Raoh sighed. "It's just such a shame," he said. "I wanted you to stay with Kashuga Lai."

At Masyu's urging, they'd launched several secret experiments at Yugino Lodge that Raoh hoped would succeed. If Masyu stayed with Kashuga Lai, there'd be so much more they could do together.

"I've always hoped that one day you'd play a central role within the Ministry of Wealth and change the current system."

Masyu's eyes softened. "That you felt this way about me has been a tremendous support. I thank you."

He lowered his voice and said firmly, "I'm leaving so I can do things that can't be done if I remain on the inside. Although no signs are evident yet, I'm sure that dangerous times are coming. I promise I'll find a way forward that will save us from a descent into hell."

Life in the Five Peaks Army couldn't have been easy, but within a year, Masyu had been promoted to lead a troop of one thousand cavalry. Although he could easily have risen to senior rank within the army, he rejected that path to join the Roots, an intelligence organization under the Ministry of Surveillance that probed the political situation in the protectorates. There he'd gained the firm trust of the emperor and was appointed an inspector.

During this period of dizzying transition, Masyu continued to visit Raoh and explain to him the route he was charting to avert impending disaster. Raoh had listened to his ideas and offered suggestions and support for his plans.

Now, Masyu had discovered a key that might open a new door.

Master Raoh. I've found the real Kokun.

The shock and perturbation that had filled Raoh when he first read these words in Masyu's letter spread through him once again.

Ever since that day, a verse from the ragged, yellowed pages of Alternate Tales of the Kokun had kept floating into his mind; words whispered by the first emperor who had paled at the sight of giant yoma.

The clouds of hunger cover the sky. The earth withers. No food for the mouths of men. Oh Kokun, read the truth of all things in the wind and save all sentient beings.

If that girl was the true Kokun, would the clouds of hunger that brought famine upon the people appear once more?

In his mind, he saw once again Olie's drawing of the giant yoma eggs, a pest he'd believed was just an ancient legend. He sighed.

We must prepare.

The signs were apparent. It was best to assume the worst and get ready now.

First, we must do something about the giant yoma in Rapa.

While overtly agreeing with Iilu's approach, he would have to implement secret measures to prevent the insect's spread to other areas.

He heaved another sigh and rose slowly. As he stepped from the hidden room, he was enveloped in dazzling sunlight. Slightly surprised, as though he'd woken from a nap and realized it was still day, he looked out the window at the green forest.

Gazing at the familiar, unchanging scenery, he murmured to himself, "May you stay just the way you are. Now and forever."

Chapter III
Outlanders

1
Life at Yugino Lodge

Aisha was picking edible wild plants when she heard someone call her name. Turning toward the lodge, she saw Laina, who was quite short, standing on her tiptoes and waving both arms. Laina gripped something in one hand, which made it look like she was sending flag signals.

Aisha couldn't help but grin. Laina always waved both hands when calling someone. Her husband Tak often remarked that she only needed to use one, but she just ignored him.

Aisha picked up her basket and hurried back to the lodge.

"Look at how much you got!" Laina exclaimed when she saw the brimming basket. "I'll go wash them," Aisha said, but Laina shook her head.

"Let me do that. Take this to Olie instead." She held out a light woolen cloak.

Aisha put down the basket, wiped her hands on her apron, and took the garment.

"I don't mind that she wanders around," Laina said, "but she always forgets to take something to keep her warm."

The lodge was in the mountains, where it was much colder than the lowlands in which Lia Garden was located. Even now, in summer, they lit a fire in the mornings and evenings, and during the daytime carried a cloak or jacket to throw on over lighter clothing when needed.

"She's probably over at Yukiomi Wood."

Aisha nodded, hugging the cloak to her chest. "I'll go look for her."

"Thanks. Oh, and could you stop by the west field on your way back and tell Tak to bring me some oshaki berries? I asked him to do that yesterday, but he forgot. I need them to season the pickles, so tell him to remember this time!"

"All right."

* * *

Besides Aisha and Olie, the only others living at Yugino Lodge were Tak, a quiet man with a magnificent beard, his wife Laina, who, though short, was as lively as a colt, Laina's mother Ilaina, whose skin was etched with wrinkles, and Tak and Laina's tall, strong twins, Chital and Madal. Although Aisha had only been living there for half a month, she sometimes felt as if she'd been there much longer. Everyone was so relaxed and friendly, there was no need for formalities.

Olie was the same. Here, she was called just Olie, never "Lady" or "ma'am," and after living together under the same roof, Aisha had grown so comfortable with her that she could look Olie in the eye without any qualms. Whenever she remembered that Olie was probably the Kokun, the living Scent Goddess, she feared she shouldn't be treating her with such familiarity. But each time, she reminded herself of what Tak had told her the night they'd arrived.

"This is a special place," he'd said. "No one can enter the valley or woods around this lodge without permission. So, when you're here, forget about people's social status and circumstances. In this place, our gods and teachers are the plants and the sky, the stones and the earth, the bugs, birds, and beasts. They respect us, and we respect them. There's no separation. In the same way, those of us who live here respect each other without making distinctions."

Though Tak's words were intended for Aisha, Olie was beaming as she listened, her face transformed from the one she'd worn in the carriage on the journey from Lia Garden. It occurred to Aisha that here Olie could set aside the burden of being the Kokun and take a break.

Although Aisha couldn't imagine what it was like to be both human and divine, the more she came to know Olie's friendly, cheerful disposition, the more convinced she was that for Olie it must be agony to live in the vast, dimly lit palace as an object of worship, unable to speak freely or intimately with anyone.

Olie never told Aisha who she was, and no one at the lodge ever mentioned it. Still, Aisha sensed they all knew. She suspected this was why Tak had told Aisha to forget people's status and circumstances while she was here.

That was a relief for Aisha too.

I'll do what he says. While I'm here, I'll put everything aside—the pain of feigning death to flee my homeland, the sorrow of being separated from my brother, my fears for the future.

The route to the lodge from Lia Garden had been steep and rugged. Their carriage had stopped part way up the mountain at a hunting lodge where Tak was waiting. Olie and Aisha disembarked, and the carriage began lumbering back down the mountain with Olie's maidservant still aboard. Aisha and Olie would ride the rest of the way on the horses Tak had brought with him.

As soon as the carriage rolled out of sight, Olie's face relaxed. To Aisha's surprise, she swung herself onto her horse with the ease of a country girl and started up the mountain path. Tak gazed after her with the affection of a father watching his daughter.

Olie guided her mount with a sure hand, occasionally breaking into song. She had a beautiful voice.

The song was unfamiliar, and Aisha guessed it was from Rigdal, the Kokun's homeland. Although she couldn't understand the words, it was a joyful tune, and by the time the lodge came into sight, Aisha was humming along with her.

Once they reached the lodge, Olie changed into clothes that were easy to work in and showed Aisha around the building and its surroundings. When the sun began to set, Olie stepped into the kitchen to help Laina prepare dinner, as if this was the most natural thing for her to do.

As she bustled about the kitchen, she filled Aisha in on details like which dishes were whose and which ones Aisha could use. The peaceful, cheerful scent she exuded eased Aisha's jitters at being in unfamiliar surroundings, helping her to forget her nervousness.

The lodge smelled of forest. Its deep fragrance had permeated the roof and walls of the building and merged with the smell of wood crackling on the hearth, jogging memories of Aisha's home. Enveloped in these familiar scents, she'd slept soundly from the night she arrived.

Life at the lodge resembled life in Aisha's village. Apart from supplies, which were delivered every few days by a fixed team of porters, they lived on what they gathered from the forest or grew in the fields. They also raised livestock, and Tak and his sons were busy from morning until night.

When they finished their evening meal, the men retreated to the study to write or do other work, so they only saw the women at breakfast and dinner. Although they weren't talkative and opportunities to talk were rare anyway, the men always smiled at Aisha when their eyes met.

In contrast, Laina was extremely talkative, her mouth moving as fast as her busy hands and feet. A hard worker, she rose before dawn and went to the cellar to start milling the rice they would eat that day, using a foot-powered mill. The household woke to the rhythmic thump of the pestle pounding the rice.

Rice cultivation wasn't possible where Aisha had grown up near Tohula Ila, and she'd never seen a foot-powered mill before. She was surprised at how strenuous it was. The thought that Laina, who was close to sixty, did this every morning before cooking the rice for them to eat, made Aisha feel guilty. "Can I help?" she asked timidly.

Laina beamed with pleasure and clapped her on the shoulder. "Well, if that isn't the sweetest thing to say! But with those skinny legs of yours, you're going to have a hard time of it. Let's start by taking turns. Besides, at my age, if I slack off, I'll lose what strength I've got."

Laina was right. The rice pounder was much heavier than Aisha had expected, and within a short space of time, not only her legs and hips, but also her back and stomach muscles were aching. As she'd been the one who'd offered to help, she couldn't bear to give up. Gritting her teeth and drenched in sweat, she kept pumping the pedal. When Laina insisted on taking over, warning Aisha with a laugh that she'd come down with a fever if she pushed herself too hard, Aisha felt almost dizzy with relief.

Although she didn't come down with a fever, the next day her body ached all over, especially her legs.

Despite being of royal blood, Aisha hadn't been pampered as a child. Her father often went away with Jiiya on trading trips. Left behind, Aisha had helped her mother with the daily chores from an early age. After both her parents died, she did most of the housework herself. Still, the Makishi had helped a lot, and, in retrospect, she realized her life had been easy compared to life at the lodge.

The work here seemed endless. Once they milled the rice, they not only had to cook it, but also mix the bran with water to make livestock feed. Aisha began helping with these chores too, learning from Laina how they were done.

When Master Raoh had sent her to Yugino, he hadn't assigned her any specific tasks. She'd asked Tak what she should do, but he'd just said, "All in good time."

She was at a loss, until one night Olie gently told her, "I brought you here to ease your mind, so just relax and enjoy this place. Everyone will feel much better if they know you're happy."

So that's why I was sent here.

Although Aisha was surprised that everyone would be so considerate to a stranger sent to the lodge under unusual circumstances, Tak and his family went on with life as usual, without paying her, or Olie for that matter, any special attention, and Aisha gradually realized there was no point in worrying about it.

The days flew by. Each morning, she rose before dawn to mill the rice and spent the rest of the day taking care of the livestock, cleaning the lodge, washing clothes, picking wild plants, cooking, and helping Laina with any other chores.

Olie's days were much the same, an endless series of mundane tasks that she tackled calmly and methodically. The person Olie spent the most time with was probably Ilaina.

Though Ilaina was tiny and her face was lined with wrinkles, her eyes were always sparkling. Despite being over eighty, she had no trouble climbing the mountain paths or steep stairs. She'd clearly passed on her boundless energy to her daughter.

Ilaina's main job was taking care of the pigeons.

From the moment Aisha had arrived at the lodge, she'd been aware of the smell of pigeons, but when Olie led her to the attic, her mouth dropped open. The large space had been converted into an aviary and was lined with pigeon holes housing dozens of birds.

Their warmth and scents filled the dimly lit room. Ilaina, her nose and mouth covered with a cloth, was bustling back and forth, carefully sweeping up pigeon droppings and feathers with a short-handled broom.

In addition to the pigeon coops, there were makeshift bookshelves in one corner and a large desk at the back, along with a brazier and tea things.

A pigeon flew in through the window, its wings flapping

noisily. Ilaina put down her broom and approached it, making clucking sounds, then grasped it deftly in both hands, removed a thin tube from its leg, and put the bird in one of the coops.

"They're carrier pigeons, aren't they?" Aisha whispered to Olie, but before Olie could answer, Ilaina looked up and beckoned Aisha over.

When she approached, Ilaina drew out a small letter scroll from the tube and handed it to her. The page was densely covered in writing, but Aisha couldn't read any of it.

"That's not Umalese. What country is it from?" Aisha asked, handing it back.

Ilaina cast her an impish smile. "It's not from any country."

Olie came over, and Ilaina placed the letter scroll in her outstretched hand. She read it wordlessly, a faint flush creeping up her cheeks. As she watched Olie, Ilaina's smile deepened.

2
The Yukiomi Tree

Olie loved walking in the woods and would wander off whenever she had a little spare time. There was no need to fear any bandits, but the woods were full of other dangers. Every time Aisha saw her casually stroll off into the trees on her own, she couldn't help thinking Olie was truly the Lady Kokun, the one who knows all things.

Although the forest was deep, there were not that many paths, and it would be easy for Aisha to find Olie by following her scent. With the cloak in her hand, Aisha picked up the scent trail. As Laina had predicted, Olie had chosen the path that led to a dense grove of yukiomi trees.

It was a clear day, and the sun shone white on the meadows around the lodge where the sheep and cattle grazed. Once Aisha entered the trees, however, the forest canopy blocked the light like a ceiling. For a moment, she was robbed of sight, but her eyes quickly adjusted to the darkness, and she could make out the narrow path ahead dappled with sunlight falling through the leaves.

It seemed Olie had passed along the path some time ago; her scent was fading. But as Aisha proceeded along the path, the trail grew stronger, and by the time she reached the large grove of yukiomi trees, she could detect Olie's scent quite clearly within the fragrances on the wind. When it was so strong that she could close her eyes and see the scent halo of Olie's body, Aisha caught sight of her standing among the trees.

She was staring at a lone yukiomi tree, her figure softly

illuminated by the clear light that filtered through the canopy. The innocent tranquility in her expression pierced Aisha's heart.

To be worshipped as the Lady Kokun must be such a heavy burden.

This thought held Aisha back from speaking, and she stood gazing at Olie with the cloak hugged to her chest.

Olie's eyes remained fixed on the tree, as if she were oblivious of Aisha's presence.

Probably because I'm downwind, Aisha thought.

Eventually, Olie sighed and turned, running a hand through her hair. Her brows rose. "Aisha!" she exclaimed. "How long have you been there?"

Aisha bobbed her head. "I'm sorry to have startled you."

Olie stared at her for a moment, then laughed. "It's me who should be apologizing," she said. "You've brought me my cloak."

She hurried over and took it from Aisha. "Did Laina complain very much?"

"A little."

With a laugh, Olie reached out and poked Aisha's cheek with her finger. "Thank you for bringing it."

Aisha blushed. "Uh-huh," she stammered, trying to hide her embarrassment. At a loss for what to say, she blurted out the first thing on her mind. "What were you looking at?"

Olie put an arm around Aisha's shoulders. "Come," she said.

She led Aisha to the spot where she'd been standing and pointed to the tree in front of them. "Do you think there's something different about this tree compared to the others?"

It looked like an ordinary yukiomi tree, still quite slender. *It probably isn't that old,* Aisha thought. Its bark was peeling in places, but other than that, she couldn't see anything unusual about it.

The fragrance that wafted from it, however, seemed slightly different from the other trees.

"Is it sick?" she asked.

Olie's eyes widened ever so slightly. "What makes you think that?" she asked.

"It's just a feeling, but it seems to be whispering, 'Help me.'"

Olie remained silent for a few moments, then nodded. "Yes. This tree has suffered." Looking at the trees surrounding it, she continued. "Do you see how the yukiomi grow more densely here than in the rest of the forest?"

Aisha glanced around and nodded.

The bark of the yukiomi was unique. Patches of faintly luminous white lichen clung to the trunks, so that from a distance it looked as if the bark was covered in snow. The stand of yukiomi was densely packed, with only narrow spaces between the branches in the canopy. The trees looked quite cramped.

"Tak was concerned about how densely the trees grew here. He told me he tried to thin them out a little to let the breeze through and the sunlight in. But he was so busy, he only managed to thin one spot and never got around to the rest of the grove."

Olie placed a hand on the tree in front of her. "Some yukiomi get a blight that peels their bark, and when this one started peeling, Tak felt bad each time he passed it. He expected it would die and thought if he'd been able to give it more sun, it wouldn't have been stricken with blight. But then he noticed something strange."

Olie pointed to a spot a slight distance away. "Look there," she said.

Following her finger, Aisha saw a glade. The sun shone brightly on the grasses, but looking closely she noticed that the trees were of different thicknesses, and the fragrances that wafted her way seemed oddly disparate.

"What do you think? Is that clump of trees over there healthy? I'm sure you can tell."

Aisha shook her head. "This grove here smells calmer and healthier than that one."

Olie nodded. "That's right. Tak was very surprised. Where he'd thinned the trees to improve airflow and bring in more sunlight, some trees did grow thicker and taller, but others got sick or were infested with pests.

"In contrast, in the part of the forest where we're standing, the trees grew more uniformly, and the grove seemed healthy. Not only that, but . . ."

Olie reached out to stroke the bark of the tree. "This one didn't die. Even though its bark is peeling, and it's clearly sick, it survived."

Aisha stared at the tree in front of her. Unlike that of a robust tree, its scent voice was feeble, a call for help.

As she sniffed the air, however, she began to pick up a different fragrance, a gentle one. It wafted from both the weakened tree and the other yukiomi around it. In response to the plea for help, multiple scent voices were intertwining like threads, softly wrapping the suffering tree.

"The other trees," Aisha whispered. "They're helping it."

Olie's brows rose slightly, and she gazed at Aisha without speaking for so long that Aisha began to wonder what she was thinking.

At last, she nodded. "Yes . . . You feel it too, do you? Tak said the same thing. He told me the roots of yukiomi are connected underground, and the other trees are probably helping it."

Tears sprang into her eyes. "It's strange, isn't it? This world is a heartless place. Trees can't move and if their bark peels off, they must die where they stand. Yet sometimes others will reach out like this to help and protect the weak."

Her voice sank to a murmur. "I think about that every time I come here. About what it means to help one another. About what we're protecting when we extend a hand instead of abandoning the weak."

She shifted her gaze to the sun-filled glade. "Although a tree that stands alone, hogging the sunlight, looks happy, it's cut off from others and must survive on its own, exposed to the elements. It may in fact be lonely."

3
The West Field

After parting with Olie, Aisha headed for the west field to pass on Laina's message. Although she'd been given general directions, it was her first time to go there, and she was a little worried about whether she could find it. As she followed the mountain trail Laina had told her to take, the breeze brought the smell of ashes and earth, letting her know she was getting close.

When Aisha had heard they'd recently burned off some land and planted buckwheat, she remembered one of the Makishi women telling her long ago that buckwheat seeds were sown while the ashes in the field were still hot.

Aisha had wondered if they could survive. When she'd expressed her concern, the woman had laughed and told her the seeds were like little babies that would grow quickly when put down to sleep in a warm bed.

"The mountain's our mother," the woman explained. "When we burn off the trees and other plants, it makes a nice warm bed to grow buckwheat and beans and millet. After that, we thank the soil and let it rest a few years. Trees and plants start growing, wild and free, 'til the great forest is back. It helps us, giving us mushrooms and medicinal herbs that cure sore tummies. Once it's had enough rest, then we burn it again to make a bed for the beans and buckwheat. That's how the land nurtures us.

"The mist that covers the valley helps too, watering the seeds. Because the ground is warm, the tender shoots that poke their heads out of the soil stay warm and grow real fast."

The woman's words ran through Aisha's mind as she walked until she came to a break in the trees and stepped out into the sunshine.

She stopped and blinked. *Is this a field?*

The land before her was covered so thickly with various grasses, she couldn't tell where the field was.

In the distance she could see Tak bending down, hard at work, but there was no sign of the twins. Clearly, it was the west field, but it was planted not just with buckwheat but with a diverse array of other plants.

Captivated by their varied scents, she closed her eyes and bowed her head. Instantly, another world rose in her mind, different from the one she saw with her eyes.

Eyes still closed, she headed toward Tak, walking through a world shaped by the fragrances of different crops, the insects clinging to them, and all the living things in the ground, while avoiding those areas where the aroma of buckwheat was stronger.

She felt Tak turn toward her as she drew near and opened her eyes. He was looking at her with concern.

"Aisha? What's wrong? Aren't you feeling well?"

Aisha smiled and shook her head. "No, I'm fine. The sun was so bright, it made me a little dizzy, that's all."

Tak's face relaxed. "The sun's strong here," he said. Glancing behind her, he asked, "Did you come alone?"

"Yes. Laina said not to forget to bring back some oshaki berries today."

"Ah!" Tak exclaimed with a laugh. "She asked me to do that, yesterday, didn't she?"

After taking a towel from around his neck and wiping his sweat-drenched face, he pointed to a shrub growing on the edge of the field. "That's oshaki. Could you pick a little and take it to her for me? I might forget again."

"The brown berries?"

"That's right."

"She's going to use them to make pickles, so should I just pick a few?"

"Yes, it's just for flavor. A handful will do."

Aisha nodded and made her way to the shrub he'd pointed at. The berries grew in thick clumps under the shiny green leaves, giving off a pungent fragrance.

She picked enough to fill her palm and slipped them into the pocket of her apron. Her eyes fell on the shrub's roots, and she paused, surprised to see that no weeds grew around them. She crouched, and touched the earth, then frowned. A different scent stung her nose.

This bush . . .

It was proclaiming its boundaries, stridently, like a jay defending its territory.

With her face so close to the soil, she began to pick up multiple scent voices she hadn't noticed before. Without rising, she turned toward the field and gasped. It was so noisy!

The scents in her mother's vegetable patch by their house in West Kantal had been so hushed, it was almost a letdown to smell them. Perhaps because the garden was well-tended and kept free of weeds. But this field was as noisy as a flock of little children, some huddled close playing together happily, others screaming at each other to stay away.

As she focused on the different scents wafting in the air, she detected something strange in the middle of that uproar.

A starkly different smell was emanating from the soil around a patch of grasses a short distance away. Nothing else grew near it, and the patch was surrounded by empty space. The fragrance was stronger than that of oshaki and had a far more menacing shriek as the plants asserted their territory.

Wait a minute . . . I've smelled this somewhere before . . .

The overpowering scent that intimidated the other plants summoned a memory. An image of a vast expanse of rice fields viewed from a carriage window rose in her mind, and she cocked her head.

Could it be? But those plants were already ripe with grain while these ones are still immature . . .

At that moment, Tak came up. He'd probably noticed she was crouching on the ground. "Are you all right?" he asked. "Did you get dizzy again?"

Aisha jumped to her feet. "No, I'm fine," she said. Pointing to some plants that gave off a gentle scent, she asked, "That's buckwheat, isn't it?"

Tak's eyebrows shot up when he saw where she was pointing. "Yes, but I'm amazed you recognized it."

So I was right, Aisha thought.

She turned and pointed to the patch with the intense fragrance. "And that bunch over there, that's ohaleh, right?"

Tak frowned and stared at her.

Aisha's stomach clenched with the realization that she shouldn't have said that. She'd asked without thinking, but now remembered that he probably couldn't distinguish the scents of either buckwheat or ohaleh.

"You recognized them even though they haven't developed any ears of grain yet," Tak said. "That's impressive. Have you worked on a farm before?"

Aisha shook her head. "No, I haven't."

"Is that right?" Tak gazed at her silently, then finally said, "Did you pick some oshaki?"

"Yes. Is this enough?" Aisha showed him the contents of her pocket.

Tak smiled. "That's plenty."

"I'll head back now then," Aisha said, ducking her head in farewell.

Tak nodded. "Be careful on the path. The sun sets early in the mountain forest."

He shifted the hoe in his hand, turned and began to walk

away, when he stopped suddenly and looked back at her. "Aisha, did you happen to see Olie on your way here? She told me this morning she might drop by sometime."

"Yes, I did. She was looking at the yukiomi."

"Ah, I see." He smiled. "I guess she'll turn up soon then."

Aisha shook her head. "I think she'll be a little longer. She said she was going to Blue Creek to see the yukagi. The blossoms will be at their peak."

Tak's face clouded. "To Blue Creek? To see the yukagi?"

"Yes."

His face turned grim. "I forgot to warn her not to go there."

"Why? What's wrong?"

Tak groaned. "The last few years there have been richiyaga, poisonous red moths, in that area. They used to be found only in the lowlands. In this season, their larvae may be on the flowering trees."

"Are they dangerous?"

"The moths aren't so bad, although the dust on their wings can cause a rash. It's the larvae that are frightening. They're the same color as the bark, and if you touch one by mistake, the toxins will make the skin all over your body swell and turn bright red. Some people have difficulty breathing and even die."

Aisha's scalp tightened and her forehead grew cold. "Is there an antidote?"

"Boiled oragilu root." He paused and looked at Aisha. "Do you know tossala?" he asked, translating the word oragilu for her.

Aisha's eyes widened. "Yes. Do you speak Kantalese?"

"Just the names of plants really. But as I was saying, when someone's exposed to red moth toxins, a tea made from boiled tossala root works. It must be drunk as soon as possible though, which means it's a race against time. If it's given too late, it won't work."

Tossala . . .

The Makishi had often used a medicinal solution made from boiled tossala root. *Poisonous moths for which tossala is a remedy. Larvae that look just like sticks.*

An image rose in her mind, and she blurted out, "Richiyaga, poisonous red moths. You mean like muchiyari, spotted moths?"

Tak nodded. "Yes, that's right. Richiyaga are called muchiyari in Kantalese."

As soon as she heard this, Aisha relaxed.

Is that all? Just muchiyari.

The spotted moth had a distinctive smell, and their larvae had a particularly unpleasant odor. Olie, the Lady Kokun, would be sure to notice, so there was no need to worry that she might touch one.

Aisha almost blurted this out, but stopped herself in time, remembering that the Makishi hadn't been able to detect the scent of moths. She would have liked to put Tak's mind at ease, but to try to explain would likely be a waste of words.

"Aisha."

"Yes."

"I'll head to Blue Creek. Please run back to the lodge and tell Laina to prepare some oragilu tea just in case."

"All right. I'll do that." Aisha bowed and left the field. It would be pointless for Laina to make the solution, but it couldn't be helped.

When she entered the forest, it seemed darker than before. The light of the sun on the treetops had a reddish tinge to it now.

The thought that Tak would be relieved when he got to the river and found Olie safe flitted through her mind. *Olie is so good at pretending to be a normal person that everyone forgets she's really the Lady Kokun.*

She walked along without hurrying, and by the time she reached the lodge, the sun was setting. The breeze carried an unexpected scent, and she stopped in surprise, turning toward the source.

A strange, shadowy shape moved through the darkening forest. Aisha gasped to see it was a man carrying someone in his arms.

Masyu!

Gritting his teeth, Masyu strode rapidly toward her clutching Olie to his chest, her head resting on his shoulder. Even from this distance, Aisha could see that Olie's face was badly swollen.

4
Exposed

The sunset was fading by the time Tak reached the lodge. When he'd failed to find Olie at the river, he'd searched all over before heading back. He paled when Aisha described Olie's condition.

"Has she drunk some oragilu?" he asked.

"Laina's just making it now."

Tak nodded and hurried toward Olie's room, but Aisha didn't follow him. Just the thought of Olie's swollen face sent shivers up from the pit of her stomach.

How could Olie have failed to detect the spotted moth larvae? How could Masyu have found her and brought her back?

Nothing made any sense. Terrified that Olie would die, Aisha couldn't stop shivering.

The powerful aroma of simmering tossala root wafted from the kitchen.

I should have run back.

She couldn't help blaming herself for being so slow. Over and over, she heard Tak's voice saying that the medicine should be taken as soon as possible; that if given too late, it wouldn't work. Her face twisted.

Lady Olie. I'm sorry. I'm so sorry.

Laina emerged from the kitchen, bearing a steaming pot and a towel, and hurried toward the back room.

"Laina! You forgot the bowl and tub!" Ilaina appeared from the kitchen with the forgotten items in her hands, rushed after Laina, and disappeared into the far room.

It was long after dark when the twins returned, but Olie's symptoms still hadn't abated. After hearing what had happened, they went to her room to see how she was, only to come back to the living room where they sat by the fireplace and gazed blindly at the unlit hearth.

Aisha crouched in the doorway, her back turned toward the room, and gazed out at the black forest. No one thought to make dinner or even realized the room was dark. Time alone kept passing by.

It was not until late in the evening that Laina emerged from Olie's room. Walking into the living room, she exclaimed, "Goodness! What were you thinking? You haven't even lit the fire!" She clucked her tongue and began lighting the candles.

"How is she?" asked one of the twins.

Laina turned. "Mom thinks she'll be okay now." Fatigue was evident in her voice. "The swelling, pain and itchiness have all gone down, so it looks like she took the oragilu in time."

The twins heaved a loud sigh in unison. "What a relief," they said, then rose and wandered into the kitchen mumbling about being hungry.

Aisha knew she should get up and start making the meal, but she had trouble standing. When she finally got to her feet, her legs were wobbling.

Thank the gods. She's alive . . .

With this thought, tears suddenly welled in her eyes. She tried to swallow her sobs, but couldn't. Shoulders shaking, she burst into tears.

"Aisha!" Laina hurried over and wrapped her arms around her. "You poor thing. You must have been so worried. But it's all right now."

Laina's warm embrace smelled of tossala. Wrapped in that scent, Aisha wept, her shoulders heaving.

That night, dreams plagued her sleep. The scariest dream

came to her at dawn. She and Olie were walking through a field full of grain under a strangely bright, yellowish sky.

Many times, she said, "This grain smells like ohaleh, doesn't it?"

But Olie just kept walking through the grass, giving no indication as to whether she'd heard.

At the end of the field was a stream. The stream with the spotted moth larvae. Aisha tried to run so that she could stop Olie, but her legs were so weak she struggled to make any headway.

"Lady Olie!" she screamed. "Lady Kokun! Please! Wait!

"Lady Kokun?" she heard Olie say faintly. "Who's that?"

Olie turned slowly toward her, backlit by the sun. She had no face.

Aisha woke drenched in sweat and let out a long breath in the darkness. From downstairs she could hear a dull thumping. Laina was milling the rice.

Aisha wiped the sweat from the back of her neck, rose, and changed out of her nightgown. Climbing down the stairs to the cellar, she made out the vague shape of Laina in the blue light of early dawn.

"I'll take over," Aisha said.

Laina turned. "You're up, are you? That's good. I've been cooling the medicinal tea in the kitchen. It should be ready now. Could you take it Olie's room for me? It's on the counter."

Inwardly, Aisha cringed, but she nodded and went back to the kitchen.

A fire had been lit in the oven, casting a dim glow over the room. She put the pot and a tea bowl on a tray. Various noises drifted down from upstairs. Everyone seemed to be waking up.

The shutters were still closed, and the living room was pitch dark, but Aisha made her way through to the corridor without bumping into any furniture and headed towards Olie's room.

Scents were shaded by distance, changing their depth and potency. Although they were subtle and wavered when someone moved, she'd always been able to make out the objects around her and their location by the shading of their scent, at least when she was indoors. It was as natural to her as seeing with her eyes.

As she drew nearer to Olie's room, the smells within became clearer. She sensed Masyu rise and approach the door, so she wasn't surprised when it opened with a faint click before she'd even knocked.

His features were indistinct in the dim light, but she thought he looked thinner. He raised a finger to his lips, and Aisha nodded and passed him the tray, trying to make as little noise as possible.

She heard the bed creak faintly and then Olie's weak voice. "Laina . . .?"

The meaning of Olie's question hit Aisha like a thunderclap. Her head jerked up, and she stared at Masyu. In the dimness, she sensed him gazing steadily down at her. She backed away, then turned and fled.

She heard shutters being opened in different rooms as she dashed along the hall and down the cellar stairs, just missing Tak as he came down from the second floor and went to the sink.

"Laina," Aisha said. "I'll take over now."

"Oh, thanks." Laina climbed down from the foot mill.

Immersed in the varied sounds and scents of the lodge waking up, Aisha kept pumping away at the mill, her thoughts in a turmoil.

* * *

Olie cradled the bowl from which she'd just drunk the medicinal tea while watching Masyu open the shutters. The coolness of the pottery against her feverish hands was soothing.

After he'd opened the window to let in the breeze, Masyu walked slowly around the foot of the bed and sat down on a chair beside it. "How're you feeling?" he asked.

"Much better than yesterday." Olie raised a hand to her face. "Still a bit swollen though."

Masyu reached out and tenderly stroked her cheek with his knuckles. "Is it itchy?"

"A little, but not bad. It just feels a bit stretched and stiff. How about you?"

"I'm fine. I wasn't exposed much in the first place."

Olie gently wrapped her fingers around his warm hand and lowered it.

"It wasn't Laina who brought the medicine, was it?"

"No."

"Aisha?"

Masyu nodded.

Olie closed her eyes for a moment. Opening them again, she murmured, "I guess the secret's out." She smiled ruefully. "I knew I couldn't hope to conceal it for long, but it hasn't even been a month."

"Did you read the messages I sent by pigeon mail?" Masyu asked quietly.

Olie nodded. "Yes, I did. Aisha's bright and strong-minded, too. I think she'll accept the task you want her to do, but . . ."

She looked down at his hand in hers, half shadowed and half illuminated by the white morning sunshine. "I don't want to drag her into this," she said.

After arriving at the lodge and reading Masyu's messages outlining what he hoped Aisha would do, Olie's first thought had been for herself: *He's trying to rescue me.*

Of course, she knew that wasn't all, but as she learned more about Aisha's ability, she couldn't help thinking how everything might change if only this girl would help.

Deep down, I'm hoping she'll agree to it too.

But the closer Olie became with Aisha, the more she hated the thought of plunging this pure-hearted young woman into the same hell she was living. Aisha hadn't been singled out as the Kokun. Left alone, she could lead a normal life.

"Because of her circumstances," Olie said, "and her character, too, she won't be able to refuse if you tell her what you want. It's not fair to make her think she voluntarily chose such a cruel path when she really has no other choice."

Masyu, who'd been listening silently, asked, "But don't you think getting involved might actually help her?"

Olie looked up in surprise. "Help her?"

"Yes. Her life is already a lonely one. Though in a different way from yours."

Olie gazed at him wordlessly.

"Although her ability far surpasses mine, I still have some idea of what it's like to live in a world no one else understands. You must pretend that you live in a world no one understands, but Aisha actually lives in that world. Helping each other might be a kind of salvation for you both, one you can't get any other way."

Olie stared at him intently. He always said things she wasn't expecting. Things that made her see a different angle, as if flipping over a cloth to reveal a pattern on the under side that was invisible from the surface.

A lonely life . . .

That might be true. She recalled the expression on Aisha's face the first time they'd met in the dimly lit infirmary at Lia Garden; how pale she'd looked, racked by the anguish of being unable to share with anyone what kept her awake at night.

When she thought I understood . . .

A sharp pain stabbed Olie's conscience at the memory of how Aisha's face had lit up. *Because she thinks I'm like her.*

She'd deceived Aisha in a terrible way. *I was so caught up in my own loneliness that I didn't see hers.*

She looked at Masyu. She had loved this man for so long. She thought she knew a lot about him. Yet even so, she'd assumed the frown that occasionally crossed his face was just the irritation of someone with a keen sense of smell who'd always been more sensitive than others. It had never occurred to her that loneliness lay there too.

"You say she won't be able to refuse," Masyu said, gently taking the bowl from Olie's hand and placing it on the bedside table. "I think that will depend on how it's presented. I intend to propose she try it out first, and let her know she can quit any time if she feels she can't do it."

Olie raised her brows. "Quit in the middle? Isn't that too risky?"

"It's dangerous, yes, but I don't think she's the type to give up on something once she's decided to do it."

Olie blinked. "That's unusual. For you to trust someone so completely."

Masyu gave a lopsided smile. "As you said, she's in no position to commit treachery."

"But if that's the only reason . . ." Olie said with a frown.

"Yes, if that's the only reason, then she might betray us if my brother threatened to kill her younger brother. However . . ." Masyu paused and gazed out the window, where the sky was growing brighter.

"Her grandfather," he continued, "was driven from his throne because he rejected ohaleh. At a fundamental level, we share something in common."

Olie gazed at his face, lit up now by the morning sun.

Masyu and Aisha had both been raised in the remote Tenro Mountains of West Kantal. A strange connection. At this, a thought suddenly occurred to her. "You two look alike, you know."

Masyu's eyes shifted back to her face. "You see a resemblance?"

"Yes." Olie laughed suddenly. "And you both did the same thing in the middle of the night."

A smile lit Masyu's eyes. When he smiled like that, she could catch a glimpse of his old self. She felt her tension dissolve as she watched his face. "Knowing you, you've already thought this through from every possible angle."

She squeezed his hand where their fingers interlocked and sighed. "All right. I've made up my mind. I'll commit myself to this too."

Masyu said nothing, but his expression softened.

"Is this your last day here?" Olie asked.

"No. I can stay another two or three days."

"Still, the sooner the better. Let's talk with her today."

5
Breakfast

Laina ladled freshly cooked rice onto a large platter, slipped a fluffy omelet over top, drizzled it with a salty sauce made from chopped herbs steeped in chicken broth, and placed the platter on the tray Aisha was holding.

While she swiftly filled another tray with small serving dishes, fragrant tea, fruit and other things, she glanced at Aisha and said, "You go on ahead and take that. I'll bring this one myself."

As Aisha walked down the corridor bearing the steaming breakfast, Tak stepped out of Olie's bedroom.

"Ah, Aisha." He hurried toward her. "Olie wants to have breakfast with you. I'll take this in, so you go and get your own breakfast and bring it to her room."

Aisha looked at him, perplexed. "With . . . me?"

"That's right. Here, let me have that." He took the tray from her hands and headed back to the room at the end of the hall.

Aisha stood staring blankly after him.

"Aisha? What's up?" asked Laina, who was bearing down on her with the other tray.

"Tak says Olie wants to eat breakfast with me . . ."

"She does? Better go get your breakfast then. No, no, that's fine. I'll take this tray to her room. You go on and get yours."

Aisha returned to the kitchen with her feelings in a jumble.

How am I going to face her?

Should she pretend she hadn't noticed? But Masyu would surely realize she was uncomfortable. Maybe they wanted her to join them so they could find out if she knew.

She closed her eyes with a sigh, then opened them again.

No use thinking about it.

She put her own breakfast on a tray and headed for Olie's room. The door opened and Tak and Laina came out. As she passed them in the corridor, Tak reached out and patted her on the head, as if she were a little child in need of encouragement.

Startled, Aisha turned to look after him, but he just kept going without looking back, following Laina into the kitchen.

For some reason, hot tears rose in Aisha's eyes. She blinked them back and took a deep breath, then continued walking down the hall.

When she reached the door of Olie's bedroom, it opened, and Masyu beckoned her inside. The window had been opened wide, and the bright room smelled of morning dew. The aroma of breakfast mingled with the fragrance of dew-wet grass and seikoso, quietly filling the room.

Olie had changed and was sitting in a chair. Masyu took the tray from Aisha and transferred the dishes from it onto a table that had been temporarily set up.

"Sit here," he said, gesturing towards a seat across from Olie. Aisha pulled out the chair and sat in it, while Masyu took a seat a little distance away.

Once they were all settled, Olie said, "Aisha, I'm so sorry I was careless and gave you such a fright." Her eyelids and cheeks were still swollen, but she looked far better than the day before.

Aisha rose and bowed deeply. "It's me who should apologize," she said. "If I'd told Laina sooner, you wouldn't have suffered as much. I'm so sorry."

Olie shook her head. "No, Aisha, it wasn't your fault. Please raise your head."

Aisha looked at her, and Olie smiled. "No more apologizing, okay? Let's eat. Look at this platter of rice. Just like Laina to fill it so full. It's too much for Masyu and me, so let's share it. Masyu, you start. Take as much as you want."

Masyu shook his head. "You two go first. I'll take what's left."

"That's no good. Aisha will be too shy to help herself before us. You and I will have to go first."

Masyu grinned. "So, you won't accept me being too shy."

Picking up the serving spoon, he took some rice and egg, followed by Olie. There was still a lot left.

"Won't you have a little more?" Aisha said. "Laina already heaped my plate with food, and I can't eat it all."

"Just take as much as you like," Masyu said. "I'll eat what's left."

Perhaps because he was out of uniform, he looked completely at ease, not at all like the man she'd first met.

"Oh, by the way," he said. "I stopped by the farm where Milucha and Mister Uchai are living. They're both doing very well."

Aisha's heart leaped, and she leaned forward. "Thank you! Did Milucha complain a lot?"

Masyu smiled. "No, not at all. The couple who run the farm weren't blessed with many children. They just have one, a boy, but he seems to be a genius at playing. Milucha spends the whole day playing with him, so much so that Mister Uchai made a face and said he'd better start teaching him how to work."

Aisha pictured Jiiya and her brother and burst out laughing.

"They sent letters with me. If you want to write back, I'll deliver them for you." He rose, took a thick envelope from the shelf behind him, and handed it to her.

Aisha opened it eagerly and spread out the pages. The first was scrawled with letters as lively as Milucha. All it said was, *I'm doing well. Aisha, how are you?*

The remaining five pages were densely covered in Jiiya's perfect script, which could have been used as a worksheet for handwriting practice. Aisha decided to read Jiiya's letter later and returned both to the envelope.

She'd been worried about her brother and had been wondering constantly how he and Jiiya were doing. Now that she knew they were just the same as always, she felt as if a hard lump inside had melted away.

"Thank you so much," she said, bowing her head. "I'll write a reply today, so please deliver it for me." Masyu smiled and nodded.

They helped themselves to some of the fresh fruit and vegetables, chatting as they did so. Once they'd all taken as much as they wanted, Olie raised her hands to the heavens, then to the earth, and gave thanks to the gods of both.

"Now," she said. "Let's eat."

Aisha waited for Olie and Masyu to start, then picked up her spoon. She mixed some of the fluffy egg with the rice, which had absorbed the sauce, and took a bite. The delicious fragrance of seasonings filled her nose. The savory sauce of chopped herbs marinated in chicken broth fused with the rich flavor of the freshly prepared omelet. It was the perfect complement for the sticky rice, which had been cooked to retain the shape of each grain.

Aisha thought she wasn't hungry, but with the first bite, she realized she was ravenous and couldn't stop eating. For some time, they all concentrated on their food. When they finished, Aisha poured the tea.

"Ah, that was delicious," Olie said as she reached for her tea cup. "Laina's special sauce is so versatile. I'd never eaten upland rice before I came here. Teela, where I come from, is a mountain basin where they grow ohaleh in paddy fields, so I was surprised the first time I ate native rice grown on dry land. To be honest, ohaleh has a deeper flavor. But you said you'd never eaten it, didn't you?"

"That's right," Aisha said. "We ate wheat and buckwheat, which have always been grown in mountain fields."

Olie smiled. "And what a strange coincidence that it was

Masyu's cousins who brought your family the wheat and buckwheat you ate."

Aisha started to nod, but then stopped and looked at Masyu.

"It's okay," he said quietly. "Olie knows everything."

Aisha stared at him. "Why?"

Masyu put his cup down on the table. "I owe you an apology."

Aisha watched him wordlessly.

"That night in the forest, I only told you part of the reason why I saved you. There's another reason that I haven't shared." His expression was inscrutable. "For a long time, I've wished there was someone like you in this world."

"Someone like me?"

"Yes. Someone like you, who can know all things from their scent."

Aisha glanced swiftly at Olie. A sad smile rose to Olie's lips. "I hear the larvae of richiyaga, or muchiyari as you call them, have a distinctive smell," she said.

Aisha said nothing.

"You can smell them, can't you?"

Aisha's pulse began to race. She nodded, her face rigid.

Tears rose in Olie's eyes. "I can't," she said.

6
A Travel Journal

A tear slid down Olie's still reddened cheek.

"I've always had a keen sense of smell," she said. "But I've never been able to smell spotted moth larvae. Or someone on the other side of a door."

She smiled with tears still pooled in her eyes. "You know I'm the Kokun, don't you?"

Aisha nodded, her gaze unwavering. Olie nodded too. "I thought you did. Looks like I was right. Did you pick up my scent when I was behind the bamboo curtain?"

"Yes."

Olie sighed. "That's an amazing ability. To detect my scent behind the screen at the far end of that huge hall, and then to remember it."

She glanced at Masyu. "When I read the letters he sent me, I realized why you behaved the way you did . . . And I knew if we lived at the lodge together, sooner or later you'd realize I didn't have the same ability as you. But what an embarrassing way to reveal my secret. The blossoms were so beautiful, I just wanted to bring back a sprig to put in my room."

Aisha stared at her, barely able to breath. More than shock, what squeezed the air from her chest was the sense that she shouldn't be hearing such a confession.

"I'm sure you know by now, but I'm no goddess, not by any means." Olie's voice quivered. "I was only thirteen when the Kokun's emissaries came to my village to conduct the Search for the Departed Spirit and find the reborn Kokun. When they declared me the Lady Kokun incarnate, my life changed forever. I was elevated instantly to the position of a living goddess and taken from my family and my homeland and brought to the Kokun's palace, whether I liked it or not."

Olie's gaze was unfocused, as if she was looking at something far away.

"At first, I thought: if the Kokun's emissaries say so, it must be true. I must be the Kokun incarnate. But somehow it didn't feel right. Even when we got to the palace, I had no memory of the building whatsoever. I was so anxious. I felt like an imposter and was terrified that someone would find out and expose me as a fake, not the real Kokun at all."

She wiped tear stains from her cheeks. "The first half year was very stressful. But eventually, Master Raoh began teaching me the truth about the Kokun, a little at a time. I was shocked, but relieved too. Because it meant I wasn't the only imposter."

A bitter smile rose to her lips. "Aisha, the Kokun is like a beautiful statute of a goddess that has been given an important role to play. The history of how that came about is complicated, and even if I told you, it would be hard to grasp at first. Let me just say that, except for the first one, none of the previous Kokun were divine beings who could understand all things from their scent."

Masyu shook his head. "I doubt that even the first Kokun was a goddess . . ." His eyes gleamed with a strong light. "She probably came from a foreign land."

He rose, removed his rucksack from a peg on the wall and took out a small book. Pushing aside the plates, he quickly wiped the table and placed the slim volume in front of Aisha. The title on the cover was A Travel Journal, and the yellowed, furry paper suggested he'd read it many times.

"This contains the contents of a manuscript my father had," he explained. "The original document is locked away in the palace library, which is managed by both Houses of Kashuga, the old and the new. No one can read it without permission from the emperor or one of the heads of the Houses of Kashuga.

"Of course, making a copy is forbidden, but my father transcribed it anyway. He always carried it with him. When I was a boy, I saw him reading it under a tree once. Because it was a travel memoir, I asked him whose travels it was about. He smiled and said it was about our ancestor's journey.

"Two years after he sent me to the capital, he disappeared. We still don't know where he went. I hoped the manuscript he treasured so carefully might give me a clue, but I couldn't find it among his books. Perhaps he had it with him when he vanished.

"I asked Master Raoh to show me the original. It's written in the ancient classical language, so it took me a long time to decipher the meaning. But I read it until I understood it thoroughly, then translated it into contemporary language and made this booklet.

"Do you know the story of how the Umal Empire came into being? The epic of the first emperor?" he asked.

Aisha nodded. "Yes, my father told me. The tale of our imperial ancestor Arailu and his companion Amil Kashuga, founder of the House of Kashuga. Together they went to the divine land of Ohaleh Mazula, found the Lady Kokun, and brought back ohaleh rice."

"That's right." Masyu nodded.

Olie began to recite in a soft, singsong voice.

"Long, long ago, in a tiny mountain kingdom called Umal, famine gripped the land, growing worse with each passing year. Many died of starvation. Arailu, the king's youngest son, longed to save his people. He shut himself away in the frozen mountains and prayed for a hundred days. On the hundredth day, a light appeared in the sky, pointing in a certain direction.

"Believing this was a divine message, Arailu set off with his friend Amil. Eventually, they came to Mount Yugila, the gate to the gods, which shone white during the day and blazed like a flame at night. Deep into that mountain they traveled 'til they came to Ohaleh Mazula, the land of the gods.

"Even in the harshest depths of winter, spring flowers bloomed profusely there. Although the divine city was filled with luxurious mansions, no people could be seen except for one beautiful girl who lived in a palace surrounded by a vast garden filled with flowers.

"The girl promised to give the sturdy young outlanders a rice so hardy it could grow in the coldest place if they would but vanquish the monster that had captured her and seized this land, then take her away with them.

"Arailu and Amil fought valiantly to free her and together, all three escaped from Ohaleh Mazula. The seed rice, which she had brought woven into a hair ornament, grew well even in frozen ground and wasteland, yielding a great harvest. Freed from hunger, the people of Umal grew healthy and bore many children, and the kingdom flourished.

"In time, Arailu united multiple clans, becoming their king, and subjugated surrounding lands to acquire a vast territory. In this way, Umal, which had been but a small mountain kingdom, grew into a vast empire blessed with the bounties of earth and heaven."

As Olie finished her recital, a breeze blew through the window and ruffled her hair. Masyu reached out and pulled the book toward him.

"Like the founding myths of any country, there are numerous versions. I've read them all, but this travel journal is the shortest and dullest. There's no mention of Arailu praying in the mountains, receiving a divine message, or battling a monster in Ohaleh Mazula. All that's written here is a record of their travels.

"And for some reason, it only describes the journey home from the land of the gods. But I'm guessing my father believed this record was the closest to what really happened. And I think he was right."

Masyu flicked the book open. It opened at the page he was looking for, as if he'd referred to it many times. "This memoir was written by Yosh, the great-grandson of Amil Kashuga, who accompanied the first emperor on his journey. When he was old and blind, Amil summoned Yosh and had him record his memories of that journey. But the record stopped part way back to the capital, and was left unfinished."

"Did Amil pass away on the way back?" Aisha asked.

Masyu shook his head. "No. Amil Kashuga died in the fifty-eighth year of the imperial calendar. The final entry in this book is dated five years before that."

Masyu flipped to the last page and showed her. It was clearly dated the fifty-third year of the imperial calendar.

"The last entry ends when they reach the Yuino Plain that spread out on both sides of the Manasu River. The Yuino Plain was the first place the Umalese grew ohaleh rice, but when the first emperor Arailu reached it, it was just a wasteland. It says here: 'stretching before them was a barren plain across which a cold wind blew.'"

The Yuino Plain . . .

Aisha recalled the endless fields of rice she'd seen from the window of the swaying carriage. It was not far from there to the capital.

"It does seem odd, doesn't it?" Aisha said. "If he was going to record his journey that far, then why not finish it up with his triumphant return to his beloved homeland."

Masyu nodded. "Exactly. But what intrigued me even more was the beginning of the memoir.

"When Amil and the emperor returned, having barely escaped alive from the land of the gods, it says they emerged into a grassy meadow scattered with white rock protruding from the ground. Along a trail of white stones like dadoula, they met an ascetic descending from a high and distant mountain peak. The pilgrim was shocked to see the two men and asked them how they'd come to this forbidden place.

"What caught my interest was the description that the white stones in the trail resembled dadoula."

Masyu began reciting the words so effortlessly, Aisha realized he knew them by heart. "'On the high mountain peak where no trees grow lies the trail of great white stone, deeply cracked like dadoula. Below the mountain, the river runs through the valley, greener than jasper. An ethereal land, where rivers and lakes appear and disappear even in the lowlands.'"

These words revived a distant memory, and Aisha's eyes narrowed.

A trail of white stones. Deeply cracked. Valley bottom. Green river . . .

A story she'd heard as a child from some young Makishi men who'd returned from pilgrimage to the top of a mountain came back to her.

"It sounds like the Tohula Ila," she murmured. Raising her eyes, she saw Masyu smile.

"I was shocked too when I first read this. Dadoula is the ancient form of the words dohula ula, meaning cracked rice cake. It wouldn't be surprising if Amil Kashuga, who grew ohaleh rice and ate pounded rice cakes, used the expression 'dohula ula' to describe to his great-grandson a trail of cracked white stones high in the mountains surrounding Tohula Ila, the Great Ravine."

Masyu paused and took a sip of his tea, which had grown cold. "Tohula Ila is west of the capital, but in the tale, it says that Arailu and Amil went east. I've had many opportunities to travel the eastern lands where the story of the first emperor is set, but I've never come across a valley that fits this description. I think my father did the same thing. Over a longer period of time. And I think he came to a certain conclusion."

Masyu gazed at Aisha. "Ohaleh Mazula, the land of the gods, is in the west, not the east. The description in the epic tale was false, written to conceal the way to the land of the gods. When Amil Kashuga realized he was nearing the end of his life, he decided to leave a fragment of the truth for future generations and asked his great-grandson to record his memoir."

"Ah," Aisha said, exhaling slowly. "So that's why your father visited Tohula Ila and . . ."

Masyu nodded. "Yes, that's why he came to Tohula Ila. And that's how he came to meet my mother, and why I was born."

The morning light shone through the window, illuminating his tanned face from his forehead to partway down his cheeks.

"My mother was the daughter of the chief of the Azaleh clan, which lives in one of the remotest areas, even among the Makishi. They're storytellers who have kept alive many oral traditions. As you know, the Makishi are a stubborn people who live by a code outsiders don't even know exists. The Azaleh clan, in particular, is bound by many taboos.

"A person's lineage determines which tales they can learn and recite, and which they can't recite or even listen to. My grandfather on my mother's side was a direct descendent of the Azaleh clan founder and had the authority to tell of the forbidden land, the most secret of the ancient tales."

A wry smile crossed Masyu's face. "When I read this memoir and realized why my father had come to Tohula Ila, I had very mixed feelings. I wondered if that's why he'd approached my mother, you see."

Olie, who was peeling a shiny red lomi fruit, spoke up. "I've told you before, but even if your father initially approached your mother for that reason, the fact that she accepted him shows their feelings for each other were mutual."

She looked at Masyu and smiled. "After all, her clan hated outsiders, yet they still let her marry him, and from that, you were born."

Masyu ran a hand over his face. "I wish I hadn't been so naïve at fifteen. If only I'd talked more with my father and grandfather while I still could."

He sighed, then continued. "When my father told me to become my uncle's foster son and a male descendant of the Kashuga Lai, I was furious. It just seemed so selfish. I loved life in the mountains. I didn't want to leave my clan and become part of the Kashuga family that had spread the cursed grain."

Masyu looked at Aisha. "You know the Makishi hate ohaleh and call it the cursed grain, don't you? As a child, I was ashamed that my father was the son of one of the heads of the House of Kashuga. Still, none of my clan ever said anything negative about my father, probably because my mother's people had accepted him as part of their family. Looking back on it, I should have asked my grandfather why. He was the key storyteller among the Azaleh. He could've answered some of the questions others couldn't.

"If only I hadn't been so immature. I was furious with my father, and with my grandfather, who'd let my father make that decision, and I left home without speaking to either of them. If I'd asked, I might have gotten a piece, or even a fragment of a piece of the puzzle I so desperately want to solve."

Olie's hands paused as she peeled the lomi fruit. "Masyu's father and his grandfather both disappeared and still haven't been found."

"What? Your grandfather too?"

Masyu nodded. "They both vanished when I was seventeen. I got permission to return home and searched the mountains repeatedly with the village men, but we couldn't find them.

"My mother was a superb tracker, better than me. If she'd searched, we might have succeeded, but unfortunately, she wasn't well then, and couldn't join us.

"According to her, it was my great uncle, my grandfather's older brother, who went missing first. He went into the mountains, and when he didn't return after three days, my father and grandfather went after him. The men of the clan tried to go too, but my grandfather stopped them and only took my father."

The voices of Tak's sons came through the open window. They were probably letting the goats out from the livestock quarters under the house. The sound of clucking noises could be heard on the wind.

"When I came home discouraged, having failed to find them, my mother told me not to bother searching any more. She said if we'd looked that hard and hadn't found them, they must have gone somewhere they could never be found.

"She looked drained and exhausted, and somehow I felt she'd been expecting this to happen some day."

Masyu stroked the cover of the book with a tanned hand. "That night, my mother took me to my father's study, a small hut he'd built beside our house. My mother called it his 'den,' half teasing, half complaining. Because he spent so much time on the road and what little time he was at home, he usually spent holed up in that hut, like a hibernating bear. Only my father was allowed inside. When he was away, the door was kept locked, so I'd never been inside before.

"As a child, I was overcome with curiosity. Many times, I tried to get a peek, but without success. But when my mother led me there that night and unlocked the door, I didn't want to look."

Masyu paused for a moment before continuing. "It was remarkably tidy and well organized. The shelves were filled with books and my father's journals. He'd told my mother that if he ever disappeared without telling her where he was going, she should give me access to his study. On the condition that I never took anything out of it.

"I stayed in that study for three days, starting from that night, and read my father's journals. I didn't bother to look at any of the books because I knew I had to return to the capital soon.

"My father had many journals and deliberately omitted things from his entries. There was no way I could grasp everything he'd written in just three days. Still, several grabbed my attention.

"One was about my maternal great-uncle, the first to go missing."

Masyu raised his eyes from the memoir and looked at Aisha. "When we were in Jookuchi's tent, you asked me if I was a litaran, didn't you?"

"Yes."

"What made you say that?"

An image flashed through Aisha's mind: an elderly man striding deep into the forest, trailing the scent of fragrant blue grass.

"Because you smelled of seikoso," she said.

Masyu smiled. "Did you know that seikoso is odorless?"

7
Origins

"Odorless?" Aisha repeated, struggling for a moment to understand what he meant.

Masyu nodded and looked at Olie.

She pulled a small, delicately embroidered pouch from her robe. Instantly, the fragrance of seikoso filled the room. She pressed her nose against it and sniffed, then looked at Aisha. "To me, it just smells like cloth."

Aisha's eyes widened. "What? But that's impossible. It has such a strong smell."

The scent of spotted moth larvae was faint enough that she could understand Olie being unable to detect it, but she was astounded to hear she couldn't smell the powerful fragrance permeating the room. It was like being unable to see the table right in front of them.

"You really can't smell it? Even though it's so strong?" Aisha turned to Masyu. "You can smell it, can't you?"

Masyu nodded. "Yes, but not as strongly as you seem to."

Aisha blinked. "Really? But it does have a smell, right?"

"For you and me, yes," Masyu said slowly. "My mother could smell it too. But the rest of my family insisted it was odorless. I've never met anyone who could smell it other than my mother. And now you."

Are you a litaran?

Mouth agape, Aisha stared at Masyu, recalling the shock on his face when she'd asked him that question.

"You thought I was a litaran because I smelled like seikoso, right?"

"Yes."

"Who told you what the word litaran means?"

"A Makishi woman." She related how she'd gotten lost in the forest and collapsed in a field full of blooming seikoso. When she explained that an elderly litaran had saved her, a look of astonishment spread across Masyu's face.

"When was that?" he asked. "How old were you?"

"I think I was about six."

Masyu and Olie looked at each other. Excitement suffused Olie's face.

"What?" Aisha asked.

Masyu turned to her and said, "The man who saved you was my great-uncle."

Aisha gasped. "You mean the first man who went missing?"

"That's right. He was the only litaran among the Makishi at that time. If you were only six and it was the season when seikoso bloom, you might have seen him just before he disappeared. You said you collapsed in a glade with a spring. And seikoso flowers were blooming there, right?"

"Yes."

"Then . . ." Masyu fell silent, staring off into space.

"Then what?" Olie asked impatiently.

"It seems we were looking in the wrong direction," said Masyu.

"What do you mean?"

Masyu looked at Olie. "My great-uncle used to wander in an area we call Ho Ila, meaning Misty Ravine, so we used that valley as our starting point and searched all around it. But if Aisha met my great-uncle on the day he disappeared, then he was walking in the opposite direction from Ho Ila."

Olie cocked her head. "It could have been a different day."

"Besides," Aisha interjected, "if he saved me on the day he went missing, the woman who brought me home would have told someone when she heard you were looking for him."

Masyu shook his head. "Although the Azaleh told other

Makishi when my father and grandfather went missing, I'm sure they would never have said anything about my great-uncle disappearing."

"Really? Why?"

"To any Makishi who didn't belong to the Azaleh, like the woman who brought you home, my great-uncle was just a lonely litaran living in accordance with his vows. But for the Azaleh, he was taboo. The Azaleh have sayings like 'to mention something is to make it appear' or 'speak of something and it will follow you.' So they're reluctant to mention anything considered forbidden or taboo."

The room suddenly grew dark. The breeze blowing through the window turned chilly and carried the scent of rain. The voices of the twins hastily rounding up the goats could be heard outside.

Masyu rose and went over to close the window. Although the window panes were good-quality glass that let in plenty of light, once closed, the room became even darker.

The smells inside sharpened as everyone's faces blurred in the dim light. Just as the color of a bonfire becomes clearer when the sun sets, so too the scent contours stood out in the darkness.

"Aisha," Masyu said, "there's a flint box in the cupboard behind you. Could you please get it and light the lamps?"

Aisha took out the flint and lit the wicks. Oddly, the lamplit room made her feel as though it was already evening. Too impatient to wait until Masyu had sat in his chair again, Aisha asked, "What do you mean by taboo? Was he untouchable?"

"No, it wasn't like that." Masyu pulled out his chair and seated himself. "He lived among us like any other member of the clan."

Lacing his fingers together, he recounted the tale. "When I was a child, my great-uncle often played with me. He was quiet and gentle, and an expert at finding medicinal herbs. But I found it strange that he lived alone.

"Some elder members of our community had lost their spouses, but they always lived with their children, or a brother or sister. My great-uncle, however, lived alone. I never heard anyone say he'd had a wife or children, and nobody, not even my grandfather or my mother, ever mentioned his family.

"Once, I asked my grandfather why he didn't come and live with us, but he just looked at me sternly and warned me never to ask my great-uncle that question. My grandfather's look was the same one he used whenever I asked something I shouldn't, something that touched upon our clan's taboos. So, I never mentioned it again, and I never asked my great-uncle."

The wind whistled, and a gust shook the window pane.

"It was only after reading my father's journals that I understood why my great-uncle was taboo. It also gave me an inkling of why my grandfather consented to my parents' marriage . . ."

Masyu paused, mixed emotions crossing his face. "My mother wasn't his daughter . . . She was the daughter of his brother, my great-uncle."

Aisha's eyes grew round. Masyu laughed dryly. "Where I come from, it isn't unusual for people to raise the children of their kin. My mother's circumstances, however, were . . . highly unusual."

Large raindrops began striking the window.

"When he was a youth, my great-uncle disappeared once. He went into the mountains searching for precious medicinal herbs and didn't come back for over ten years. Everyone assumed he was dead. They even held a funeral.

"One very windy night, however, he returned to the village wearing clothes unlike anything his clansmen had ever seen. His hair had grown long, and he had two girls with him."

The wind shook the windows, and the rain washed down the glass.

"When he was asked where he'd been, he couldn't answer. In fact, he seemed to have forgotten how to speak and just stared blankly at everyone's faces without responding to their questions.

"He was in no shape to raise two children, so my grandfather, whose third son had just been born, adopted the two girls. My great-uncle lived with his parents, my great-grandparents, who were still alive then. Gradually, he regained the ability to talk and work, but for some reason, he became very distressed whenever he saw the two girls, so my grandfather decided to raise them himself, rather than giving them back.

"At the time, however, life was very hard for the Azaleh. For two years in a row, both the buckwheat and the wheat crop failed, and my grandfather, who was still quite young, had a hard time feeding five children. I'm guessing that's why he ended up raising only my mother. There was no mention in my father's journals of when or where the other girl disappeared to."

The drumming of the rain intensified, and the lamps flickered in a gust of wind that seeped through a crack.

"I didn't even know there was another girl, and my mother never mentioned her. I suspect my grandfather and the other Azaleh never talked about her because they had doubts—or, more accurately, because they were afraid of—where those two girls might have come from."

Masyu's vacant eyes were fixed on the shadows of the dishes dancing in the flickering light.

"There's a strange tale that has been passed down among the Azaleh. Sharing the story isn't taboo, and when I was a child, my grandfather recited it to me like a folktale.

"Azaleh is surrounded by thickly forested mountains. Sometimes people went into the forests and never returned, but according to that tale, occasionally someone who went missing suddenly reappeared many years later.

"All of them came back wearing unfamiliar clothes with long, unkempt hair but a clean-shaven face. And they all brought back a girl.

"Some seemed to have lost their wits. They appeared vacant, as if they'd left their soul behind, and died soon after their return. Others lived longer and would suddenly regain their memory of going missing, as if they'd retrieved a piece of their soul. After that, they'd begin wandering off as if they were searching for something.

"These people never took a wife. They lived alone and wandered the mountains on their own, as if hoping they could retrieve something they'd lost in return for giving up a normal life. They always carried a pouch of fragrant blue grass on them, and people who suffered some misfortune and wished to supplicate the gods copied this custom. Such supplicants came to be called seiya litaran, meaning 'bearer of seikoso.'"

Masyu paused and took a breath, then plunged on. "The girls brought back from the other land were all strikingly beautiful and clever, but they usually died young before having children, and even those who lived longer never married.

"That was the tale my grandfather told me. When I first heard it, I asked him where those people had gone when they went missing. But he just shook his head slowly and didn't answer."

"Speaking about that place was taboo then," Aisha murmured.

Masyu raised an eyebrow, then nodded. "That's right. It wasn't taboo to share the story itself, but it was forbidden to speak of where they'd gone or what they'd done."

Aisha's mouth felt dry, and she took a sip of her cold tea. While listening to Masyu, a thought had occurred to her, and it made her heart ache. Like a flickering flame, an image of her short-lived mother's beautiful face rose in her mind. The words she'd said when Aisha had explained what happened echoed in her ears.

Ah . . . So that's why you smell of seikoso . . .

In a hoarse voice, Aisha asked, "Was your mother one of the girls your great-uncle brought back from the forbidden land?"

Masyu nodded, his eyes fixed on hers.

"Is she still alive?"

"No, she died when I was nineteen. She was only thirty-five."

A pain stabbed Aisha's heart. She took a deep breath and said, "My mother died young too. She was thirty-four. She . . . could smell seikoso too."

The room was silent except for the sound of wind and rain.

"When you asked me if I was a litaran," Masyu finally said, "I felt as if I'd been struck by lightning. Things that had never occurred to me before filled my brain. One of them was the thought that we might be cousins. I'm guessing that's what you're thinking now too."

Aisha nodded.

"I think we probably are," Masyu went on in a low voice. "We can both smell seikoso. And so could our mothers. And we've both got a much keener sense of smell than others. How about Milucha?"

"Nowhere near as keen as mine, but it's much sharper than my father's or Jiiya's."

"I see. So perhaps women develop a keener sense of smell than men. Regardless, when you put everything together, it seems likely we're cousins. Still, it's unclear whether the two girls my great-uncle brought back with him were sisters, so we may or may not be blood kin."

Aisha stared at him blankly, feeling as if her head had gone numb.

"There's no certainty. After I read my father's journals, I searched for the other girl, but couldn't find a single clue. Maybe my mother knew, but I couldn't bring myself to ask her. I finally made up my mind to ask the next time I went home, but it was hard to get leave, and she died before I saw her again."

He sighed. "There are so many things I wish I'd asked. In the end, I never asked her anything important . . . My uncles told me that when your family moved into the forest, my mother sometimes took food to your house, so maybe she knew that your mother was her younger sister, but there's no way of knowing now. We never thought of you as anything other than the exiled family of the true king."

Aisha recalled the faces of the Makishi women who had brought them food. She'd often seen her mother talking with them. Had one of them been Masyu's mother?

"If your mother was the other girl," Masyu said, "then, for some reason, my grandfather must have entrusted her care to someone who was close to Keluahn, whom the Makishi considered their beloved king. We've no way of finding out now though."

Olie, who had listened silently throughout, frowned. "Masyu," she said sternly. "Why did you begin with that story? Starting off like that will influence Aisha's feelings."

"What?" Aisha said, looking at Olie. "What do you mean 'influence my feelings'?"

Olie opened her mouth, but Masyu cut her off. "I'm about to ask you to do something dangerous. Olie is afraid that now you've heard this story, it'll be hard for you to refuse."

He looked at Olie. "I didn't tell her with that in mind. Either way, I would've had to tell her. Whether I told her that tale first or not, it would still influence her decision."

Olie's frown deepened. "That may be true but . . ." She sighed. "I really hate that about you, you know."

Masyu laughed, and Olie raised her brows. "What?" she said.

"Oh, nothing, nothing. Just something silly."

"That only makes me want to know more. What?"

Masyu gave a rueful smile, as though conceding defeat. "I was just remembering that when we were young, I used to tell you all the time, 'It's just fine if you hate me. It'll be a problem if you like me.'"

Olie threw him an exasperated look. With a sigh, she turned

to Aisha. "I'm sorry to butt in, but I don't like . . . or, more accurately, I have reservations about telling you all this."

Perplexed, Aisha exhaled slowly. "I don't know yet what that dangerous thing is," she said.

"That's true. Sorry." Olie sighed again and shook her head. "Although it's annoying, Masyu's right. The order we tell you things probably won't make any difference . . ."

She paused and looked straight at Aisha. "But there's one thing I want to make sure you keep in mind when you hear what we have to say. Please know that you're free to accept or reject it as you wish. No matter what you do, don't accept it because you're worried about Masyu or me, or that we'll think badly of you if you don't.

"I'm telling you this straight from my heart. Please remember: I would never put you in a position where you feel forced to do something against your will."

8
The Road the Emperor Traveled

The lamp flickered with a spitting sound.

Aisha started to rise, but Masyu gestured for her to stay seated. He walked over to the cupboard, took out a can of oil, and began filling the lamp.

"The reason I told you about my great-uncle first was because I wanted you to understand my father's train of thought."

He put the oil can back on the shelf and closed the cupboard door firmly, then returned to his seat.

"Using Amil Kashuga's travel memoir as his guide, my father came to Tohula Ila. I don't know how he met and married my mother, or when he realized that her uncle was really her father. But I think he formed a certain hypothesis when he found out that she'd been brought back from the forbidden land."

From what Masyu had told her so far, Aisha guessed what he was going to say next. "That Ohaleh Mazula, the land of the gods, is somewhere in Tohula Ila?" she asked.

Masyu nodded. "Yes. My father guessed that the place the Azaleh call the forbidden land was actually Ohaleh Mazula, and that those who went missing had accidentally found their way into it, lived there, and then returned. I think he also suspected that the same thing had happened to the first emperor and Amil Kashuga as well."

Aisha glanced quickly at Olie, a sudden thought occurring to her. "And they brought back a girl too!"

Olie nodded slowly. "Yes, they did. The first Kokun."

Thunder rumbled in the distance, rolling toward them across the dark heavens.

"But . . ." Aisha frowned and cocked her head. "If that's true, why wasn't the story told like that? Was the first emperor trying to respect the Azaleh taboo which calls that place the forbidden land?"

"That's the point that bothers me," Masyu said. "They didn't convey the facts as they were. Why? Was it because it was taboo to speak of the land of the gods, just as it's taboo for the Azaleh? Perhaps, although there's no way to confirm that. However, my father suspected there was a different reason."

"A different reason?"

"Yes. My father thought that the Umalese and the Makishi share the same roots."

Aisha blinked. "The same roots? You mean they're the same people?"

"Yes. You may think that's far-fetched, but when I read my father's idea, I thought it could very well be true. And that reminded me of something.

"About a month after I first came to the imperial capital, I attended a funeral for an elder related to the House of Kashuga. I'm guessing you've never been to an Umalese funeral, but it includes a rite called Sending Off the Soul. It's conducted at twilight and is intended to guide the soul back to its homeland. A priest climbs up onto the roof of the deceased person's home and chants a prayer while facing the setting sun. The words he chanted gave me a very strange feeling."

Masyu closed his eyes and began reciting in a low singsong voice.

"Oh, soul that has cast off the burden of the body, listen well.
Soar high into the heavens, like the birds of Alushai,
and seek the river, the shining river that reflects the heavens.
Follow the river of light 'til you come to the great Manasu River.
Oh, soul, that has cast off the body and flies lightly, listen well.

When you reach the Manasu River, rest on the hill called Maguli.

Refreshed, fly onward, to where the light of the great heaven sets.

Cross the hill called Mishula, the fields of Todoma, the wide river of Iama,

westward, westward, fly . . ."

Masyu opened his eyes. "The reason it gave me such a strange feeling was because I recognized the places the priest was chanting.

"Not long before, I'd crossed the River Iama, cut through the fields of Todoma, passed over Mishula, and made my way up the tributary of the great Manasu River to the capital.

"In other words, if the deceased followed the directions the priest was chanting, their soul would have retraced the route I'd taken to the capital in the opposite direction. It seemed odd that the home of an Umalese born and raised in the capital would be found in that direction.

"I asked the squire, who'd been assigned to help me adjust to my new life, about it, but what he told me was also a surprise."

"What did he say?"

"Although he was a native Umalese, he said he didn't recognize any of the places in that prayer except the Manasu River. Every time he heard all those unknown names being chanted, such as the hills of Maguli and Mishula, he was afraid that when he died, his soul might get lost on its way. He was quite serious."

"Maguli, Mishula . . ." Aisha whispered, cocking her head. "I don't know those hills either. Did I pass them on my way here from West Kantal?"

Masyu smiled. "I'm sure you've heard of Mahuli and Meesha, haven't you?"

"Yes . . . What? You mean those hills?"

"That's right. In Umalese, the words Mahuli and Meesha become Maguli and Mishula."

Perplexed, Aisha reflected on what he'd just said. "But . . . Maguli and Mishula . . . Those place names aren't West Kantalese, right? If so, then how did you know?"

A light gleamed in Masyu's eyes. "They don't exist in the West Kantalese language. However, they do exist in the language of the Makishi."

"They do? But—"

"You wouldn't have known because when the Makishi go down the mountain and talk to the people there, they speak West Kantalese. With a very thick accent, but it's still understandable, right?"

"Uh-huh."

"But when we talk among ourselves, we speak the language of the Makishi."

"The Makishi have their own language?"

"Yes. Although the West Kantalese might understand some of it, it's still quite different. In our village, my father spoke the Makishi language, not Umalese.

"When I first arrived in the capital and heard everyone speaking Umalese, I was surprised because it sounded somehow familiar. It seemed closer to the language we Makishi spoke than Western Kantalese. Some words are pronounced differently, but once I learned the pattern of variations, I was able to speak it fluently. For example, pronouncing Maguli as Mahuli is a typical change in Umalese.

"So when I read my father's idea that the Makishi and the Umalese might have the same roots, I thought he could be right. Later, when I read this travel journal, I became even more convinced."

He picked up the book. "Why did Amil Kashuga record his travels going away from, rather than toward, Tohula Ila? What if it was because Tohula Ila was not the destination, but the starting point?"

Aisha gasped and stared at him.

"My father's hypothesis was this: Long ago, due to a cold summer or some other reason, famine threatened the people who lived in Tohula Ila. By chance, two young men went missing, eventually returning with a girl from the forbidden land. They also brought with them some ohaleh seed rice.

"Ohaleh rice is extraordinarily resistant to cold. What's more, it can even be cultivated in Tohula Ila, where normally rice won't grow. Those miraculous seeds probably saved the lives of the people who lived there.

"But then something happened. It's not clear when, perhaps a few years after their return, or perhaps more than a decade later. Whatever it was, it made some people hate ohaleh and call it the cursed grain. My father suspected the Makishi split into two groups at that time.

"One group chose to stay in the valley and never grow the cursed grain again. The other, led by the first emperor, Arailu, and Amil Kashuga, set off with the Kokun on a journey to find a new land, taking with them ohaleh seed rice."

Masyu flipped to the last page of the thin volume and began to read.

"The mighty Manasu River has many tributaries. The great plain, which the Ramalese call the Yuino wasteland, is blessed with abundant water, but it is a barren land of short summers . . ."

He raised his head and said, "The place the emperor and Amil reached was a plain with a plentiful water source that could produce bumper crops if only the plants could withstand the cold."

A thought occurred to Aisha and she whispered, "If so . . ."

Masyu urged her with his eyes to continue.

"Then maybe the memoir didn't stop partway through the journey. Maybe it stopped there because that was the end of the road . . ."

Masyu broke into a smile. "Very perceptive!"

He waved the well-worn book in the air. "That's what I thought when I read this too. That Amil Kashuga and his people settled on the Yuino Plain first, and the capital was built in its current location later. And that Amil may have intentionally left the ending hanging as a hint that they'd settled there first."

Aisha imagined a group of people standing on the desolate plain. The heavens dark, but the horizon bright. The wind cold enough to cut the skin. With them, they bore seed rice that could grow even in that frigid clime.

There must have been women and children there too. They would have been anxious about settling in this unknown land so far from home without any allies.

"Were there any other people living on the Yuino Plain at the time? Or bandits that might attack them?"

"There were probably people living there already," Masyu said. "Historical records indicate there was a small kingdom called Ramal somewhere around the Yuino Plain when the empire was founded. The Ramalese were the first to pay allegiance to the emperor, and together they built the empire.

"In those days, that region was colder than it is now, and there were some years when it remained winter almost year-round. I'm not sure Ramal could really be called a kingdom. It was just a group of people surviving mainly on livestock herding because they couldn't grow grain."

"Ramal . . . You mean the Ramal cavalry Ramal?"

"That's right. The Ramalese form the core of the imperial cavalry. For generations, many have served in important posts as loyal retainers. Originally, they were horsemen who grazed their herds of sheep and horses on the Yuino Plain. I'm guessing the first emperor and his followers were able to expand their territory by gaining dominance over the Ramalese and thereby acquiring a cavalry."

Aisha frowned. "But . . . if they were horse riders, wouldn't they also have been skilled fighters? How could the emperor and his people subjugate them when they were essentially encroaching on Ramalese territory? The Ramalese must have been much stronger than they were."

A light kindled in Masyu's eyes. "It was the Kokun who subjugated the horsemen, despite their military might."

"How?"

Masyu glanced at Olie. She nodded and began to speak. "That story is recorded in both The Kokun's True History and Alternate Tales of the Kokun. Although the accounts of most stories are quite different in each of these books, the story of the Ramalese is the only one that's almost identical, which means it's probably close to the truth."

She moistened her lips and began to recite slowly with downcast eyes. "One night, long, long ago, when a blizzard had been blowing for three solid days and three solid nights, there came a knock at the door of the Kokun's palace. The maidservant opened it to find a group of ten Ramalese accompanied by their women and children.

"So cold and starved were they that they could not speak, and so the Lady Kokun invited them inside to sit by the fire. She added water to a pot of freshly cooked rice to make a soft porridge and flavored it with precious salt. This she gave them, and they ate it hungrily.

"The children devoured the porridge in a flash and cried for more, but the fathers warned them sternly that their bellies had been empty for too long; they should not fill them all at once.

"The leader of the company bowed low before the Lady Kokun and thanked her. 'My name is Haldoon Roi Ramal,' said he, 'chief of the Roi clan.'

"With tears in his eyes, he told her their tale. The Roi were a fierce nomadic people, renowned for their bravery as the shields of the king, but this past winter, the king's favorite horse had been devoured by a wolf while the clansman guarding it slept. Enraged, the king seized the clan's territory and exiled them to this barren land.

"Their food had run out just before the blizzard came. The children were freezing, and the Roi clan thought they would all perish, when they glimpsed a light in the distance. This they followed and came to the palace.

"The Lady Kokun took pity on them and let them stay with her people. When they saw the storehouses of the Umalese, the horse riders were astonished. There were seven great buildings filled with golden grains of unhulled rice. The Umalese shared this rice unstintingly, nourishing the clan generously, so that by the end of winter, they had completely regained their health.

"Come spring, the Roi clan helped till the hard, frozen ground. They had never used a plow, but they fixed harrows made by the Lady Kokun to their horses and tilled the ground so that the rice fields became fertile. In the fall, they worked side by side to harvest the abundant ohaleh.

"When they saw the ohaleh rice grow hardily in the frozen ground, the Roi clan knew that the Umalese were blessed by the gods and that it was the power of the living goddess, the Lady Kokun, that had saved them.

"They bowed down before her and begged her to let them stay and live under her protection forever. The Lady Kokun accepted their request.

"But there was one man among the Roi, Haldoon's uncle, Woonun, who had wicked thoughts. Wishing to restore his prestige among the Ramalese, he slipped away after the harvest and went to the king, telling him that he'd found a land where golden rice grew even in the harsh cold.

"The king, whose people had long suffered from famine, was overjoyed. Guided by Woonun, he led a thousand horsemen to attack Umal. But when they reached Umal, they found the palace, the castle, and all the houses empty. There was no one to be seen anywhere in the capital.

"The seven storehouses were also empty save one. In it was a mountain of seed rice and beside it a heap of fertilizer, as if to say, grow your own rice.

"As the king, his senior vassals and Woonun entered that great storehouse, Haldoon stepped from behind the mountain of seed rice and declared in a ringing voice, 'Listen well, oh greedy one, who repaid with betrayal the kindness and mercy shown by the Lady Kokun to our freezing, starving people. And you also who responded to this wicked man with your own avarice.

"'The living goddess, the Lady Kokun, has declared she will give you one chance to repent. This ohaleh seed rice is the grace of the goddess. If sown by the pure of heart who align their will with the will of the gods, it will bear golden harvests even in frozen ground. But if sown by those with evil in their hearts, it will bring misfortune. Oh, chief vassals, listen well. You will know when the harvest time comes whether this king you follow can truly bring you happiness.'

"Thus spoke Haldoon. The fierceness of his anger and his majesty made the Ramalese freeze in their tracks. He strode through their ranks and disappeared into the distance.

"When spring came, the king of Ramal and his men plowed the frozen fields and planted the seed rice left in the storehouse. The ohaleh rice flourished despite the cold summer and yielded such a bountiful crop in the fall that even seven storehouses could not hold it. The king rejoiced and declared to his people that the gods had proved he was their rightful ruler.

"But when they threshed the grain, the people were dismayed to find that the husks were empty, yielding not one grain of rice. Filled with awe, they held the empty chaff in their hands. Now they knew. The man they had revered as king was empty, without substance.

"Confronted with irrefutable proof of divine will, the people abandoned their king. They tied him and Woonun to the back of a horse and sent them off into the great plain where the snow was flying.

"Suddenly, a beautiful woman mounted on a white horse emerged through the driving snow. Gently she touched the horse on which the two men were tied. It bowed its head and followed her. Speechless, the Ramalese stared at her as she led the two sinners back to them.

"She came to a halt within their midst and said softly, 'There is no need to punish those who have repented. Those who wish to live under my protection and cultivate the golden rice should respect and pledge allegiance to the king of Umal.'"

As the narrative came to a close, Aisha let out a long breath. "I wonder why the husks were empty," she murmured.

Olie and Masyu exchanged glances. Olie inclined her head, and Masyu turned to Aisha. "The empty rice husks are probably a metaphor," he said. "In fact, all seed rice yields grain. As I'm sure you know, however, even though you can eat the harvested grain, you can't use it for seed rice. It will grow, but it won't ripen and bear new grain. Ohaleh brings not only prosperity but also servitude."

In Aisha's mind, Masyu's voice overlapped with that of her father talking about her grandfather.

He called ohaleh the rice of joy and sorrow.

"There's one closely guarded secret concerning ohaleh—how to make seed rice," Masyu continued. "Only the Kokun, the emperor, the heads of the two houses of Kashuga and their direct descendants know. If anyone else learns of it, that person along with the one who told them will be executed on the spot without trial."

Masyu spoke calmly, but the ruthlessness of this statement took Aisha's breath away.

Masyu watched her steadily. "What I want to ask of you is closely related to the secrets of ohaleh, including the seed rice. So, if you listen to what I'm going to say and decide to accept my request, you'll be living in constant danger of execution."

Aisha said nothing.

"Once you've heard what I have to say, if you decide you don't want to get involved in something so dangerous, then please say so. We'll just conclude that this conversation never took place. But you'll have to swear not to tell anyone, no matter what happens."

Masyu's scent altered, growing more complex. As she observed his scent and the expression rising in his eyes, Aisha realized why he was willing to let her decline even after sharing such dangerous information.

He holds everything that matters to me in his hands. Milucha, Jiiya . . . and me. If he wants to get rid of any or all of us, he can do whatever he wants and blame it on unrest in West Kantal.

That was a terribly cold thought. But at the same time, it meant she could trust him to keep his word and let her decline at anytime. She'd never be able to tell anyone whatever secrets she learned here. Everyone in this room was absolutely confident of that, which was why Masyu and Olie wouldn't mind if she decided to refuse once she heard their request.

The secret of ohaleh rice.

The rice her grandfather had rejected. The rice of joy and sorrow that had impacted so many lives, including her mother's.

She looked at Masyu. "Tell me," she said.

* * *

The weather in the mountains was always unpredictable. By early afternoon, the sky that had been so dark before, was clear and sunny.

Aisha passed through the forest, inhaling deeply the fragrance of the trees and plants that had soaked up the welcome rain, and stepped out into the western field. Although she'd moved swiftly, her hair, face, and clothes were damp from the water dripping off the underside of the leaves.

A phrase her mother had often sung when Aisha was a child came back to her now.

Showers fall in the forest shadows when the rain in the fields has stopped.

The fragrance of the western field was as lively as ever. Tak was bending over something in the ground.

"Tak!" Aisha shouted.

At the sound of her voice, he straightened and looked her way, then waved. "Hey there!"

Aisha walked over to him and examined the green ohaleh shoots. They were growing more slowly than in other areas. When she'd stood here before, she'd thought their scent seemed weaker than other ohaleh plants. This time the difference was even clearer.

Something's soothing them.

The soil here smelled quite different from that in the ohaleh cultivation areas she'd passed through. Some element in it seemed to have changed the nature of the earth and suppressed ohaleh growth. Its scent, which usually clamored to assert its territory, felt more peaceful.

She closed her eyes and focused on the varied fragrances wafting from the soil and drifting on the wind. Within that bouquet, she recognized several familiar plants.

"Ichi weed, shiluma weed, okino weed," she muttered.

Opening her eyes, she saw Tak gaping at her.

He tried to say something, then cleared his throat and started again. "Can you really identify those plants just by standing there? Even though I only added a little of each to the fertilizer spread on this plot?"

Aisha nodded.

He took a deep breath. "I see. And can you also tell what those plants are doing?"

Searching for the right words, Aisha answered hesitantly, "They're suppressing ohaleh growth. As well as diluting its powerful scent. It's strange, but when mixed into the soil, those plants seem to alter the fragrance of the ohaleh."

She closed her eyes and inhaled deeply. Opening her eyes again, she said, "Except for the ichi weed . . . I can't quite explain it, but its smell seems selfish and rebellious. Like it's unwilling to work with the others. Its scent is interfering with the fragrances of the other plants, so they aren't as effective as they might be. If you want to suppress ohaleh, maybe you should try adding a different plant to the mix instead of ichi weed."

A deep flush crept slowly up Tak's face. He raised his hand to rub his cheek, then remembered it was still covered in dirt and hastily wiped it on his clothes.

"Well, I'll be . . ." he breathed. A smile spread across his face, one of genuine delight.

At the sight of it, a hot rush of emotion coursed through Aisha's chest. Joy. Warm and deep, such as she'd never experienced before.

9
The Rice of Joy and Sorrow

"It took me a long time to figure out the combination of these three," Tak said, lifting each one from his basket. "But you say ichi weed isn't needed after all. It's funny, because it did the best job of slowing down the rice seedlings' growth."

He passed a stalk of it to Aisha, and she took it in her hands. Its scent was indeed strident, much like ohaleh and oshaki. "Did you add the others to the mix because ichi weed alone wasn't enough?"

"That's right. Ichi weed by itself couldn't completely suppress ohaleh growth. But when I mixed these other plants into the fertilizer along with it, it not only slowed down ohaleh growth but also allowed other grains planted alongside it to sprout. I was thrilled to have found something that worked."

Tak rolled the ichi weed across his palm. "Normally, when ohaleh ripens, every other type of grain planted nearby withers and dies. Even when ohaleh is uprooted and removed from the field, no other grain will grow unless all the soil is removed and replaced."

He sighed and gazed at the ohaleh. "Sometimes this plant seems like a monster," he murmured.

He glanced at Aisha. "I heard your grandfather was Keluahn, the king who rejected ohaleh."

Aisha stiffened, but Tak smiled. "Don't worry," he said. "Maybe you already know this, but I'm Raoh's cousin. We've always been close, ever since we were kids, and so we tend to confide in each other, even about things that are confidential. As this is the kind of life I lead, me knowing what's going on isn't going to change anything."

He ran his eyes around the field as he spoke. "I can't remember when I first heard about the king of West Kantal being dethroned for refusing to introduce ohaleh, but I do remember how surprised I was. I thought he was a visionary leader."

Aisha stared at him open-mouthed. She'd never heard anyone speak about her grandfather that way before.

When she thought of her parents, her own situation, and the many people her grandfather had essentially sentenced to death, she felt she should protest. But at the same time, she couldn't help feeling a quiet warmth spread through her chest.

Tak returned his gaze to Aisha. "I've heard the Makishi of West Kantal detest ohaleh and claim it's cursed. Did your grandfather believe that too?"

A breeze wafted past, and the scent of ohaleh deepened.

"I don't know," she said. "He died when I was very young. I barely remember him. But . . ." Recalling her father's face, she said, "I was told he called ohaleh the rice of joy and sorrow."

Tak's expression changed. "That's a good way of putting it," he said.

The sun, which had taken on a reddish hue, shone softly on his face. "Although I said ohaleh seems like a monster, it's also a treasure. It's terrifying to think what would happen if it suddenly disappeared. Yet, it's still a monster. It changed the soil, and people too, making them depend on it alone . . ."

He placed the stalk of ichi weed back in his basket. "What a fix we're in. Our ancestors should never have built an empire based on a single crop. Although there's no point in complaining about that now."

Aisha pictured the majestic imperial palace in the capital; the towering edifice that seemed to stand upon golden waves of rice. The thought of what would happen should the cornerstone, ohaleh, be removed made her feel faint. The enormity of the loss it would incur filled her with a futility that surpassed even fear.

Without ohaleh, the empire would collapse. Yet few dreamed this could ever happen. Masyu, however, had said the time was near at hand.

* * *

"Along with Amil's travel journal," Masyu had told Aisha, "my father always carried a copy of the Alternate Tales of the Kokun. In it, there's a passage that reads: 'The clouds of hunger cover the sky. The earth withers. No food for the mouths of men. Oh, Kokun, read the truth of all things in the wind and save all sentient beings.'"

Although Masyu recited these words plainly, they gave Aisha goosebumps. She felt as though she'd heard them somewhere long ago.

"When the first emperor Arailu tried cultivating ohaleh in the Amaya wetlands in the south, a pest called giant yoma proliferated, destroying the ohaleh crop."

"What? You mean there are pests that can destroy ohaleh?" Aisha exclaimed.

Masyu nodded. "Yes, giant yoma are the only insects ever known to have damaged ohaleh crops, which is supposedly impervious to pests. At the time, the fields were burned immediately, which prevented them from spreading. But the passage I just recited is attributed to Arailu. It's said he paled when he saw giant yoma and muttered those words as if he'd seen the insects before."

Masyu stroked the tabletop with his fingers. "My father thought the sight of giant yoma jogged a memory for Arailu: a memory of a catastrophe in his homeland. My father wondered if a giant yoma outbreak triggered a massive famine. That might explain why the Makishi called ohaleh the 'cursed grain.'"

"His homeland? You mean in Tohula Ila?"

"Yes. There's one place there that has many species of yoma. We call it Rii Chiyai, meaning the warm hollow. It's a large depression with hot springs bubbling up from the ground nearby. When I was young, my father took me there once. We found traces of an old waterway that indicated people had once drawn hot spring water into the depression. When we saw it, the canal was dry, but my father said our ancestors probably cultivated the land there; that, when the climate was colder, they might have used the hot spring water to grow crops. Now, however, cultivating that area is forbidden."

"Forbidden? Why?"

"I don't know. But I'm sure my father must have been very excited when he learned farming was prohibited there."

Aisha's brow furrowed.

"In the Koshi Regulations, which were drawn up by the first Kokun," Masyu continued, "there's a rule that shisha weed should be added to the fertilizer when high temperatures and heavy rain cause yoma species to proliferate. I'm guessing that rule was made to prevent an outbreak of giant yoma."

Masyu spoke slowly, enunciating his words. "Yoma populations can explode under hot and humid conditions. I think that in such situations, if ohaleh hasn't been weakened by adding shisha to the fertilizer, yoma that eat it may mutate. The conditions in that warm, humid basin would resemble those in hot and rainy growing areas."

Aisha's eyes widened as she realized what Masyu meant.

He nodded. "I think the first Kokun tried growing ohaleh in that basin, and as a result, giant yoma appeared, followed by a disaster that caused mass starvation. Ohaleh withers other grains, so if those pests devoured the ohaleh crop, people would've had nothing left to eat."

"But . . ." Aisha cocked her head. "Vegetables still grow even if they're planted near ohaleh, don't they? And there are wild boar and deer in the forests of Tohula Ila. Surely, there would have been other things to eat?"

Olie piped up. "That's exactly what I thought when Masyu first told me his idea. Giant yoma reportedly don't eat vegetables, so an infestation alone wouldn't explain why the emperor said 'the earth withers.'"

"I know," Masyu said. "It seemed odd to me too when I read my father's journals. People in those days didn't have to pay taxes, and there would've been plenty of game to hunt. Even if giant yoma consumed the entire ohaleh crop, it shouldn't have caused a famine.

"But if they'd already been cultivating ohaleh in Tohula Ila for a number of years when this happened, the kingdom's population could've swelled to the point where they couldn't feed everyone just with vegetables grown in the fields and food gathered from the forest."

Masyu stroked the cover of the memoir. "As I studied my father's journals, I realized he didn't say the disaster was a giant yoma outbreak. Rather, he believed an outbreak served as a catalyst; that something else occurred because of the infestation. Something so terrible, the emperor lamented there was no food for the mouths of men."

"Something else . . ."

Masyu nodded. "What it was, I don't know. I don't think my father did either. But he believed a giant yoma outbreak triggered something catastrophic."

Aisha cocked her head once more. "But even if a disaster occurred in the past, there hasn't been one since. Why was your father so afraid it might happen again?"

"Because parts of the Koshi Regulations, ones he believed were related to giant yoma, were being revised," said Masyu. "Even the directive I mentioned earlier about shisha weed, which was most likely intended to prevent giant yoma outbreaks—that one's no longer being implemented either."

"Really? Why?"

Masyu sighed. "To increase yield and make production more efficient. Yoma are found everywhere. On the plains and in the mountains, within the empire proper and the outlying protectorates. Although warm weather and heavy rain, which foster lush vegetation, can cause massive outbreaks, sometimes yoma don't increase that much at all.

"Collecting data on fluctuations in yoma populations throughout the empire is a formidable task. Although it probably wasn't so bad during the time of the first Kokun, now that the empire has vastly expanded, it's prohibitively time consuming. Using shisha reduces ohaleh yield. It also increases costs because the government must buy up any surplus shisha weed from the farmers. So, the regulation was abolished after a one-year trial period during which no problems arose when shisha wasn't used."

Aisha stared at him wordlessly.

"But the fields observed during the trial didn't have large-scale yoma infestations to begin with, which means the parameters were different. I think it's when a major yoma infestation coincides with unsuppressed ohaleh growth that something must happen."

A shiver ran up Aisha's spine. She frowned. "Yet, despite this, ohaleh growth isn't being suppressed?"

Masyu nodded.

"Then giant yoma could emerge at any time," Aisha said.

"In fact," Olie said, "they already have."

10
Evening Breeze

Giant yoma eggs were found in the Rapa district of Ogoda. Fortunately, the fields were burned off immediately, and so far, there has been no damage."

Relieved, Aisha felt the tension drain from her shoulders. "Thank goodness!" she said.

Olie shook her head slowly. "For now, at least, but we don't know how long that will last. Think about it. If giant yoma eggs have been found in Rapa, it means they could appear elsewhere too. Rapa isn't the only place where conditions are ripe for large-scale yoma infestations."

"Has there been a major yoma outbreak anywhere else?"

Olie sighed. "We don't know."

"You don't know? Haven't you checked?"

"We've surveyed some of the cultivated areas," Olie said, "but not all of them."

Masyu spoke up. "Frankly, with the current number of koshi, it's difficult to keep track of conditions in every part of the empire. When the system requiring koshi to report on fluctuations in yoma populations was abolished, Master Raoh set up a system for farmers in each village to report. However, it was hard enough even for the koshi to keep up with this work. Now that they're no longer involved, I doubt busy farmers will bother reporting detailed changes in the insect populations."

Masyu gazed up at the sky through the window. "I'm guessing giant yoma outbreaks may occur the same way landslides do. A very heavy rainstorm isn't necessarily enough to trigger a landslide. It's only when certain conditions coincide that the earth begins to shift.

"Like Olie said, if giant yoma eggs have already been found in Rapa, it means they could emerge wherever the right conditions coincide.

"After the eggs were found, we became more vigilant, so we may have bought ourselves some time. But we can't possibly keep an eye on every inch of land within the entire empire. Eventually, somewhere, the signs will be overlooked."

"Couldn't you hand out pictures of the eggs and warn villagers to watch out for them?"

Masyu smiled bitterly. "For political reasons, no, we can't. The most we can do is report on any yoma outbreaks."

He shifted his gaze from the window to Aisha. "We're infuriatingly limited in what we can do. If giant yoma emerge in the absence of effective action and aren't caught in time, if they proliferate before the fields can be burned and spread to neighboring areas, if such outbreaks occur simultaneously in different parts of the empire, the consequences will be horrific."

The light shining through the window cast a faint glow on his face. "The situation in the empire today is completely different from that of Tohula Ila in the past. A huge number of people, not only in the empire itself but also in the outlying protectorates, depend on ohaleh for their livelihoods. Even if the entire empire threw itself into combatting giant yoma once an outbreak occurred, it would take at least several years to see results.

"If we burned fields infested with giant yoma and added shisha weed to the fertilizer in all the other ohaleh fields, we might be able to prevent outbreaks from spreading. But not only is that politically difficult, if it were done throughout the empire, it would slash overall yield.

"We'd have a hard time securing enough food to feed everyone in the empire and the protectorates for just a year. Even if we used every means possible: growing other crops, livestock raising, fishing, trading, tapping stockpiles—it still might not be enough.

"Neighboring countries might see this crisis as an opportunity to attack. Under current conditions, if substantial outbreaks occurred in multiple places, it would be a catastrophe. Thousands would starve, and war would consume the land. That's the future awaiting us."

Overwhelmed by the enormity of that vision, Aisha could only stare at him. Memories of stumbling through a blizzard, wracked with hunger, rose vividly in her mind, and her skin prickled.

Olie spoke up. "Of course, it's possible the damage caused by giant yoma might be confined to a single region. But as Masyu's father feared, it might lead to an even worse disaster.

"Because we also fear that day may come, we've been secretly preparing for it. What we're doing here at Yugino is part of that. Tak and his family are searching for ways to cultivate crops that will feed people when they can no longer grow ohaleh."

Aisha recalled how Tak and the twins spent the evenings writing after they worked all day in the fields. *So that's what they've been doing.*

"Ohaleh comes from a foreign land," Masyu said quietly. "As such, it can't be understood with the knowledge we have here.

"As you know, it causes other grains to wither. It changes the soil in which it's grown. And its effect is deep and wide-reaching. Even if ohaleh is removed by the roots, other grains won't grow where it has been planted unless all the soil is replaced.

"It's the fertilizer that keeps ohaleh in check. Normally, fertilizer is used to change the nature of the soil to foster healthy plant growth, but for ohaleh, we use fertilizer to change the nature of the plant."

"The nature of the plant . . ."

"That's right. When grown without fertilizer, ohaleh flourishes and spreads at an alarming rate, taking over everything. And the grain it produces is highly toxic. Ohaleh fertilizer suppresses these traits."

Aisha blurted out the thought that had come to her as she listened. "If the fertilizer is capable of suppressing ohaleh, then couldn't you reduce ohaleh's impact on other crops by increasing or decreasing some of the fertilizer ingredients?"

Olie nodded. "Yes, that's what we thought too, so we began by investigating ohaleh fertilizer. Besides, we had some questions about the mix that's currently being used."

"Questions?"

"Yes. It was reportedly the first Kokun who taught people how to make ohaleh fertilizer, but what's being used today appears to be different from what she used."

Olie glanced at Masyu, and he began to explain. "An entry in one of my father's journals caught my eye. The Book of the People is a record of daily life at the beginning of the empire. According to my father, there's a passage in it that indicates farmers may have grown not only ohaleh, but also wheat and buckwheat during the time of the first Kokun."

"Really?"

"I was excited by this discovery, so I asked Master Raoh to let me into the palace library. I spent a whole day searching for the book until I finally found it tucked away at the very bottom of a bookshelf. It was a diary written by a low-ranking official, and my father was probably the only person who ever bothered to read it. It wasn't well preserved and was so worm eaten and tattered that it was hard to read. But it did indeed contain a few lines that suggested people were eating wheat and buckwheat."

"Which means," Aisha said slowly, "in those days they were able to grow other crops even while cultivating ohaleh."

"Exactly."

"Then why?"

“Yes, that’s the question. Why can’t we grow those crops with ohaleh now?”

Masyu paused and exhaled slowly. “In his journal, my father speculated that it had something to do with the expansion of the empire’s territory. I think he was probably right. After the first Kokun died, the empire kept growing. To expand, they would’ve had to increase ohaleh yield. They needed not only to produce more of it, but to produce it more efficiently.

“I gathered from several different entries in the Book of the People that only one crop of ohaleh was grown annually and that the yield was much smaller than it is today.”

“The first Kokun . . .” Olie said softly. “She was probably trying to control ohaleh so that it could adapt to this land. She hoped to make a crop that would yield enough to feed their small kingdom without withering other grains and destroying the native vegetation.”

“But after her death,” Masyu said, “the rulers changed direction completely. They eased restrictions on ohaleh growth. Like the revisions of the Koshi Regulations I mentioned earlier, they probably changed the way they used fertilizer to increase yield and efficiency.

“Although that meant other grains could no longer be grown, I think it was probably deliberate. Because making people solely dependent on ohaleh would consolidate their rule.”

Aisha stared at the two of them, at a loss for words.

“Aisha,” Masyu said. “We’re looking for a way to control ohaleh growth, like the first Kokun did, so that it can coexist with other crops. Of course, the empire is huge compared to when she lived. We can’t reduce ohaleh yield too drastically, which means we can’t just increase the amount of fertilizer to suppress ohaleh. So, if the first Kokun’s method of control was based on adjusting the amount of fertilizer, we can’t copy her method.

“However, we also can’t remain solely dependent on ohaleh either. That’s why we decided to start by experimenting with fertilizer. By investigating the effects of each ingredient and what happens with different combinations, we thought we could find a way for ohaleh to coexist with other crops without negatively impacting them.

"To some extent, I think we chose the right direction. Our efforts have borne fruit, and we've finally succeeded in getting buckwheat to sprout, which we've been trying to do for years without success."

"That's wonderful!" Aisha exclaimed. The news felt like a ray of light in the darkness.

Masyu's expression softened a little, but he shook his head. "The seeds may have sprouted, but the buckwheat plants withered before they ripened. We're still up against the same hard wall, unable to make any headway. Time is running out."

Aisha frowned. "Isn't the emperor doing anything about this?"

She remembered her father telling her that a ruler's mission is to save the people. It seemed strange that the emperor would do nothing when a potential disaster was looming.

Masyu and Olie glanced at each other. "No," said Masyu. "At this stage, that's not possible. Even the discovery of giant yoma eggs is just being used as a means for political machinations."

A bitter smile rose to his face. "If it were obvious to everyone that a catastrophe was fast approaching, we could probably sway the emperor. But right now, with no proof but a few excerpts from the Alternate Tales of the Kokun and my father's journals, it's a miracle to even have Master Raoh on our side."

Olie gently placed her hand on Masyu's, then looked at Aisha. "Only a handful of people foresee this crisis, Aisha. And what that handful is doing will inevitably impact the empire's very foundation. It's the longing for ohaleh, the miraculous grain, that binds this empire together. That yearning represents not only hope and desire, but also resignation to the chains of servitude."

She gave a little sigh and continued. "If we suppress the

impact of ohaleh so that other grains can be cultivated, the chains binding the people will weaken. If we succeed, it could shatter the empire's framework. Do you think the emperor or anyone else in charge of this empire would agree to that?"

The longing for ohaleh . . .

An image of the pilgrims praying fervently in the garden of the Kokun's palace rose in Aisha's mind, and a sudden thought seized her.

Without that longing, Olie . . .

"If you suppress ohaleh so that no one needs to depend on it anymore," she asked, "what will happen to you—the Lady Kokun?"

A sad smile touched Olie's face. She remained silent for a while, as though searching for words, then said calmly, "Although I'm just a figurehead, I've tried to fulfill my responsibility to protect the lives of my people. If there's any way to save them from starvation, that's the path I'll take."

* * *

The evening breeze crossed the field that Tak had worked so hard to make. Within that cool wind, Aisha could detect a variety of fragrances. Was she the only one who could smell them? Did no one else sense them?

Who am I?

Was she the real Kokun as Masyu and Olie seemed to think?

No . . .

To know all things through their scent and save all sentient beings. She didn't think she could do that. And she knew very well she wasn't a living goddess.

She recalled the sad smile on Olie's face.

Although I'm just a figurehead, I've tried to fulfill my responsibility to protect the lives of my people. She'd looked beautiful, dazzlingly so, when she'd said that.

There's neither a true Kokun, nor a fake.

If, as Masyu had said, even the first Kokun wasn't a living goddess, then the idea of a Kokun who saved humanity must have been spun from people's prayers.

How had the first Kokun lived? What had she thought, and what had she done, when she realized that the ohaleh rice she'd brought into this world might one day cause everyone to starve?

Tak put down the basket with the ichi weed and knelt on the ground to examine the young ohaleh shoots. The reddish light of the setting sun illuminated his figure.

If the first Kokun wasn't a goddess . . . then maybe she had to ponder and agonize over what to do, just like me.

She would have used her knowledge of ohaleh, and her ability to detect scents that others couldn't, to save the people, while bearing the weight of their belief that she was a living goddess who would save them.

And she made fertilizer. One that would allow ohaleh to coexist with other crops.

Aisha thought of the surprise on Tak's face and the smile that had followed when she'd told him it would be better to remove ichi weed from the mix, and her heart stirred.

Maybe there's something I can do too.

The fragrance of ohaleh on the evening breeze was strong.

The scent voices that filled the heavens and the earth. Although she didn't know all things, she might find a way forward if she listened to those voices.

I bear a great sin . . .

Her father's voice echoed in her ears. Her father, who'd been unable to dissuade her grandfather. Her mother, weakened by hunger, who'd died too young. The many lives lost because of her grandfather's actions. And Aisha herself, who'd been born at the end of all that.

Even without being a living goddess, there's still something I can do.

"Tak," she said. She crouched beside him, and he looked up, startled. "Let me help you with your work."

He gazed at her steadily, then said slowly, "Masyu told you how dangerous it is, didn't he?"

"Yes."

"I see. And you're offering even though you know the risk."

He looked at the sky, then murmured once more, "I see."

11
The Kokun's World

The mountain path was slippery in places, soaked by the rain that had fallen from midnight until dawn. Olie tread carefully so as not to fall.

For you to fall and hurt yourself would be a great way to upset everyone again.

The image of herself covered in mud from slipping on the path made her smile. She stepped through a break in the trees into the sunlight and stopped to survey the mountain field. She caught sight of Aisha working, bent over, at the edge of the field, but there was no sign of Tak or his sons.

Olie opened her mouth to call out, but Aisha turned before she'd uttered a word and shouted, "Lady Olie!" The smile that burst across Aisha's face was like a ray of sunshine, lighting up Olie's heart. She raised both arms and waved.

Compatibility was a strange thing. Although they hadn't known each other long, just being with Aisha made Olie feel happy and at ease.

"Where's Tak?" she asked when she reached Aisha.

"He said he was going to drop by the south field before coming here. Shall I go get him?"

"No, don't bother. There's no rush." Eyes half-closed, Olie inhaled the scents rising from the earth. "It's a beautiful day, isn't it?" she said.

Aisha smiled. "Isn't it though!"

She'd only been helping Tak with his work for a month, but already she was darkly tanned, and the bridge of her nose was peeling.

"Why don't you wear your hat instead of leaving it dangling down your back?" asked Olie. "Your nose is peeling badly; it must hurt."

Aisha laughed. "It does. But as soon as I put my hat on, the wind blows it off, and it's a hassle—" She broke off and turned. Waving her hand, she called out, "We're over here!"

Olie looked in the direction Aisha was facing and saw Tak climbing the southern slope toward them.

When he caught sight of Olie, Tak hurried over. "Do you need me for something?" he said. "What can I do for you?"

Olie shook her head. "No, I didn't have any specific reason for coming. It's just that I'll be leaving for the palace in a few days, and I wanted to see what Aisha has been helping you with."

"Ah." Tak smiled and looked at Aisha, but his smile quickly faded.

"Am I in the way?" Olie asked.

Tak looked surprised and shook his head. "No, not at all."

He turned to Aisha. "So, what do you think? Did you notice a change?"

Aisha glanced at Olie. "It's okay," Olie said. "I'm already familiar with the work they've been doing here, so you don't need to explain."

She knew that Tak's team had been experimenting with oha-leh fertilizer for many years. They'd begun by making five fields with closely similar conditions, which alone was a significant challenge.

Just finding suitable spots was difficult. Although the fields were quite small, they not only needed the same soil conditions but also the same exposure to sun and wind, the same volume of snow in winter, and the same availability of water. In addition, they had to be located a considerable distance from each other.

Masyu, who was still in his teens at the time, had helped make the fields. Under Tak's direction, he and the twins had first made five fields with similar conditions, followed by another five fields with different conditions. After Masyu left, Tak and his family had continued the work, eventually experimenting in earnest with crop cultivation.

As the fertilizer that was used to farm ohaleh inhibited its growth, they tried adjusting the volume and content to see if they could reduce ohaleh's impact on other grains grown nearby. This process, however, proved to be dauntingly time consuming.

In some fields, they experimented with different volumes of fertilizer, while in others, they changed the fertilizer's composition, testing many different combinations, all while trying to cultivate other crops nearby. Several years had passed, but it was only the year before that they'd had some success: a nearby field of buckwheat had finally sprouted. Unfortunately, it had failed to ripen.

Buckwheat grew even in nutrient poor soil and was quick to ripen, which made it a good crop to ward off famine. But because ohaleh also grew in such soil, fields where buckwheat used to be farmed—both in the empire proper and in its protectorates—had all been converted to ohaleh.

Was it really possible to grow other crops despite the effects of ohaleh? Olie knew that even Tak, who'd devoted himself to this project for many years, was worried.

"About the amount of hikimi used in this field," Aisha said to Tak. She pointed to a patch of ohaleh. The stalks were much thinner than normal.

"Uh-huh. Is it not enough? Should I add some more?"

Aisha shook her head. "No. A little less would be better I think."

Tak's eyebrows shot up. "Less? But then we won't be able to suppress ohaleh growth."

"It's hard to explain, but even though we need to reduce the impact of ohaleh, I feel like it's not good to suppress it too much."

Aisha was struggling to find words, and her frustration showed in her face. Olie couldn't help intervening. "Is it hard to explain because you're talking about things Tak and I can't smell?"

Aisha's brow furrowed. "I can't really say; I don't know which scents you can and can't smell. Fragrances don't have color or shape, so I can only compare them to other scents to explain. Even if I told you, there's no way for me to know if they smell the same to you."

Olie nodded. "I see. That makes sense."

"The reason I felt there was too much hikimi in the mix was because the scent changed."

"Changed? Like fruit when it ripens?"

"Oh, yes. It's quite similar to that . . ."

Watching Aisha's troubled expression as she searched for words, Olie was overcome with the desire to know what she felt when she smelled things. "Aisha," she said.

"Yes?"

"It may be hard to put into words, but could you try? For example, take this field, which is full of fragrances. When you stand in the middle of it, what do you feel?"

Aisha's eyes lit up. "Ah, that might be the fastest way to explain. Though it might be hard to understand too."

Olie smiled. "That doesn't matter. Just tell us in your own words."

Aisha nodded and closed her eyes. She took a deep breath and began to speak slowly. "The loudest scent voices right now are coming from the grasses near the buckwheat. The peak of summer has passed, and it's cooling down, so there're more aphids eating them. They keep shouting, 'Ow, ow!' It's quite noisy.

"Their screams are attracting ladybugs, which are eating the aphids. There're ants nearby, so they may start trying to chase away the ladybugs."

Olie dropped her gaze to the grasses growing beside the buckwheat.

Ladybugs . . .

Aisha was right. Ladybugs were crawling up the stalks and eating the aphids.

"The scent of the buckwheat is also changing in response to the cries of the grasses. But instead of calling ladybugs, the buckwheat's scent is telling the aphids to stay away. Like it's saying, 'Don't eat us. We taste bad.'"

With her eyes still shut, she pointed to the ohaleh. "More than the aphids though, the buckwheat seems anxious about the ohaleh. It's changing its scent as the ohaleh fragrance weakens."

Without opening her eyes, she pointed to the buckwheat. "Now I'm picking up the scent of the buckwheat's roots. It's very complex. It feels like there're millions of tiny little creatures there. I think they must be organisms that live around the roots. When the scent of the roots is strong, the plant flourishes, so I think those creatures may be supporting its growth.

"People grow buckwheat in Tohula Ila as well. One of the Makishi women took me to a buckwheat field, and this smell was very strong and clear there."

Olie and Tak listened breathlessly to her words.

"But that smell grows fainter when buckwheat is grown near ohaleh," Aisha continued, "and the plants are weaker."

Tak's eyes narrowed. "I see," he said. "So that's why the buckwheat isn't flourishing?"

Aisha opened her eyes and cast him a slightly troubled look. "Well, that's what I thought, but that may not be the only reason. Tak, the buckwheat grown in the south field withered before it grew this tall, right?"

"Uh-huh. Because we used a different fertilizer there. It couldn't suppress the ohaleh, and the buckwheat withered as soon as it sprouted."

Aisha nodded. "That's what I thought. I smelled the buckwheat in the south field first. Just now, when I looked at the scent of the buckwheat here, I realized the roots smell different.

"The scent around the roots in this patch is fainter than in Tohula Ila, where buckwheat grows vigorously, but it's still stronger than in the south field where the buckwheat withered as soon as it sprouted."

Aisha crouched and stroked a buckwheat stalk as she spoke. "The fertilizer seems to be keeping the ohaleh in check better here than in the south field. I'm guessing the organisms supporting buckwheat growth have managed to survive and are keeping it alive. But even so, the plants are still getting weaker."

Aisha touched the soil. "I've been trying for quite a while to figure out why. If the roots were the only problem, the buckwheat plants should be healthier because the ohaleh is exerting less impact. It's odd that instead they're getting weaker."

Tak watched her silently.

"This morning," she said, "it suddenly occurred to me that maybe it's because of the soil."

"The soil?"

"Yes. There're many things in the soil—some much too tiny to see. It makes sense then, that changes in those things could affect buckwheat growth. That's why I smelled the soil in the south field first. Just as I thought, it smells different from the soil in this field."

Aisha stood and looked at Tak. "Ohaleh changes the soil, right?"

"Yeah."

"I don't know how, but I think that perhaps ohaleh suppresses or weakens things in the soil that might interfere with its own growth."

She shifted her gaze to the field. "What if things in the soil that are harmful to ohaleh are also harmful to buckwheat? What if that was the one factor where the interests of ohaleh and buckwheat aligned?"

She spoke slowly, as if gathering her thoughts. "Ohaleh weakens buckwheat, but at the same time, it may also be weakening things in the soil that harm buckwheat. If so, then maybe when ohaleh is suppressed, it no longer weakens those harmful things and that makes the buckwheat plants weaker too."

Tak's eyes widened.

Her gaze still on the ground, Aisha said, "Some things that don't bother us when we're healthy can be hard to handle when we're sick, right? The soil in the buckwheat field in Tohula Ila smelled like this soil, which means there must have been harmful things there too. But in Tohula Ila, those things didn't hold the buckwheat back, and it flourished.

"The Makishi woman told me that buckwheat is strong, and I'm sure this buckwheat wouldn't have succumbed to the harmful things in the soil if it hadn't already been affected by ohaleh. But in its current weakened state, I think it finds this soil hard to live in."

Tak's cheeks were flushed. "That's a good point." His voice was unusually excited. "So that's what you meant when you said we need to suppress ohaleh, but not too much. If we want to grow crops alongside it, then just suppressing it isn't enough."

Aisha nodded. "Of course, it's still very important to suppress ohaleh because it gives off something that weakens not just the roots, but the whole buckwheat plant. However, I feel that if we knew how the soil, the roots and many other things worked together, we could make a breakthrough."

Her eyes shone. "I'd like to smell buckwheat that's growing completely free of any influence from ohaleh. I'd like to compare the smell of the soil here with soil where healthy buckwheat grows."

Tak smiled at her. "All right," he said. "It'll take a while, but I'll make sure you can compare those scents. In the meantime, I'll start changing the amount of hikimi in the fertilizer. I'll decrease it a little at a time, so please come and check the smell each time I change it."

A radiant smile spread across Aisha's face. "Of course," she said. The breeze ruffled her hair, bringing with it the scent of early autumn woods.

Watching Aisha's face, Olie thought, *She picks up myriad scents on this wind, ones I can't even imagine. Not only that, but she knows what they mean.*

When bitten, plants emitted scents that attracted the offender's natural enemies. They could summon beneficial insects and change the soil. Were such countless unseen interactions unfolding even now, at this very moment, in astonishingly complex ways?

Clouds drifted slowly across the blue sky. Staring at them without really seeing them, Olie sighed, and a coldness enveloped her.

That is the world of the Kokun.

To know all things by their scent. She felt as if she'd just caught a glimpse of what those words meant.

Her eyes met Tak's. Seeing his expression, she understood why his face had clouded when she'd told him she'd come to see Aisha work.

Aisha was looking at her too, her gaze serious and sad.

A wistful smile touched Olie's lips. "Don't worry about it," she said.

She reached out and brushed a strand of hair from Aisha's cheek and spoke the words that came to her heart. "There's a role for me to play in all this too, and I'm well aware that it's also meaningful . . ."

Feeling the warmth of Aisha's skin against her hand, she added, "Aisha, that you are here, at this time, it's like a dream come true . . ."

After that, she could say no more. Hot tears coursed down her cheeks.

Chapter IV
Ogoda's Secret

1
Giant Yoma

Yugil opened the carriage window and stared numbly at the blackened fields, feeling the warm, damp air against his face.

Blessed with a mild climate, the Rapa district of Ogoda was a rich agricultural region that yielded three ohaleh crops a year. The paddy fields should have been full of ripening grain, but he couldn't see even a single weed, let alone a blade of rice. Everything had been burned to exterminate the pests.

"It's a terrible sight, isn't it, sir," said the governor of Rapa from his seat across from Yugil. "Giant yoma eggs were first found in southern Rapa over three years ago. We thought we had burned them all off, but they soon broke out in other places. It's just been three years, but look how far the damage has spread.

"The first year, outbreaks were limited to one part of southern Rapa but by last year, they'd even reached us here. We lost our entire harvest. Several times we planted, hoping and praying that this time we would be spared, but as soon as the grain ripened, it was covered in giant yoma. All we could do was weep as we torched our fields. It's been like that ever since.

"Please inform your father, Sir Iilu Kashuga of our misery. Now that you've seen this blackened wasteland for yourself, you must surely realize the desperate circumstances of the people of Rapa. I implore you—"

"You were told to torch even the grass along the river banks," Yugil said, cutting him off. Suppressing his emotions, he turned a flat gaze on the governor. "Have you made sure those orders were carried out fully?"

The governor flushed slightly, but then nodded quickly. "Yes, sir. We burned the river banks completely—as soon as we received the koshi's directive. It wasn't easy to make people comply. The sedge that grows along the river is essential for livestock and draft animal feed, as well as for roof thatch. But I made sure they burned it all off. It was devastating for the farmers to have to destroy all the crops that sustain their lives . . ."

The governor's expression suggested this decision had been painful for him as well, but Yugil knew he'd ruthlessly punished any villagers who'd failed to follow his orders.

He kept his gaze fixed on the man's face. "For the last two years, people in four villages in southern Rapa have starved to death. This year, famine will strike villages throughout Rapa. People are beginning to flee, and some villages have already been deserted. Ogoda is mainly made up of islands. Ohaleh can't be grown near the sea, so Rapa is the granary for the entire protectorate. The price for deceiving the empire is harsh."

The governor's face tensed. Blinking rapidly, he spluttered, "Th-that is a gross misunderstanding. As I have already told you, I have never deceived the empire as the district governor! It was unscrupulous merchants who lied and sold illegal fertilizer to ignorant fools. I admit the failure to see what the merchants were doing was indeed negligent of the previous governor, and everyone who worked under him. But the previous governor has already been banished, along with his family and cohorts."

A thin smile curled Yugil's lips. "And therefore, you are absolved of any blame for this treachery?"

The governor's face froze.

Leaning forward, Yugil said in a low voice, "You've seriously underestimated me. Perhaps because I'm young?"

The governor's lips trembled. "No, sir, I would never—"

"I know not only the names of every one of those so-called unscrupulous merchants, but also their origins, their affiliated organizations, and the details of everyone associated with them."

The governor's eyes widened.

"We knew all along the scheme being plotted," Yugil continued. "Not just by Rapa district, but by the entire Ogoda protectorate, and how far it extended. We knew, yet we closed one eye. We contented ourselves with executing only the perpetrators and merely banishing the governor and his cohorts. Surely you know why, don't you?"

The governor said nothing. Yugil leaned back against the upholstery in the carriage. "If you understand, then you also know it's useless to appeal to my youthful sense of pity with such unconvincing pleas."

Yugil looked out the window once more. "It is indeed a terrible sight. This is the consequence of your actions. And it won't end here."

The governor stared at him.

"Giant yoma have wings," Yugil said. "If they cross the mountains to other districts and reach as far as neighboring East Kantal, the devastation won't stop at Rapa. A storm of condemnation will fall upon you."

With a sidelong glance at the governor's ashen face, Yugil murmured, "You've turned your backs on the gods."

* * *

A voice came from the other side of the door.

"Sir Yugil, Senior Koshi Olam has arrived."

Yugil placed his chopsticks on the table. "Come in," he said.

The door opened, and a middle-aged man strode into the room. When he reached the table, he dropped to one knee and bowed.

Yugil smiled. “Olam, thank you for your hard work. You must be tired. Have a seat.” He gestured to the chair across from him. “Have you eaten yet?”

“No, not yet.”

“Then you shall dine with me.” Yugil gestured to the servant waiting by the door and told him to bring Olam some supper.

“Thank you,” Olam said. He bowed and sat where Yugil had indicated.

An array of fresh fish, seafood and other delicacies that paired well with rice wine had been set before Yugil. Surveying the spread, Olam remarked, “That is quite the grand repast, isn’t it?”

Yugil cast him a cynical smile. “I’m sure you can tell from this what kind of man the new governor is.”

Olam nodded. “He would appear to be a typical rural bureaucrat.”

“Just so. He thinks all he needs to do is provide what he assumes is hospitality fit for an illustrious guest. Nothing more. That’s how petty he is. He has no clue what he should really do when the chief inspector comes from the Ministry of Wealth.”

Yugil grasped a piece of glossy shellfish between his chopsticks and held it up. “The closest port is Yaka. It must have cost a fortune to transport shellfish all that way and keep it this fresh. The people here are starving to death. Clearly, the governor doesn’t know how to use district funds.”

Olam’s lips crooked. “On the contrary. I expect he thinks this is the best use. Surely, he believes that pleasing you is the fastest route to rescue. You cannot blame him for that.”

Yugil grimaced. “If that’s the case, then it’s our fault too. If they think we’re the same as the foolish privileged class of Ogoda, it means we’ve failed to accurately communicate our intentions.”

“That is true, but . . .” Olam blinked as though searching for words.

Yugil raised his eyebrows and chuckled. "Am I being too naïve?"

"No, not at all. But the fact is we lack the manpower to do that."

Yugil sighed. "I guess you're right. It just seems to me that we keep putting off things that appear less important. Now they're piling up and bogging everything down. It's impeding progress."

Outside the door, a servant requested permission to bring in a tray of food.

"You may enter," Yugil said, and the servant came in bearing a tray laden with only slightly less variety of sumptuous dishes than those already arranged upon the table. Yugil and Olam cast each other a wry smile.

"It looks like this new governor will be quite a handful," Olam murmured. "I'll keep that in mind." He waited for Yugil to pick up his chopsticks, then raised his own.

"You've been traveling the mountain regions, haven't you," Yugil said. "How're things there?"

Olam's face turned grim. "The situation is dire. I'll submit a detailed report later. But the mountain villages have been hard hit too. Ohaleh is now grown on all arable land, even in the mountain areas."

"They're burning the fields?"

"Yes. We found no giant yoma in those areas two years ago, so we waited and watched. But last year, they appeared even in the mountains. To be on the safe side, we ordered the farmers to burn all the fields, including those where no giant yoma were found."

"In all five mountain villages?"

"No, we have not yet visited the two southernmost villages. They're isolated from the rest. Even if an outbreak were to occur there, it would take some time to spread. Master Raoh advised us not to be hasty, but to wait and see before we decide to burn."

Yugil's face clouded. "Master Raoh is usually right, but do you think it's safe to just stand by and watch? Wouldn't it be better to burn all the fields now for the sake of the future?"

"Master Raoh said it was a very difficult decision to make. But if we burn off everything, the number of deaths from starvation will more than double."

"True, but . . . it still might be better to torch the fields, even if it means reducing taxes."

Olam nodded. "I know what you mean, but Mijima will be keeping a sharp eye on the fields in those villages. I'm sure she won't fail to catch any signs of an outbreak."

Yugil's face brightened. "I see. Mijima is in charge. In that case, it should be all right." He paused for a moment, lost in thought, then said, "I wish I could've trained as a koshi."

Olam smiled faintly. "Your position is different from hers."

"You think so? But Mijima is the daughter of Master Raoh, head of Kashuga Oi. She may have married into the Olu Kashuga branch, but she and her older sister, Makiya, are still Master Raoh's only children. If something were to happen to Makiya, Mijima would become the head of Kashuga Oi."

"That is indeed true, but . . ." Olam shook his head. Lowering his voice slightly, he said, "A koshi's work is dangerous. You are the only child and heir. Compared to Mijima, who may or may not become head of the Ancient House of Kashuga, you are destined to become the next Minister of Wealth. That makes your position quite different."

Yugil regarded Olam's tanned face for a few moments, then said quietly, "Today when we visited the village . . ."

"Yes?"

"I saw corpses. People who'd starved to death."

Olam frowned. "The governor arranged it so you would see them, did he?"

"Most likely. I expect he wanted to appeal to my emotions by showing me how miserable the situation is."

Yugil's face twisted, and he shook his head. "It was awful. Particularly the babies and little children." He pressed his lips together and stared blankly at the table.

"It is tragic," Olam said quietly. "I've worked many years as a koshi, but I'd never seen people starve, or emaciated corpses. Until two years ago. I couldn't get those images out of my head. For a long time, they gave me nightmares."

He took a deep breath and continued. "At the same time, it made me keenly aware of my responsibility as a koshi. The lives of everyone in each protectorate and the entire empire depend upon ohaleh. Those scenes were a painful reminder of that."

Yugil gave a deep nod. "You're right. That's exactly what I thought when I was at the village. It's very different reading about these things on paper. I'd seen the reports, so I knew how many people had starved to death. But I'd never pictured them as individual faces."

His father's face rose in his mind, along with something he'd once said.

To run this empire, you must see its people only as numbers. Never think of them as individuals with faces. If you focus on their faces, you'll lose sight of the whole. When you lose sight of the whole, the empire will crumble. Never forget that. You're too easily influenced by your emotions.

Maybe that's why he wouldn't allow me to become a koshi, Yugil thought.

If he got to know the people as individuals and became familiar with their lives, he'd start caring about them. To order them to burn their fields when he knew they were starving would be distressing, and distress would cloud his judgment.

My father will be watching. He'll be assessing my response to everything I see on this observation tour. I'll have to show him I'm the kind of man who can see the bigger picture, even when confronted with a raw and painful reality. Otherwise, he'll cut me off mercilessly. It won't matter that I'm his only legitimate heir.

He suddenly recalled the pinched, anxious face of the crown prince, Odosen, when he'd ascended the throne soon after the death of his father, the emperor. Throughout the coronation ceremony, he'd kept glancing in Yugil's direction, but it wasn't Yugil he was looking at. He was looking at Yugil's father, Iilu Kashuga, who stood beside Yugil.

Up until the emperor's death, the balance of power between the faction supporting the crown prince and that supporting the emperor's younger brother, Prince Ragalan, had seemed evenly matched. When the emperor died, however, Ragalan's supporters quickly dwindled and, before he knew it, Odosen had secured a rock-solid foundation.

Yugil guessed Odosen was well aware that he owed his position to Iilu. And that even being the emperor wouldn't protect him should he incur Iilu's displeasure.

The irony of this wasn't lost on Yugil. *Like everyone else, the emperor will spend the rest of his life trying to guess what my father's thinking.*

With a sigh, he raised his eyes to Olam's face. "I haven't seen Mijima for some time. Is she doing well?"

Olam nodded. "Very well."

"Is she still traveling on her own?"

"Actually, no." Olam blinked. "She travels with an apprentice."

"An apprentice? A novice koshi?"

"No. The apprentice is already qualified. Although she came from one of the protectorates, she was given special permission to study at Lia Garden. She passed the exams, one after the other, with surprising speed."

"Oh, you mean that girl!" Yugil jumped in. "The one Uncle Masyu brought back with him?"

"Yes, that one."

"Aisha Loliki, right?"

Olam looked surprised. "You even know her name?"

An embarrassed smile suffused Yugil's face. "I was curious when I heard my uncle had brought back a relative on his mother's side . . . So, she now accompanies Mijima?"

As he recalled the one glimpse he'd gotten of the girl's face, he sighed. *How I envy her,* he thought, only to immediately reconsider. *In the midst of this tragedy, visiting the mountain villages right now must be heartbreaking.*

He picked up his chopsticks again and tackled his now-cold meal, his mind still on the girl he'd seen walking behind the petite Mijima.

"I rarely get to come this far," he said, "and if Mijima is nearby, I'd like to see her and catch up a little."

Olam didn't answer, and Yugil cast him a quizzical look. "Is there some problem with that?"

"What? Oh, no. I just remembered something I meant to report to you."

"What is it?"

Olam put down his chopsticks and took a piece of folded paper from his robe. "It's still a rough draft with only general estimates. I will prepare a more accurate report once I've finished investigating. Please have a look, and tell me what you think."

Yugil unfolded the paper and scanned its contents. It was a report on the number of deaths from starvation in all five mountain villages. Two years ago, there had been no deaths, but last year, two villages reported deaths from starvation, while the remaining three reported none.

"These villages that reported no deaths last year, are they the ones that didn't burn their crops?" Yugil asked, then paused. "No, wait. Only two villages didn't burn their fields. This village here, Yala, did it have a stockpile or something?"

Olam shook his head. "Yala is the remotest and the poorest of the five. It's inconceivable that they would have been able to stockpile any food."

"And they burned the land."

"Yes."

"Yet no one died of starvation? They were also paying taxes, right? I know many villages on the plains have fallen behind in their taxes, but I seem to remember that hasn't been the case for most of the mountain villages."

"That's correct. In the first place, Yala has very little land where ohaleh can be cultivated. The total yield is therefore much lower than the other villages. For that reason, Yala is allowed to pay taxes with specialty products, such as medicinal herbs."

"Ah yes, I remember now. Even so . . . If no one has died of starvation, is it because they can gather enough food from the forest to feed everyone?"

"No. In terms of what they can gather from the wild, the situation in Yala is no different from the other villages."

"Then what's the difference?"

"That is precisely what bothers me. Despite our investigations, there seems to be no satisfactory answer."

"What about its location? Could they be smuggling medicinal herbs to the empire proper or something like that?"

"That was my main concern, but despite a thorough investigation, I could not find any evidence of that. However . . ."

"What?"

Olam hesitated, but then seemed to make up his mind. "The village children said something odd. One of them told me that a messenger had come from the gods. But as soon as he said that, the other children looked frightened and scolded him. They said the messenger would never come back if they told someone.

"Although you cannot trust everything children say, I always listen to them. Often their words reveal secrets the adults are hiding. When I brought this up casually with the villagers later, they looked anxious."

"They clammed up?"

"That's right."

Yugil's eyes gleamed. "Interesting . . ." He paused, deep in thought.

Olam watched him silently, waiting for him to speak.

Finally, Yugil shook his head slowly. There was no trace of a smile on his face. "No, we can't just dismiss this as an interesting tale. If someone's pretending to be a messenger of the gods and trying to prevent people from starving, it could have serious consequences. We can't ignore it."

He rested his eyes on Olam's face. "Olam," he said. "Would you investigate this for me? But very cautiously."

Olam nodded. "Yes sir."

2
The Prayer Pigeon Prophet

A flicker of movement appeared in the shadows between the trees.

"Over there," Muzuho whispered, and the men behind him tensed.

A remnant of sunset still stained the mountain ridge, but the heavens were already turning the color of night. Evening mist flowed along the ground, and the shadow approaching from the forest depths seemed to waver in the haze.

Finally, a slender figure emerged at the edge of the forest and walked toward them.

When the person drew close enough for them to see, the villagers drew in a sharp breath. The figure was not only hooded, but a black cloth obscured their face. No lantern guided their way.

It was inconceivable that someone could see through that thick veil and know where to step, let alone pick out the path in this darkness. Yet the figure had walked unerringly down the mountain path and through the field toward them.

The villagers stood frozen, watching the figure approach and come to a halt in front of them. A gust of wind blew, and the figure's full-length black cloak fluttered.

"Good evening." The stranger's voice was young and female, and she spoke in the Ogoda language.

"I have come in answer to the prayer pigeon. Where is your village chief?"

Muzuho stepped forward. As he did so, the events that had led him to this point rushed through his mind like a long dream.

* * *

Some time ago, he'd heard rumors about a prophet who came bearing prayer pigeons.

Where they'd started, no one knew, but the rumors said a man with a basket of carrier pigeons and a young woman, whose face was veiled, had appeared in different villages, and that the veiled woman foretold the future with remarkable accuracy.

The first rumor said she'd found a little girl who'd gotten lost and brought her back to her parents. Other rumors followed, saying she'd caught a thief, found something someone had misplaced, or made a prediction that came true.

If that was all, Muzuho would have dismissed these as amusing tales, much like those of other fortune tellers who occasionally appeared and claimed they could find lost items. But this woman never asked for anything in return.

When the villagers, surprised and a little suspicious, asked why, she always gave the same answer: That she wasn't really the one who was helping them; that she'd been sent by someone else to do this work and had no need of riches.

"Famine is coming to Rapa," she warned them. "The day will come when a terrible pest will devour ohaleh. When that happens, if anyone wishes for help and is prepared to work hard, send off a prayer pigeon.

"But beware. If you speak of this to imperial officials, or to anyone from the empire, no help will come."

Some villages took good care of the pigeons she'd left behind, but many others forgot her once she'd gone. Since she'd never come to Olani village, Muzuho quickly forgot this story too.

When a giant yoma outbreak hit the plains of Rapa, however, shock had spread through the village. Reports on the damage done had been horrifying. Despite ohaleh's supposed resistance to pests, they had destroyed almost the entire crop.

It was then that Muzuho recalled the fortune teller. He realized with surprise that her prophesy had come true. Still, the plains were far away, and he never thought his own village would be affected.

The pests, however, hadn't stopped at the plains.

The previous year, outbreaks had occurred even in some of the mountain villages. Government officials had ordered the villagers to burn their fields, causing an uproar. Muzuho knew many people on the plains had starved to death, but last year, he'd heard they were dying not only on the plains, but also in some mountain villages.

Although, fortunately, the giant yoma hadn't reached his village yet, he was terrified when the imperial koshi came to check the fields.

Even in the mountains, ohaleh was now the main staple.

Before, the villages had grown many kinds of grain, including upland rice, yogi barley, and yogi buckwheat, but once they'd started cultivating ohaleh, no other grains would grow, even when planted. Still, ohaleh seemed like a miracle grain. It had made life far easier than they could ever have imagined possible.

When Muzuho had heard that mountain villages infested with giant yoma were being ordered to burn off their crops, he had gazed at the fields of golden ohaleh waving in the wind. The thought of what would happen if they were ordered to torch those fields sent a shiver down his spine.

Once again, he recalled the prayer pigeon prophet.

There was just one village in the mountains where no one had died of starvation, even though they'd burned their ohaleh crop: Yala. Rumor had it that Yala had kept its prayer pigeons and sent one off when the villagers first heard about what was happening on the plains.

If that were true, Muzuho thought, then shouldn't he try to get a prayer pigeon and send it off with a request for help?

Once this idea occurred to him, he couldn't sit still. If he were to act, he had to hurry.

Olani village didn't have any pigeons. If giant yoma had been able to travel all the way from the plains to the mountains, then they could easily fly from a neighboring village to Olani. They might be ordered to burn off the fields as early as next year.

Fortunately, the chief of Yala was Muzuho's relative, even if a distant one. Muzuho set off bearing a gift and begged the chief to give him a prayer pigeon.

The chief was a good man, and he listened earnestly to Muzuho's request. They had five pigeons, he said, so he would be happy to give him one.

He paused and gave Muzuho a long look. "Your village got any yogi barley?" he asked.

"Yogi barley?" Muzuho repeated.

They'd once grown plenty of it, but since they'd started growing ohaleh, they'd stopped. Or rather, they'd been unable to because it simply wouldn't grow.

"Hmm. I doubt anyone's got yogi barley seed anymore," Muzuho said. "Why'd you ask?"

The chief fixed him with an earnest gaze. "You gotta swear not to tell anyone. And not just about the prayer pigeon. About everything we've been talking about. You swear?"

"I sure do. You can count on me."

"And you'll see that none of the other villagers talk?"

Muzuho's heart beat faster. He nodded. "I promise."

The chief of Yala leaned forward and said in a low voice, "Yogi barley's what saved me and my village."

Muzuho's eyebrows shot up. "Yogi barley? You mean you grew it? But how?"

The chief of Yala opened his mouth, then seemed to think better of it. He groaned. "Even if I told you, there's no point."

"Why not? Come on. Don't be mean."

"I'm not being mean. It's just that it depends on the village, so there's no point in telling you what we did here."

"You mean the method's different from one village to another?"

The chief of Yala nodded. "That's what the messenger said."

"Messenger?"

"The prayer pigeon prophet. In Yala, we call her the 'messenger.' Because she was sent by a great being to help us."

At this, Muzuho leaned forward. "Is it true she won't accept a reward?"

The chief nodded. "She wouldn't take anything. Even though we told her it was a token of our gratitude."

"Is that right?" Muzuho still found this hard to believe. "You're sure what you did here won't save our village?"

The chief nodded. "The messenger said if any other village asks, we could tell them growing yogi barley saved us, but that's because this is Yala. There's no guarantee it'll grow anywhere else, she said. If anyone needs help, they should send a prayer pigeon and help'll surely come."

Muzuho frowned. "Well, then . . . But it still seems kind of rude not to tell. Sorry. I meant the messenger, not you."

The chief shook his head. "That's just because you haven't seen it with your own eyes. You'd understand if you met her."

He looked at Muzuho earnestly. "Whatever you do, don't doubt or underestimate the messenger. It's gonna take time to grow yogi barley. Or anything else for that matter. She'll give you detailed instructions. And those details matter.

"If you doubt the messenger, even a little, then your villagers might decide to skip a step or two. Because they think it's too much bother. That's what happened here, and it made everything a lot harder.

"That's why I'm telling you now, and I hope you'll take it to heart. As the village chief, you gotta believe and follow each step exactly. That's what counts. Don't give up. No matter how much time it takes or how much work. Not even if everyone complains. Do everything just like the messenger says. If you do, yogi barley will grow. No one in Yala starved to death. That's the best proof you could have."

The chief of Yala had leaned forward as he spoke, holding Muzuho's gaze. Muzuho was touched by his sincerity. "All right then. If you say so, I believe you."

Then a thought struck him. "But we don't have any yogi barley seeds."

"You can have some of ours."

"Really? You'd do that for us?"

Joy suffused Muzuho's face, but he added hastily, "Wait though. Yogi barley's your lifeline. You can't grow ohaleh this year. Doesn't seem right to ask you to share some of your seed grain."

The chief of Yala smiled. "No worries. At times like this, we have to help each other out. Besides, this year, we're giving yogi buckwheat a try too."

"Really?" Muzuho exclaimed.

The chief's expression grew somber. "You'll see once you get started, but it's not easy to grow new grains. You have to start by making hidden fields, so no government officials or koshi find out. You can't begin growing anything until you've done that."

* * *

"You're Muzuho, the village chief?" the messenger asked.

Muzuho nodded. "Thank you for coming so far along the mountain trails. Although I'm afraid my abode is too humble for the likes of such an illustrious visitor, please come inside and make yourself comfortable."

"Thank you."

As he led her to the house, the men, who were gathered in

front of the entrance, moved aside. Muzuho's wife, who'd been watching from the doorway, disappeared into the kitchen.

Muzuho ushered the messenger through the dirt-floor entranceway to a raised wooden-floored room with an open hearth in the center.

Without removing her black cloak or veil, the messenger took off her mountain boots and put them in a bag. She took this with her as she crossed the room and sat down in the place reserved for guests.

The village officials in the group joined them around the hearth, facing the messenger. Muzuho introduced the men one by one, while his wife and sons brought in tea and food and placed these in front of everyone.

Muzuho urged the messenger to quench her thirst; she thanked him politely but asked that the tea and plate placed before her be removed.

When the chief's wife looked at her in surprise, she said calmly, "I appreciate your kindness and am sorry to be rude, but this meeting must be kept secret. If government officials should chance to come while I'm here, even if I sneak away, they'll realize that you had a guest when they see the plate and cup."

She looked around at the seated men. "You did receive my message, didn't you?"

They nodded, and Muzuho spoke up. "Yes. But still, it seemed inhospitable not to serve you something."

Turning to his wife, he said, "Take these away." She bowed and took the dishes from the room.

Muzuho suddenly remembered something else that had been in the letter. Blushing, he rose and came to sit down beside the messenger. She waited until he was settled, then began to speak.

"Time is running out," she said, "and there's much to be done in what little time you have left. In the message I sent you,

I asked you to go and look at the western valley. Have you done so?"

"Yes, we did, but . . ." Muzuho glanced around at the men in the room. His eyes came to rest on one of them who now spoke up.

"Pardon me for being so bold as to speak for the chief, but that area's been in my family since the time of our ancestors. It's not suited for growing yogi barley. We've got a saying in the village: Yogi barley grows best where maki flowers bloom pale red, not blue. In that there valley, maki flowers are blue."

The messenger cocked her head. "Yogi barley? I don't think I wrote anything about growing yogi barley there, did I?"

"Eh? You mean we're not going to plant yogi barley?" Muzuho interjected. "The chief of Yala told me they grew yogi barley, so we thought you were looking for a place to grow some."

The messenger shook her head. "No, we won't grow yogi barley there. As you said, it doesn't grow well where maki flowers are blue. But more importantly, we don't have much time—you requested help much later than Yala village.

"What you need to grow here is yogi buckwheat. Buckwheat can be harvested sooner, and it'll grow in the soil of the west valley."

Loud protests rose from the men. The chief of Yala had given them some yogi barley seeds, but they didn't have any for buckwheat. Besides, the west valley was too close to the village. Many of those gathered felt it would be impossible to make a hidden field there.

"Begging your pardon, ma'am," Muzuho said, "but rather than the west valley—"

"You think it would be better to cultivate Ogo Valley?" the messenger interjected, bringing Muzuho up short.

That was exactly what he'd been about to say. "Um, yes. Er, we thought—"

"You thought it's farther from the village, so it would be easier to hide from government officials, that it wouldn't be as badly affected by ohaleh, and that you could cultivate a larger area?"

Muzuho swallowed his words. Their guest had known everything he was about to say in advance. She shook her head. "Ogo Valley won't do. And neither will the hollow on Mount Lokiseh or the meadow in Yumaki."

The men's voices rose in a confused babble. Every one of those places had been on their list.

"Why not?" Muzuho asked.

"They're too far from the village. Not only that, but you'd have to start by making fields from land that has never been tilled. In the west valley, you'll only have to convert your terraced vegetable plots to buckwheat."

Muzuho raised his brows. "But it's too close to where we're farming ohaleh. We can't grow buckwheat there now. Or any other grains. There're some trees growing between the vegetable plots and the ohaleh fields, but wagons carrying ohaleh pass along that road there. There's been plenty of times I had to weed stray ohaleh from those plots."

Several other men chimed in to say they'd also found ohaleh growing there.

It wasn't uncommon to encounter wild ohaleh along the roadside where government-issued seed rice was carried by horse-drawn wagons. Mice loved ohaleh, and would slip onto the wagons and gnaw their way into the seed sacks. Although strict precautions were taken, total prevention wasn't possible, and sometimes seed grain fell by the roadside and sprouted.

This was called "stray ohaleh," and the koshi instructed farmers to uproot and burn any sprouts they found. If left unchecked, stray ohaleh would spread rapidly, withering the grasses in surrounding fields so that livestock could no longer graze there.

Stray ohaleh had hard husks and small kernels. Those who'd secretly harvested and eaten it were rumored to have died painful deaths, so it was customary to carefully weed it out and burn it.

"Besides, if we plant so close to the ohaleh fields, the koshi'll find out," Muzuho protested.

The messenger shook her head. "On the contrary—" she began, only to break off and turn toward the door. She rose quickly, picked up the round straw cushion she'd been sitting on, and whispered to Muzuho, "A koshi is coming."

"What?"

"My message included instructions on what to do should this happen. Please follow them. Where's the back door?"

Compelled by the urgency of her tone, Muzuho pointed to a sliding door on the right side of the room. "Kitchen's through there. The back door's beyond."

The messenger nodded and, still carrying the cushion, slipped through the door and disappeared.

The men stared after her for some moments, then jerked around at a knock on the front door.

"It's Olam. May I come in?"

"She was right," one of the men stammered, his eyes widening.

Muzuho leaped to his feet and stepped down onto the earthen floor of the entranceway to open the door.

There in the dark stood Olam. He raised his lantern and blew it out before folding it up.

"Good evening, Chief Muzuho," he said. "My apologies for coming so late at night. I heard there was a meeting here, so I thought I would drop by."

"Ah, I see. Ah, er, pl-please come in." Muzuho managed to summon a smile to his lips as he beckoned the koshi inside. His heart was pounding so loudly against his chest that he feared Olam would hear it.

Olam bowed and stepped inside. After removing his boots in the dirt-floored entrance, he stepped up into the mat-floored room. He glanced around and smiled.

"I see all the village officials are here tonight. What's the meeting about?" he asked.

The men stared at him with rigid expressions. One of the elders cleared his throat and said, "Uh, well . . . we were just discussing the future."

"Mister Morado, is something wrong?" Olam asked. "You're sweating. Aren't you feeling well?"

"Nope, nothing's wrong. Just fine," the elder mumbled, waving a hand in front of his face. His voice trailed off.

The man beside him came to his rescue. "To be honest, Sir Olam, you frightened us. To have a koshi come visit, why, it might mean you've come to tell us we're next. That we've gotta burn the ohaleh."

At this Olam nodded. "Ah, I see," he breathed. "I can understand why you'd be frightened."

Muzuho spoke up from behind him. "Please, have a seat," he said.

Suddenly realizing that the cushion was gone, he called his wife to bring another. Inwardly, he marveled at the thoroughness of the messenger.

3
Kidnapped

In the pale blue darkness, a black shadow moved. Perhaps because it carried no lantern, the figure moved slowly, treading its way carefully down the mountain path.

Hidden behind a tree, Olam observed the shadowy movements. *Just one?*

He was surprised. He'd expected more. Soon, however, other shadows appeared behind the first.

One, two . . . three, four, five. Five more.

Like the first one, none of them bore a lantern, but each carried something in their hands or over their shoulders.

It was too dark to see their faces or identify them, but that didn't matter. Regardless of who they were, he was sure they were from Yala village.

Even before Yugil had ordered him to investigate, Olam had been looking into Yala with the help of his subordinates. That none of the villagers had died of starvation, even though they'd burned off their ohaleh crop, could only mean they were getting food by other means. If so, then the most likely possibility was that they were farming a hidden field. But they couldn't grow ohaleh without guidance from the koshi.

The distribution of ohaleh seeds was strictly controlled, as was the composition of the fertilizer. If the villagers had a hidden field, all they could cultivate would be beans, yogi barley, or yogi buckwheat.

But native species of these plants were all vulnerable to ohaleh, and although beans would still grow near it, they wouldn't yield enough to feed everyone. No matter what crops they planted, they'd need to find land a good distance away if they wanted to grow enough to feed the village.

The woods on these mountains, however, were deep, and Olam doubted any of it could be converted to farmland. Even so, he'd instructed his subordinates to search for hidden fields in likely spots far enough from the village that ohaleh wouldn't damage crops. Up until now, they'd failed to find any.

If the villagers didn't have a hidden field, then the only other possibility was that they'd found some means to secretly barter for food.

The children had mentioned "a messenger from the gods," which suggested that an outsider was in contact with the villagers. Olam had therefore stopped searching for a hidden field and instead had set a watch on the village when possible.

Searching for a hidden field could be done while the koshi carried out their normal work, but to keep an eye on the movements of the villagers was much harder with the limited number of koshi at his disposal. When he'd assigned people, it had been without much hope of discovering anything. Today, however, he appeared to have lucked out.

As he followed the men, something struck Olam as odd.

It must have been getting closer to dawn, because he could see them more clearly now. Steadily the outline of the things the figures were carrying revealed themselves to be farm tools.

So, they're not smuggling. They're cultivating a hidden field after all!

His pulse began to race.

He waited until the men returned to the village, then followed the mountain path. When he came to the end of it, he froze in astonishment.

He'd stumbled upon a hidden field in a place he'd never suspected.

How can this be possible?

He ran his hand through ears of yogi barley that were already ripe with grain, while his dazed eyes roamed across the field.

It had never occurred to him to look here because it had always been a vegetable patch. He'd assumed they were still growing vegetables in it.

Besides, just south of this spot lay the terraced fields where the villagers had grown ohaleh. Although it had all been burned off, and nothing grew there now, it had been cultivated close by until very recently.

Has enough time passed since they burned it off? No. That's not possible.

The power of ohaleh to wither other grains was astonishing. Every koshi knew that, for some reason, no other grains would grow near a former ohaleh field, even years after ohaleh cultivation had ceased.

It might have been possible if all the soil were removed and replaced, but most areas with soil suitable for farming were already planted with ohaleh. It had a frightening ability to change the soil, not just of the field in which it was planted, but of the surrounding fields as well.

In areas that hadn't been affected by giant yoma, ohaleh production would have to be given priority. So even if the villagers had searched throughout Ogoda, they would've had a hard time gathering enough untainted soil.

Olam and his fellow koshi had proposed bringing soil from the empire proper to replace the soil in the burned fields in Ogoda and save the people of the protectorate from starvation. Their proposal, however, was rejected. Not only was the cost and labor involved prohibitive, but the empire had decided not to provide relief to Ogoda as punishment for covertly producing its own fertilizer.

Although the lord of Ogoda had begun replacing the soil in some places, priority was given to the main grain producing areas, which did not include the mountain villages.

As the price of soil had soared, it was inconceivable that Yala villagers could have afforded to replace the soil here themselves. And even if they had, such activity wouldn't have gone unnoticed.

So then how could they possibly have grown this yogi barley?

Olam shuddered. The seriousness of this violation made his stomach churn.

Having spent many years of his life as a koshi, he was well-versed in martial arts and was particularly cautious when inspecting the protectorates. Although they'd pledged allegiance to the empire, the protectorates still sought to strengthen control over their own territory.

For a few short moments, however, he let his thoughts distract him. This opportunity wasn't missed by those who were lying in wait.

By the time Olam noticed the men rushing toward him, he'd lost any chance to flee.

He managed to block a rope flung toward him and knock it away with his arm, but the next moment his body was struck with weighted ropes thrown from all sides. These wound around him, immobilizing him, and he was dragged to the ground.

Sharp blades of yogi barley scraped his cheeks and arms as he rolled across the field. Gritting his teeth, he looked up at the men towering over him, backlit by the rising sun. He glared at the tattooed faces of the fierce Ogoda warriors surrounding him.

* * *

Catching Uraili's scent, Aisha rose and went to the entrance of her hideaway. She waited for Uraili to knock, then opened the door. He stepped inside, bringing with him a cold, rain-wet wind.

Face tense, he skipped the greetings and blurted out, "Is

Masyu here?" His wet hair was plastered to his forehead and cheeks.

"No. He left for the capital this morning because something came up."

Uraili's face fell.

Aisha brought him a thick towel, then took his sopping rain cloak. As she hung it up to dry in the earthen-floored entranceway, she said, "I'll pour you some tea. We need to warm you up before anything else."

Uraili nodded and stepped into the main room.

The hideaway, a refurbished inn for traveling merchants, had enough rooms to accommodate five or six people. Masyu had prepared similar houses in different places, and Aisha used them when she was acting as the messenger in between her work as a koshi.

Uraili had also joined Masyu's band of trusted comrades. As a protectorate inspector, he couldn't devote himself to Masyu's work full-time, but, right now, both he and Masyu were stationed in Ogoda, and his support was invaluable.

Over the course of many years, Masyu and Raoh had worked together to handpick members who could carry out the plan they'd devised for surviving the anticipated catastrophe.

The first members recruited were Raoh's daughter, Mijima, Tak, and Tak's family. They, along with Masyu, formed the core members of the team and had been involved the longest.

Uraili and Oloki, who had forged strong bonds of trust with Masyu over many years of serving as comrades in arms, had joined the band when the giant yoma outbreaks began in earnest. They were not only skilled in martial arts, but had also mastered a number of other crafts that made them indispensable.

Even with Masyu and Sir Raoh, the band numbered only twelve people, but they all understood the importance of their mission and were fully committed, despite the risk of being accused of treason.

Only Mijima, Tak, and Tak's family, however, had been told that Olie, the Kokun, was a member, or the real reason Aisha had joined the band. Uraili and Oloki had not been told.

Masyu seemed to feel it wasn't yet time to tell the two men about his and Aisha's sensitivity to smell either; it was a delicate matter inextricably linked to the Kokun's existence. He had merely told them he believed Aisha was his cousin on his mother's side.

When they'd heard this, their eyes had widened in surprise, followed by a look of understanding. They'd likely assumed this was why Masyu had risked so much to save Aisha and her brother.

Oloki, the dog handler, was taciturn, and his face didn't reveal much. Uraili, on the other hand, was very expressive. From the time Aisha had first met him in West Kantal, she'd found him to be deeply compassionate. Since she'd begun working with him, she'd often thought life as a warrior must be hard for him.

She put a spoonful of honey in the hot tea and handed it to Uraili, who was sitting huddled by the hearth to warm up. He thanked her and took a sip, then heaved a deep sigh.

"What happened?" Aisha asked.

Uraili grimaced. "Olam's been captured," he said.

"Captured?"

"I just got news from a spy we planted among the Dawn of Ogoda. Apparently, Olam stumbled onto the hidden field in Yala and was attacked there."

The color drained from Aisha's cheeks as she pictured Olam's gentle face framed by graying hair.

A senior koshi related to the Kashuga Lai, Olam worked for Iilu Kashuga and his son Yugil, but Aisha had a deep respect for his wisdom as a koshi and was drawn to his personality. Her stomach knotted at the thought of him being kidnapped.

She was also disturbed by where he'd been caught. "So, he discovered the hidden field, did he?" she asked.

Uraili nodded gravely. "I didn't think he'd find it because Oloki told us he and the other koshi were searching elsewhere, just as we'd planned. However . . ."

Aisha frowned. "I wonder why they would kidnap him. If that's where he was captured, it means the Dawn of Ogoda knew about the hidden field."

Uraili groaned. "I don't know. I think there're two possibilities. One is that they followed Olam with the intention of kidnapping him and that's how they came upon the hidden field. The other is that one of the Yala villagers is involved with the Dawn of Ogoda, and they attacked Olam so he couldn't report on what he'd discovered. In that case, it means they also know about the messenger. We don't need to be too worried about that yet because the villagers know very little. Still, we'll have to be even more cautious from now on."

The Dawn of Ogoda were a band of warriors who sought independence for the protectorate, but the exact nature of their organization was shrouded in darkness. Publicly, the lord of Ogoda insisted it was a group of traitors, who would be punished when caught. According to Masyu, however, the ringleader was quite likely one of the lord's own kin.

Although the band's goal was independence, for the time being, they were making no move to start a rebellion. Instead, they made sporadic raids against the trading posts of Umalese merchants who used their imperial authority to ruthlessly pressure Ogoda merchants, or against imperial agricultural officials who extorted money from Ogoda farmers and used it to bribe people in the imperial government and curry favor. As such, the empire hadn't paid much attention. It was only after the guano smuggling incident that the imperial government had begun to keep an eye on their movements. Because any action that could lead to independent cultivation of ohaleh threatened its rule and was thus an act of treason.

The emperor had ordered the Ministry of Wealth, led by Iilu

Kashuga, to investigate the Dawn of Ogoda. He'd also transferred Masyu from West Kantal to the Ogoda protectorate so that Masyu could keep an eye on the situation.

Aware that Masyu was close to Raoh, the head of Kashuga Oi, the emperor often used him in this way to maintain a balance and prevent appearing biased toward one House or the other.

Masyu could not have hoped for anything more ideal. He'd foreseen the terrible damage giant yoma would wreak on Ogoda's ohaleh crop and had already launched his plan to save the farm villages by having Aisha pose as the 'prayer pigeon prophet.'

"Where's Olam now? Has he been hurt?" Aisha asked, her face still pale.

Uraili shook his head. "I don't know. Our spy couldn't locate him. As for whether he has been harmed, we don't know that either. But Olam is a senior koshi. I'm sure they know that retribution will be horrible if they kill him. I doubt they'd be so foolish as to do something that would have repercussions for the entire protectorate."

"You don't think that's precisely why they might kill him?" Aisha asked.

Uraili raised his brows.

"Just to capture a koshi is a serious crime," Aisha went on. "Wouldn't they think it was better to erase all evidence that they'd done so?"

Uraili didn't answer, but she could see from his face that he was worried. He stared into his teacup and remained silent for a while.

Finally, he said, "If they captured him because they wanted to conceal the existence of the hidden field from the empire . . . then, yes. It's likely they'd want to eliminate him. However, I doubt they'd kill him right away.

"If they were just worried about him telling the empire of

the hidden field, they could've killed him and buried him there. That they've kidnapped him suggests they want to keep him alive so they can use him in some way."

Either way, Aisha thought, *it won't change the fate awaiting him.* She looked down and bit her lip. *I never dreamed it would come to this . . .*

For the last few years, she'd been solely focused on saving the people of Ogoda from famine.

To teach mountain villagers how to make and farm hidden fields was dangerous, but the rulers of Ogoda had failed to find a way to save their people from this tragedy. To be able to alleviate the people's suffering in any way made her happy; she felt as if she were saving her own self.

The devastation in the farming villages infested with the pests was horrifying. Through her work as a koshi, Aisha had become painfully familiar with what it meant to starve to death.

She could now understand how her father had felt.

Even if ohaleh was a yoke for subjugation, she didn't think she could have refused it; not if it meant exposing people to the risk of starvation. Each person afflicted had only one life to live. If they lost it, they'd never get it back.

Although she couldn't erase the deaths and hardship her grandfather's decision had caused, she at least wanted to help whoever she could, here and now.

But the context of the tragedy unfolding in Ogoda was complex, and just wanting to save people wasn't enough to keep famine away. The root of the catastrophe was deeply enmeshed in the empire's structure of domination over the protectorates.

For the Umal Empire, ohaleh was a miracle grain that had allowed it to extend its territory without fighting any battles. Now, however, a mere insect threatened to effortlessly overturn the very basis of imperial control. News that swarms of pests capable of destroying ohaleh had appeared in Rapa threw the entire empire into a maelstrom of shock and fear.

When the first giant yoma eggs were discovered, the koshi had been able to circumvent an outbreak by burning the crops in all the surrounding fields. In addition, Master Raoh had given strict instructions to watch for large yoma infestations and, where fields needed to be burned, to make sure the farmers were compensated. Thanks to these measures, no giant yoma were seen for some time.

In the last few years, however, many regions had been experiencing higher humidity and heavier rains, which made it much more difficult to monitor pests effectively. Substantial yoma infestations had broken out repeatedly in southern Ogoda, which was warmer than other regions. In one of Ogoda's cultivated areas, giant yoma eggs were overlooked, and an outbreak had occurred.

After that, the pests spread with startling speed.

The koshi tried various kinds of pesticide but were unable to eradicate them, leaving them no choice but to torch all the affected ohaleh fields.

Ohaleh was now the only kind of grain that would grow in Ogoda. For the local people, the order to burn their ohaleh crops was equivalent to being sentenced to death by starvation. Already, they were starting to realize that if they'd never become a protectorate or grown ohaleh, this tragedy would never have happened.

Before they'd been given ohaleh, the Ogodians had grown a variety of crops, including yogi barley and yogi buckwheat. While these grains had much smaller yields, they'd at least produced enough to survive on. Once Ogoda had adopted ohaleh, however, these other grains would no longer grow, and the people were now plunged into abject terror.

The empire had proclaimed to all that this catastrophe was the result of Ogoda's treasonous behavior. Pests would never have attacked the ohaleh crop if it had been properly cultivated. Instead, Ogoda had covertly produced its own fertilizer, which was expressly forbidden, and used it to grow ohaleh.

That, the empire claimed, was what had triggered the giant yoma infestations.

The Ogodians currently believed these claims because they knew their rulers had indeed broken the law to make fertilizer.

For the time being, the empire could probably keep control over the protectorates with this reasoning because everyone outside of Ogoda wanted to believe it was true: after all, if that's what had caused the appearance of these pests, then only Ogoda would be affected.

But if any giant yoma outbreaks occurred within the empire proper, the imperial government's argument would lose its credibility.

Both the emperor and Iilu Kashuga were surely aware of this, yet they continued to blame Ogoda and to insist no pest damage would occur if people followed the correct cultivation methods.

"The empire's like a herd of cattle," Masyu had said to Aisha. "Even if the leader sees danger ahead, it's not easy to make the whole herd change direction. And changing direction itself can be damaging. That's why the emperor's trying to find a way forward without altering course. Even if it provokes more criticism from the protectorates, he'll probably never admit the empire is at fault. Instead, he'll keep blaming Ogoda and insist that these giant yoma outbreaks were triggered by faulty Ogodian fertilizer. He'll say the ohaleh grown with it made the yoma mutate."

With a sigh, Masyu had concluded, "Using that logic, he may be able to convince people the empire's not to blame. But that won't solve the root of the problem. And the people will starve."

Three years earlier, their experiments with fertilizer at Yugino Lodge had finally borne fruit: They'd succeeded in growing indigenous yogi barley and yogi buckwheat.

When Aisha had started posing as the prayer pigeon diviner to help the mountain villages in Ogoda, Olie had sent her a message by carrier pigeon. It was just one word written in code: Thanks. Aisha had carried it with her ever since.

She would never forget the cries of joy and the smiles that wreathed the villagers' faces when they saw the barley in their hidden fields bear grain.

Although her work was fraught with danger, not once had she regretted it.

But . . .

She'd never thought her actions could expose Olam to danger. Fear and panic seized her, and she bit her lip again.

It may be too late, but even so, if there's any hope at all, I've got to do something.

She raised her face and looked at Uraili. "I'd like you to go to Madam Mijima."

Uraili cast her a puzzled look. "Why?"

"What if we make the Dawn of Ogoda believe that Sir Olam is not the only koshi who knows about the hidden field?"

Uraili's eyes lit up. "I see," he said.

Aisha knew they'd have to be careful about how they let this information out. Otherwise, the Dawn of Ogoda might realize there was a secret agent in their midst. But Uraili was used to manipulating information.

Uraili, however, frowned. "You're right, it might help save Olam's life, but . . ." He shook his head, and his eyes slid away from Aisha.

"I can't do that on my own initiative," he said. "I'll have to send a carrier pigeon to Masyu first and wait until I get a response."

Before he'd even started explaining, Aisha had realized the same thing.

If they rescued Olam, he'd tell the Kashuga Lai about the hidden field. It wouldn't take long for Iilu Kashuga to find out what they'd been doing in Yala. If so, everything they'd secretly worked so hard to achieve would come to nothing.

The villagers would be punished, and Aisha would be exposed, putting not only her life, but the lives of the entire band of comrades, in danger. Moreover, they might be robbed of any further chance to carry out their plan for averting the catastrophe.

What would Masyu say if he were here?

An icy chill spread through Aisha's breast at the thought.

For the Dawn of Ogoda to eliminate Olam, who'd discovered the hidden field, was almost too perfect a solution.

Masyu and the band of comrades could get rid of him without lifting a finger. And even if the hidden field were discovered, they could make it look like the Dawn of Ogoda were the ones who'd told the villagers to make it. After all, it was the Ogodians who'd made forbidden fertilizer, so it wouldn't be strange for them to make a hidden field as well.

A grim thought crossed her mind, and she rubbed her bloodless fingers.

Was this scenario masterminded by Masyu in the first place?

She didn't want to believe he could be so cold and calculating. At the same time, however, she couldn't believe someone as meticulous as Masyu wouldn't have taken steps when he first launched this dangerous venture to avert any suspicion falling on them if they were exposed to the Kashuga Lai.

If this was one precaution he'd taken, Uraili's message wouldn't save Olam.

Aisha thought furiously as she watched Uraili take a piece of paper and begin writing a message to fit in the tube.

Even if it were possible to do so, they probably shouldn't save Olam. Many lives would be lost if they did. Besides, he might be dead already. And even if he wasn't, she was limited on her own.

All this, she understood, yet the desire to save him kept rising inside her, like water brought to a boil in a pot over the fire. The force of it shook her body.

She couldn't bear the thought that what she'd done might get Olam killed. She'd worked so hard to save people's lives, and she couldn't forgive herself for failing to realize that her actions could lead to something like this.

Uraili's voice broke through her thoughts. "I'm going to send off a pigeon."

He rose and flung on his still dripping rain cloak. "Thanks for the tea," he said, and left.

Aisha stared blankly at the door as it closed behind him. As her nose followed his scent fading into the distance, a thought formed in her mind.

At least I can find out if Olam's all right.

Even if he'd been killed, she could bury him and say a prayer.

Maybe she was just trying to make herself feel better, but she didn't want him to die without anyone at least knowing where he was.

She rose and began to prepare.

4
The Chase

By the time Aisha reached the hidden field, the rain had stopped, but the wind was still strong.

She stared at the field bathed in the late afternoon sun and fought back the despair that seeped through her.

Rain changed the scent of everything: the trees and grasses in the forest and the soil in the fields. The wind pressed against her, bearing the wet-fur smells of different creatures and other scents. But among them, she couldn't find Olam's.

I wonder where he was attacked.

She walked slowly along the border between field and forest, until she came across an area where boots appeared to have trampled the soil. They might have been the prints of men from Yala village, but the ground had been violently churned up. Some dug into the earth quite deeply.

An image of booted men, their feet sinking into the muddy field as they lifted Olam, rose in her eyes, and her heart began to race.

She crouched on the ground to catch the scents better; an unexpected smell teased her nostrils. A faintly sweet aroma came from one set of footprints.

Pishal?

Pishal was an expensive baked sweet that contained the spice known as pisha, a valuable trading good that certainly couldn't be bought in the mountain villages. Once, Uraili had given her a few pieces of pishal when he'd received some. He'd said wealthy people in southern port towns where the trading ships stopped served it at weddings and other celebrations.

This recollection touched something buried in Aisha's mind. She narrowed her eyes.

What could it be?

Something related to pishal; something she'd felt was odd. She searched her memory, and suddenly an image came back to her with the smell of horse and straw.

That's it!

She'd smelled pishal once before in a mountain village. Not Yala, but Agila, which was nearer the plains. She'd smelled it when she'd passed a horse-drawn wagon loaded with ohaleh straw and had wondered who could have pishal in such a remote place.

A horse-drawn wagon. Carrying rice straw.

She felt her pulse quicken.

No one would think it strange if a merchant gathering straw or thatch turned up in a village. And the straw gathered would be piled very high. Now that ohaleh was being burned off, such merchants might be gathering undergrowth and fallen leaves instead of straw for compost, but even so, their wagons would be perfect for concealing and transporting someone.

Aisha rose and set off at a run.

The mountain paths in this area were wide enough for a small wagon, but too narrow for a large one to pass. If the men had carried Olam to a waiting wagon and loaded him onto it, the most likely place would be where the mountain path joined the road, behind the third waterwheel hut.

Village waterwheels were only used at specific times, and as the third waterwheel was farther from the village, it wasn't used as much.

She would've liked to go straight there to check it out, but she couldn't go near Yala, unless she was posing as the messenger. Yala wasn't in her jurisdiction as a koshi, so if she turned up like this, the villagers would wonder what she was doing there. When she'd come to the hideout today, she'd deliberately made a wide detour around the village for that very reason.

But there was still something she could do. There were only two roads leading out of Yala to other places. She didn't know which the men had used, but the one that headed toward the plains went through Agila, the village where she'd smelled pisha before. Fortunately, Agila was within her jurisdiction as a koshi, and no one would wonder if they saw her there. Praying that she was right, Aisha decided to gamble on this direction.

She smelled horse from up the road. It was a relief to know that her borrowed mount, which she'd left in the woods, was still waiting there for her and hadn't been attacked by wolves.

By the time Aisha reached Agila, the sun was beginning to set, and the roofs of the houses, thatched with ohaleh straw, shone golden in the rays of the westering sun. Although rice straw normally didn't last as long as reeds when used for thatching, ohaleh straw, which gave off a powerful scent even though it was dried, not only kept pests away, but was also highly durable, outlasting reed thatch. Observing how the thatched roofs seemed to envelop the houses, protecting them, Aisha rode toward the village square.

Suppertime was approaching, and the square was almost empty, but there were still a few merchants packing up their goods. Catching sight of a footwear merchant she knew, Aisha dismounted and approached him, leading her horse.

The merchant looked up and smiled when he saw her. "Madam Koshi, you've been working late."

Returning his smile, Aisha bobbed her head and said, "You too. With that rainstorm, it must have been freezing."

"I'm used to it," he said. He laid a hand on the box of goods he'd just closed. "Were you looking for shoes?"

"No, I'm sorry, not right now. I'm looking for a rice straw merchant. Did you see any today?"

"A rice straw merchant? Hmm, let me think." He paused for a moment, then said, "No, I'm sorry. I don't remember any."

"That's all right. I'm sorry to interrupt your work."

She turned away from the stall, wondering what to do next. The sun was already disappearing behind a mountain ridge, and the long shadows of the houses stretched across the square.

It suddenly hit her that this was like looking for a single strand of straw in a field. Her heart sank. Sighing, she was about to swing herself back into the saddle when she heard a voice behind her.

"Madam Koshi."

Turning, she saw an old man dressed in ragged clothes. It was a beggar she sometimes saw in the square scrounging things from shoppers.

"Would you be lookin' for a straw merchant now?"

"Yes. Did you see one?"

The man grinned. "And if I did, would you be giving me a reward then?"

Aisha looked him in the eye and said, "If you can prove you aren't lying just to get a reward, I'll give you one copper coin."

The old man wiped the grin from his face. "I saw one all right," he said. "That's no lie. This straw merchant, he comes from the village. His mother lives here, so whenever he comes, he gives her some money. He's a good son, who makes his ma glad. If I go begging there after he's been by, she always gives me something."

Aisha took a copper coin from the bag slung across her chest. The old man's eyes lit up, and he extended his hand, but Aisha closed the coin in her fist. "I'll give you two coins if you'll show me where his mother lives."

The old man beamed. "Follow me!"

It was a small house that he led her to, but the windows were paned with glass. One of them was slightly open, and Aisha caught a whiff of expensive wax candles, which were only sold in the city, unlike the tallow candles used by most villagers.

She also smelled pishal.

Keeping the joy that welled up inside off her face, she gave the old man three copper coins.

She watched him as he returned to the village square with a pleased look on his face, then knocked on the door.

A few moments passed, and the door was opened by a short, elderly woman. The aroma of pishal intensified.

"Who are you?" the woman asked.

"I'm sorry to bother you at this hour. I'm a koshi. There's something I'd like to ask you."

The puzzled look on the woman's face deepened. "Oh? What is it?"

"I hear your son is a straw merchant."

"Yes."

Aisha said the first thing that came into her head. "I'm researching what straw merchants are collecting instead of straw these days. I'd like to talk with your son. Is he home?"

The old woman shook her head. "Oh no, he lives in the district capital. He's not here."

"Ah, I see. I heard he was in the village today. That's why I came."

The woman smiled. "Oh, yes, he came this morning you know. I was surprised because it's not his usual day, but he said he was passing through. He brought me some pishal."

"Oh, pishal. It's so good, isn't it?"

"It is! And he knows I love it, so whenever he comes, even if he's just passing through, he always brings me some."

Aisha stared at her for a moment, at a loss for words. "He's . . . very kind, isn't he?" she finally stammered.

A bright smile spread across the woman's face, and she nodded. "Yes, he's such a kind boy. I'm so blessed with a son like him."

Her kind boy was probably involved with the Dawn of Ogoda. That thought made it hard for Aisha to look at the woman's smiling face.

"I'd like to ask your son some questions," she said hurriedly. "Would you mind telling me where he lives in the capital?"

The woman looked uncertain, and Aisha forced a smile. "There's no need to worry. It's nothing that will cause him any trouble."

The woman's expression relaxed, and she told Aisha he lived on Ashoro Street. "I've never been myself though," she added. "But he told me if I ever needed him, I should go to that street and find the yard where lots of wagons are parked. Can't miss it, he said. Do you know Ashoro Street?"

Aisha nodded. "Yes, I've passed by it before."

"What's it like? Must be a big road, I guess."

"Yes, indeed."

The woman looked like she wanted to say more, but Aisha bobbed her head in thanks and bade her farewell.

As she returned to the square where she'd left her horse hitched to a post, Aisha was filled with sadness. She couldn't believe the woman's son could afford to put expensive glass panes in his mother's windows, buy her wax candles from the city for daily use, or give her pishal each time he saw her just on a straw merchant's income. He was probably making extra on the side by gathering information for the Dawn of Ogoda.

If that connection were exposed, he'd be arrested on serious charges. When she thought of how his mother would feel, she balked at the idea of sending him before the judge.

A blue darkness was settling over the village. She could only vaguely make out the outline of her horse. The chill evening breeze brought the aroma of dinner cooking. Birds chattered as they flew to their nests, crossing the darkening sky, which was still tinged with pale yellow.

Overcome with a sudden fatigue, Aisha came to a halt and

gazed at the shadowed square. She wanted to go back to the hideout and sink into a chair by the fire.

She grasped the reins of her horse. Her koshi bracelet jangled against the harness. With that sound, Olam's face sprang into her mind, bringing her up short.

The situation was so complex, she wasn't sure if she should look for him or not. Perhaps she was subconsciously searching for a plausible excuse to give up.

She gripped the reins and swung herself up into the saddle.

The wind seemed to have picked up again. Feeling it on her face, Aisha turned her horse toward the capital.

5
Taken Alive

She was used to riding through the mountains in the dark, but by the time she reached the capital, the night was well advanced.

On the main street, light and the sound of voices spilled from the few taverns that were still open, but Ashoro Street was sunk in darkness, and there was no one to be seen as she turned down the dim avenue. Several cats, startled by her horse, leaped onto a wall and fled.

She found the wagon yard easily. Although she'd been down this road once before, she'd paid no attention to the wagons. This was her first time to take a close look at the yard.

She counted more than ten wagons lined up beyond the gate. Covered by heavy waterproofed cloth, they looked like hulking beasts in the darkness.

When she swung herself down from her horse and her feet hit the ground, Aisha almost cried out. Her legs and back were excruciatingly stiff. Riding was an inextricable part of a koshi's work, but today's journey had been a long one. Her horse looked tired too, and it smelled strongly of sweat. Feeling sorry, she whispered an apology in its ear and stroked its neck before hitching the mount to a hook in the fence.

There was no gate at the entrance to the wagon yard, just a heavy bar placed across it. The wagons were large and, as this was the only exit, the bar was enough to prevent theft.

Aisha ducked under it, ignoring the sharp twinges this caused in her aching muscles, then began walking slowly among the wagons.

The wind tugged at the waterproof coverings so that they billowed and deflated with a flapping noise, as if they were breathing. A variety of scents wafted from the wagons, and Aisha inhaled them, letting them tell her where each wagon had been that day.

When she reached the third one, she came to an abrupt halt. She caught a whiff of pishal. And something else.

Olam!

His scent came to her from inside that wagon. Although it was mixed with fallen leaves and compost, it was unmistakable.

A wave of emotion swept through her, making her tingle all over. The thin thread of pishal she'd followed all this way really had been connected to Olam.

Many different scents came from the wagon, not just from the floorboards, but also from the wheels. She closed her eyes and sniffed. The smells stimulated her brain, flooding her mind with one vivid scene after another. One image was so unexpected that her eyes flew open.

A huge chiasa tree shining in the late afternoon sun.

The internal affairs agency?

After Ogoda became a protectorate, the empire had requisitioned the villa of the former king as an office for imperial officials, who supervised the Ogodians ruling the protectorate. The building was surrounded by a garden that had once been enjoyed by the royal family.

Aisha had been there many times because anyone, including the koshi, who came to Ogoda on imperial business needed to visit the agency for their work.

The scene evoked by the smell from the wagon wheels was of a particular chiasa tree. She saw it, swaying in the breeze, and a cluster of warehouses beyond it. Tomuchi shrubs, which bore small red berries, grew around the base of the tree. In this season, the berries covered the ground along with chiasa leaves.

If she'd only smelled chiasa, the wagon could have picked up the scent anywhere. That this scene had come so vividly to mind was probably because the scent of chiasa was mingled with the smell of berries.

But that's impossible . . .

Was Olam imprisoned in one of the warehouses behind the protectorate's internal affairs agency?

It seemed unlikely when the place was always bustling with imperial officials. People were constantly going in and out, many of whom would know Olam, and Aisha found it difficult to believe he could be hidden there.

But the scent's freshness troubled her. It was so clear she was almost certain it was from today.

I won't get anywhere by just standing here thinking.

She turned on her heel and ran back to the street. There was one hideout near the internal affairs agency. She could leave her horse there to rest, and walk to the building.

She swung herself up onto her horse and whispered in its ear, "We're almost there now. Just a little farther."

With a sigh, the horse shook its head and began plodding forward.

* * *

The moon shone faintly on the surface of the river.

Eyes half closed, Aisha sniffed the wind, following the path that ran along the bank between the river and the outer wall behind the government building.

She couldn't enter the offices this late at night, but if Olam were being held in one of the warehouses, she might be able to pick up his scent, depending on the wind direction. Even if she couldn't identify which building he was in, if she could confirm he was somewhere on the grounds, she could make up an excuse to go in tomorrow and figure out where he was being held.

The wind was strong, and when it blew across the wall, she

could smell things clearly. But it wasn't steady, and obstacles changed the direction of its flow. It would help if she could find a spot as close as possible to the warehouses where nothing blocked the wind's path.

Ah, the chiasa tree . . .

But with that scent came another—one she wasn't expecting—and she stopped abruptly.

Oloki?

There was no mistake. The scent of Oloki, the dog handler, was wafting toward her from inside the wall. The scent of his dog was fainter, which meant he hadn't brought it with him.

He must have come looking for Olam, too.

Relief flooded through her. Oloki was a master tracker. If he'd already come this far, then Masyu would soon know.

But she hadn't smelled Oloki or his dog in the hidden field. Or anywhere along the route she'd traveled for that matter. Had he found his way here by different means?

A gust of wind rustled the leaves. When it brushed against her cheeks, Aisha stiffened.

It had only been a short gust, but in that moment, an image had flashed through her brain. Men, many of them—with swords, bows and arrows, oily nets.

Aisha closed her eyes and focused on the smells.

It was difficult to pin down the location with the wind being so changeable, but figures of men shimmered in her mind.

She was certain that multiple warriors lurked somewhere on the other side of the wall. Yet there was no sign of tension in Oloki's scent. Had he brought the other warriors with him to help free Olam?

No, that's wrong.

They wouldn't need nets for that. Nets were used for capturing people. Which meant Oloki was their target.

And Oloki didn't know.

Once she realized this, Aisha sprang into action. She took a deep breath and whistled through her fingers, sharp and loud. The signal to run.

The shrill sound echoed through the night. She sensed the shock that shot through the figures on the other side of the wall. After that, everything happened in quick succession.

A grappling hook landed on top of the wall above Aisha, and a head appeared. The top of the wall was covered in spikes to deter intruders, but the shadowy figure wore iron mesh gloves and deftly vaulted over the wall to land on the path.

Oloki raised his head and stared at Aisha in surprise. But there was no time to talk.

Two other men vaulted over the wall after him. Aisha drew a small metal throwing blade from her belt and hurled it at a man who was coming up behind him. It struck the man's right shoulder, and he fell to the ground as though he'd been punched.

Without stopping to look, Aisha ran forward. As she passed Oloki, she whispered, "Run!"

For a second, Oloki turned around, ready to fight, but when he saw more men on the wall, he muttered, "Sorry!", and set off at a sprint, without looking back.

If he stayed, they would both be killed, and his legs were much faster than Aisha's.

Listening to his receding footsteps, Aisha faced the men who barred the path in front of her. She felt no emotion, not even fear; just a fierce urgency, like a trapped animal.

The men advanced. Their daggers, the weapon of choice for Ogodian warriors, gleamed pale white in the darkness.

Their scent pressed closer.

Aisha drew her own dagger and yelled, parrying the strike of one warrior, then another and another. They were powerful men, and with each strike, her arm went numb. Still, she kept moving with dizzying speed, focused solely on buying as much time as possible.

Fortunately, the path along the riverbank was narrow, with

the wall on one side and a steep drop to the river on the other, so that the men could not get past her to chase after Oloki.

But their blows were swift and sharp, and it was getting harder to deflect them. Her hand was slippery with sweat. When she blocked the next thrust, her dagger flew from her hand.

The warrior's eyes gleamed.

Just as Aisha was sure she was about to die, a voice rang through the darkness.

"Take her alive!"

The warrior flipped his dagger in mid-strike to hit her with the hilt. Aisha tried to block the blow, but he moved too fast, and the hilt struck her in the stomach. She felt as if something inside her had burst, and she crumpled to the ground. As she gasped for breath, they grabbed her arms and forced her to her feet.

"Where's the other one?"

"Nagim went after him, but he might have got away."

Although she heard the words, she couldn't think. All she could feel was pain. A horrible stench approached. A cloth that reeked of it pressed against her face, and she fainted.

6
The Royal Mother

In the intermittent darkness, smells came and went. *Pishal.*
Olam.

Her body rattled and jolted. Something hard hit her above the ear, but although it hurt, she couldn't wake up. Pain ebbed and flowed.

The shaking changed to a strange rocking sensation she'd never felt before. It made her feel sick, yet even her nausea seemed like something happening in a dream.

How long she was out she didn't know, but when she finally came to, the first thing she noticed was a raw smell she couldn't recognize.

"Are you all right?" a voice asked.

A warm hand touched her shoulder, and Aisha opened her eyes.

She saw Olam. There seemed to be a window behind him because his face was backlit and hard to see, but she could still tell that he was worried about her.

Just the sight of him was comforting, and she breathed a little easier.

"I'm . . . okay." When she spoke, pain stabbed her stomach, and she winced.

"Are you hurt?"

"They hit me in the stomach, so it hurts a bit. But I'm okay."

She tried to sit up, and Olam supported her with his arm. Noticing that her legs felt strangely heavy, she looked down and saw iron shackles on her ankles. These were chained to a post. Olam was also shackled.

There was a window high up in the wall, and dust motes danced slowly in a ray of light that shone into the large empty space.

The clearest thing was the strange raw odor, along with the smell of dried fish.

"Is this a dry goods warehouse?" she asked.

"Seems like it," Olam said, "although it's not being used right now."

He readjusted his position to sit cross-legged. "You were brought here yesterday, but I guess you don't remember, do you?"

Aisha's eyes widened. "Yesterday?"

"Yes. So, you don't remember. You woke up several times and were taken to the washroom by a female guard. You drank some soup and had some other liquid too."

Aisha blinked. She had no recollection of this at all. "I don't remember anything."

"I thought as much. It was the same for me. They told me I'd woken up several times too, but I had no memory of if. It's a strange drug they use."

Aisha remembered the horrible smell. "They used it on you too?" she asked.

"Yes, when they caught me. I lost consciousness right away. They also made you drink something each time you woke up, so I'm guessing they did that to me as well."

He sighed. "I was very surprised to see you here when I woke. Where—or I guess—why did they catch you?"

She couldn't tell him she'd been looking for him. Unable to think of a response, she remained silent. Olam seemed to guess there was something she couldn't tell him as a koshi from the Kashuga Lai.

"If you can't tell me, don't worry. I'm sorry I asked."

"Thank you," Aisha said.

She bowed her head, then looked at him. "I don't know if it is all right for me to ask either, but what about you?"

He didn't answer right away, and she thought he wasn't going to, when a look of determination came into his eyes.

"I have a favor to ask," he said in a low voice. "It may be impossible for me, but you might be spared. If you get out of here, please tell Yugil that something terrible has happened."

The words began to pour from him, as if a dam had broken. He told her about finding the hidden field near Yala village, about how the villagers had been able to grow yogi barley even though the field was close to where they'd cultivated ohaleh.

"I don't know how they were able to do that," he said, "but if Ogoda has developed that kind of technology, the stability of the empire will be in jeopardy."

Aisha had sensed people approaching while he talked, but although she wanted to warn him, that would mean explaining how she knew. As she hesitated, she heard the door open behind her, and three burly warriors entered, accompanied by a woman.

Two of the warriors stationed themselves beside the door, swords drawn, while the other approached them with the woman. This warrior placed his naked blade against Olam's neck, letting him know his head could be cut off at any moment, and nodded to the woman.

She took out a key, then knelt and swiftly unlocked the shackles that bound Olam and Aisha.

"Put your hands together in front of you," she said.

They did so, and she deftly handcuffed them. After making sure the cuffs were secure, she slipped two ropes from her shoulder and put one around each of their necks.

The two warriors by the door came over. Each of them grasped one of the ropes. Pulling Aisha and Olam after them, they walked toward the door.

The wind blew through the open doorway, and as it struck Aisha, she stopped.

"Keep moving!" her captor barked, yanking on the rope.

Aisha began walking again. When she stepped outside, she was enveloped in blinding light and there before her lay a sight she'd never seen. A huge expanse of blue water filled her vision, the surface of which surged toward her, as though it were peeling itself away.

Waves . . .?

She knew they were waves, but the way the water undulated and surged was unmatched by any waves she'd ever seen on a lake or any other body of water.

"Wha—What's that?"

Olam looked at her in surprise. "What's what?"

"This thing, right in front of us."

"Ah," Olam said. "That's the sea. I guess you've never seen it before."

"The sea!" It made sense, but it was still a shock to be confronted with something she'd only heard about.

Koshi didn't travel to the islands. Although ohaleh was resistant to both cold and pests, it was vulnerable to briny air and withered quickly when planted near the sea. Because ohaleh didn't grow on the islands, there was no need for koshi to come and offer advice, or to monitor cultivation.

Some parts of the empire proper faced the sea too, but the islands there weren't habitable. Ogoda was the only place within the empire's territory where people lived on islands.

Although the kingdom of Mazalia, which bordered on Ogoda, had some very large islands, it wasn't an Umalese protectorate. The islands within Ogoda's territory were smaller, with little flat space for cultivation. There was nowhere they could plant ohaleh without it being exposed to the sea breeze.

Thus, Aisha wasn't the only koshi who'd never seen the sea.

"Get a move on!"

The warrior pulled Aisha's rope, and she stumbled forward.

The wind blowing from the sea had a raw smell that differed from dried seafood. It was somehow pleasant. The ground beneath her feet was covered in white sand that seemed to go on indefinitely, and the sun reflecting off it hurt her eyes.

She kept walking, hearing the crunch of the sand and feeling it shift and slide underfoot.

They were led up a high dune. When they reached the top, she saw a city spread out below. With their white walls and flat roofs, the houses looked like rows of white boxes. Between the city and the dunes was a grove of trees, which leaned toward the city in crooked, twisted shapes like old women with sore backs.

A short distance from the city stood a castle. Spotting the flag fluttering from a turret, Olam muttered, "The royal flag of Gilam Island. So, that's where we are."

Although not as knowledgeable as Olam, Aisha knew where the island was located and what kind of ruler it had.

With a heavy heart, she looked at Olam, and saw the same dark thought reflected in his eyes.

As they neared the castle, a strange scent teased Aisha's senses. Her head jerked up. With the first whiff, she felt as though a giant hand had caught her heart and squeezed it. An inexpressible dread coursed through her. Overwhelmed, she staggered.

"Are you all right?" Olam asked.

"Yes," she gasped, but she could barely speak. She pressed her lips together and kept trudging until they reached the castle.

As they stepped from the outer brilliance into the interior, she was momentarily blinded. The unnerving scent slithered toward her through the darkness like a billowing swath of smoke.

The warrior leading Aisha must have felt her pace drop because he jerked the rope irritably; she walked faster.

They finally came to a door, in front of which they were made to stand.

"We have brought the captives," one of the warriors said.

The door slowly opened inward. Instantly, the smell grew stronger.

The room before them was large and bright. The left wall faced the outside, and sunlight streamed through large floor-length windows, which were paned unstintingly in expensive glass. The view, however, was blurred, perhaps because the glass was so thick.

A woman, short and slender, stood near the window. Her black hair, flecked with white, was gathered in an elegant bun accented with a single expensive but tasteful hair ornament.

"Bring them here," she said in a soft voice.

The warriors quickly obeyed, leading Aisha and Olam to a spot not too close, then grabbing them roughly by the shoulders to make them halt.

The woman turned slowly toward them.

Aisha had known what to expect ever since she'd seen the flag on the turret, but still, a chill ran through her when she saw the woman's face up close.

"You're . . ." Olam said.

"Yes. I am the Mother of the Dawn of Ogoda," the woman said with a faint smile. "I suppose you think you're doomed now that you've met me and know who I am."

This noblewoman was none other than Milia Ogoda, ruler of Gilam Island and mother of Agua, lord of Ogoda.

The Ogoda protectorate encompassed multiple islands, each of which had its own ruler, and they had always vied for supremacy. It was Milia's father, Malagua, who had united them as the kingdom of Ogoda.

After the death of her husband, who had married into her family as Malagua's successor, Milia had raised their son Agua on her own and supported him as the king, and now the lord, of Ogoda. She continued to wield a strong influence over Ogoda's affairs even now that it had become a protectorate.

"Don't worry," she said. "I've no intention of killing you. This is a beautiful island. Not a bad place to spend the rest of your life, is it?"

She flicked her eyes to the warriors, and they removed the ropes from the prisoners' necks.

"I'd like to remove the handcuffs for you too, but let's wait a little longer. I wouldn't want you to try something so foolish as taking me hostage."

The warriors stepped back, but they didn't sheath their swords.

Olam spoke, his voice hoarse but firm. "You must know very well what it means to kidnap a koshi, so why did you?"

"Because I had to, of course," she responded bluntly. "We've been looking for an opportunity to kidnap a senior koshi for ages. But that we caught you when you discovered the hidden field was incredibly good fortune, don't you think?"

Olam frowned. "Good fortune? To harm a koshi is a heinous crime equivalent to rebellion. The empire has surely launched a search to determine our whereabouts. If you, the mother of the ruler of this protectorate, is behind this, then Ogoda—"

"Your whereabouts?" she interjected, cutting Olam off once again. "You'd better pray they don't trace you this far then. We have good eyes and ears you know. If we sense that the search might reach this far, you'll end up at the bottom of the sea."

A smile rose to her refined features. "We are seafarers. The sea is our highway. We're deeply versed in the currents and tides. We know what kind of current flows where and how it changes. What we dispose of in the sea will never wash ashore."

The light pouring through the windows glinted white on her hair ornament.

"If they can't find you, then even the empire, as tyrannical as it is, can never prove we've captured a koshi."

Aisha barely heard their conversation. The powerful stench

from outside kept washing over her. It felt like a thick cloth was pressed against her face, making it difficult to breathe.

Milia seemed to notice how pale she was. "Are you all right?" she asked. "As I told you, we're not going to kill you right now. There's no need to faint on us, is there?"

Aisha looked up and stared blankly at her face. "What did you say?"

Milia raised her brows. "Hasn't the drug worn off yet?

Aisha shook her head.

She knew what was outside those windows. And having come this far, she could guess what they were doing, and why. But she couldn't understand how it was possible.

She stared at Milia and said the first thing that came into her mind. "Did you create the Dawn of Ogoda to save your people?"

Milia looked searchingly at Aisha for a moment, as though taken aback by this question. "Yes," she said finally.

"How are you going to do that?"

Milia gave Aisha a long considering look, then turned, crossed swiftly to the windows, and pushed them open.

Olam gasped at the sight that spread before them.

[Continued in Volume Two]

About the Author

A fantasy writer and cultural anthropologist with a PhD from Rikkyo University, Nahoko Uehashi is an associate professor at Kawamura Gakuen University. Her research focuses on the Indigenous peoples of Australia. Her books include *The Beast Player* and the multivolume *Moribito* series. She lives near Tokyo.